THE MOST BEAUTIFUL
WOMAN IN TOWN
& OTHER STORIES

THE MOST BEAUTIFUL
WOMAN IN TOWN
& OTHER STORIES

Charles Bukowski

Edited by Gail Chiarrello

First published in Great Britain in 2008 by
Virgin Books Ltd
Thames Wharf Studios
Rainville Road
London
W6 9HA

Published in the United States in 1983 by City Lights Books,
San Francisco

The stories in *Tales of Ordinary Madness* and *The Most
Beautiful Woman in Town* originally appeared in *Open City,
Nola Express, Knight, Adam Reader, Pix, The Berkeley Barb*
and *Evergreen Review*.

A catalogue record for this book is available from the
British Library.

ISBN 978 0 7535 1377 4

Typeset by TW Typesetting, Plymouth, Devon
Printed and bound in Great Britain by
CPI Bookmarque Ltd, Croydon, CR0 4TD

1 3 5 7 9 10 8 6 4 2

Mixed Sources
Product group from well-managed
forests and other controlled sources
www.fsc.org Cert no. TT-COC-002227
© 1996 Forest Stewardship Council

The Random House Group Limited supports The Forest Stewardship Council (FSC),
the leading international forest certification organisation. All our titles that are
printed on Greenpeace approved FSC certified paper carry the FSC logo.
Our paper procurement policy can be found at *www.rbooks.co.uk/environment.*

CONTENTS

The Most Beautiful Woman in Town   1
Kid Stardust on the Porterhouse   8
Life in a Texas Whorehouse   14
Six Inches   23
The Fuck Machine   34
The Gut-Wringing Machine   45
3 Women   55
3 Chickens   63
Ten Jack-Offs   73
Twelve Flying Monkeys Who Won't Copulate Properly   80
25 Bums in Rags   86
Non-Horseshit Horse Advice   95
Another Horse Story   100
The Birth, Life and Death of an Underground Newspaper   105
Life and Death in the Charity Ward   126
The Day We Talked About James Thurber   135
All the Great Writers   143
The Copulating Mermaid of Venice, California   151
Trouble with a Battery   158
卐   163
Politics is like Trying to Screw a Cat in the Ass   170
My Big-Assed Mother   174
A Lovely Love Affair   179
All the Pussy We Want   189
The Beginner   195
The Fiend   200
The Murder of Ramon Vasquez   206
A Drinking Partner   216
The White Beard   223
A White Pussy   229

THE MOST BEAUTIFUL WOMAN IN TOWN

Cass was the youngest and most beautiful of 5 sisters. Cass was the most beautiful girl in town. ½ Indian with a supple and strange body, a snake-like and fiery body with eyes to go with it. Cass was fluid moving fire. She was like a spirit stuck into a form that would not hold her. Her hair was black and long and silken and moved and whirled about as did her body. Her spirit was either very high or very low. There was no in between for Cass. Some said she was crazy. The dull ones said that. The dull ones would never understand Cass. To the men she simply seemed a sex machine and they didn't care whether she was crazy or not. And Cass danced and flirted, kissed the men, but except for an instance or two, when it came time to make it with Cass, Cass had somehow slipped away, eluded the men.

  Her sisters accused her of misusing her beauty, of not using her mind enough, but Cass had mind and spirit; she painted, she danced, she sang, she made things of clay, and when people were hurt either in the spirit or the flesh, Cass felt a deep grieving for them. Her mind was simply different; her mind was simply not practical. Her sisters were jealous of her because she attracted their men, and they were angry because they felt she didn't make the best use of them. She had a habit of being kind to the uglier ones; the so-called handsome men revolted her – "No guts," she said, "no zap. They are riding on their perfect little earlobes and their well-shaped nostrils . . . All surface and no insides . . ." She had a temper that came close to insanity; she had a temper that some called insanity.

Her father had died of alcohol and her mother had run off leaving the girls alone. The girls went to a relative who placed them in a convent. The convent had been an unhappy place, more for Cass than the sisters. The girls were jealous of Cass and Cass fought most of them. She had razor marks all along her left arm from defending herself in two fights. There was also a permanent scar along the left cheek but the scar rather than lessening her beauty only seemed to highlight it.

I met her at the West End Bar several nights after her release from the convent. Being youngest, she was the last of the sisters to be released. She simply came in and sat next to me. I was probably the ugliest man in town and this might have had something to do with it.

"Drink?" I asked.

"Sure, why not?"

I don't suppose there was anything unusual in our conversation that night, it was simply in the feeling Cass gave. She had chosen me and it was as simple as that. No pressure. She liked her drinks and had a great number of them. She didn't seem quite of age but they served her anyhow. Perhaps she had a forged i.d., I don't know. Anyhow, each time she came back from the restroom and sat down next to me, I did feel some pride. She was not only the most beautiful woman in town but also one of the most beautiful I had ever seen. I placed my arm about her waist and kissed her once.

"Do you think I'm pretty?" she asked.

"Yes, of course, but there's something else . . . there's more than your looks . . ."

"People are always accusing me of being pretty. Do you really think I'm pretty?"

"Pretty isn't the word, it hardly does you fair."

Cass reached into her handbag. I thought she was reaching for her handkerchief. She came out with a long hatpin. Before I could stop her she had run this long hatpin through her nose, sideways, just above the nostrils. I felt disgust and horror.

She looked at me and laughed, "Now do you think me pretty? What do you think now, man?"

I pulled the hatpin out and held my handkerchief over the

bleeding. Several people, including the bartender, had seen the act. The bartender came down:

"Look," he said to Cass, "you act up again and you're out. We don't need your dramatics here."

"Oh, fuck you, man!" she said.

"Better keep her straight," the bartender said to me.

"She'll be all right," I said.

"It's *my* nose," said Cass, "I can do what I want with my nose."

"No," I said, "it hurts me."

"You mean it hurts you when I stick a pin in my nose?"

"Yes, it does. I mean it."

"All right, I won't do it again. Cheer up."

She kissed me, rather grinning through the kiss and holding the handkerchief to her nose. We left for my place at closing time. I had some beer and we sat there talking. It was then that I got the perception of her as a person full of kindness and caring. She gave herself away without knowing it. At the same time she would leap back into areas of wildness and incoherence. Schitzi. A beautiful and spiritual *schitzi*. Perhaps some man, something, would ruin her forever. I hoped that it wouldn't be me.

We went to bed and after I turned out the lights Cass asked me, "When do you want it? Now or in the morning?"

"In the morning," I said and turned my back.

In the morning I got up and made a couple of coffees, brought her one in bed.

She laughed. "You're the first man I've met who has turned it down at night."

"It's o.k.," I said, "we needn't do it at all."

"No, wait, I want to now. Let me freshen up a bit."

Cass went to the bathroom. She came out shortly, looking quite wonderful, her long black hair glistening, her eyes and lips glistening, *her* glistening . . . She displayed her body calmly, as a good thing. She got under the sheet.

"Come on, lover man."

I got on in.

She kissed with abandon but without haste. I let my hands run over her body, through her hair. I mounted. It was hot, and tight. I began to stroke slowly, wanting to make it last. Her eyes looked directly into mine.

"What's your name?" I asked.

3

"What the hell difference does it make?" she asked.

I laughed and went on ahead. Afterwards she dressed and I drove her back to the bar but she was difficult to forget. I wasn't working and I slept until 2 p.m. then got up and read the paper. I was in the bathtub when she came in with a large leaf – an elephant ear.

"I knew you'd be in the bathtub," she said, "so I brought you something to cover that thing with, nature boy."

She threw the elephant leaf down on me in the bathtub.

"How did you know I'd be in the tub?"

"I knew."

Almost everyday Cass arrived when I was in the tub. The times were different but she seldom missed, and there was the elephant leaf. And then we'd make love.

One or two nights she phoned and I had to bail her out of jail for drunkenness and fighting.

"These sons of bitches," she said, "just because they buy you a few drinks they think they can get into your pants."

"Once you accept a drink you create your own trouble."

"I thought they were interested in *me*, not just my body."

"I'm interested in you *and* your body. I doubt, though, that most men can see beyond your body."

I left town for 6 months, bummed around, came back. I had never forgotten Cass, but we'd had some type of argument and I felt like moving on anyhow, and when I got back I figured she'd be gone, but I had been sitting in the West End Bar about 30 minutes when she walked in and sat down next to me.

"Well, bastard, I see you've come back."

I ordered her a drink. Then I looked at her. She had on a high-necked dress. I had never seen her in one of those. And under each eye, driven in, were 2 pins with glass heads. All you could see were the glass heads of the pins, but the pins were driven down into her face.

"God damn you, still trying to destroy your beauty, eh?"

"No, it's the *fad*, you fool."

"You're crazy."

"I've missed you," she said.

"Is there anybody else?"

"No, there isn't anybody else. Just you. But I'm hustling. It costs ten bucks. But you get it free."

"Pull those pins out."

"No, it's the fad."

"It's making me very unhappy."

"Are you sure?"

"Hell yes, I'm sure."

Cass slowly pulled the pins out and placed them in her purse.

"Why do you haggle your beauty?" I asked. "Why don't you just live with it?"

"Because people think it's all I have. Beauty is nothing, beauty won't stay. You don't know how lucky you are to be ugly, because if people like you then you know it's for something else."

"O.k.," I said, "I'm lucky."

"I don't mean you're ugly. People just think you're ugly. You have a fascinating face."

"Thanks."

We had another drink.

"What are you doing?" she asked.

"Nothing. I can't get on to anything. No interest."

"Me neither. If you were a woman you could hustle."

"I don't think I'd want to make that close a contact with so many strangers. It's wearing."

"You're right, it's wearing, everything is wearing."

We left together. People still stared at Cass on the streets. She was still a beautiful woman, perhaps more beautiful than ever.

We made it to my place and I opened a bottle of wine and we talked. With Cass and I, the talk always came easy. She talked a while and I would listen and then I would talk. Our conversation simply went along without strain. We seemed to discover secrets together. When we discovered a good one Cass would laugh that laugh – only the way she could. It was like joy out of fire. Through the talking we kissed and moved closer together. We became quite heated and decided to go to bed. It was then Cass took off her high-necked dress and I saw it – the ugly jagged scar across her throat. It was large and thick.

"God damn you, woman," I said from the bed, "god damn you, what have you done?"

"I tried it with a broken bottle one night. Don't you like me anymore? Am I still beautiful?"

I pulled her down on the bed and kissed her. She pushed away and laughed, "Some men pay me that ten and then I undress and they don't want to do it. I keep the ten. It's very funny."

"Yes," I said, "I can't stop laughing . . . Cass, bitch, I love you . . . stop destroying yourself; you're the most alive woman I've ever met."

We kissed again. Cass was crying without sound. I could feel the tears. That long black hair lay behind me like a flag of death. We enjoined and made slow and sombre and wonderful love.

In the morning Cass was up making breakfast. She seemed quite calm and happy. She was singing. I stayed in bed and enjoyed her happiness. Finally she came over and shook me, "Up, bastard! Throw some cold water on your face and pecker and come enjoy the feast!"

I drove her to the beach that day. It was a weekday and not yet summer so things were splendidly deserted. Beach bums in rags slept on the lawns above the sand. Others sat on stone benches sharing a lone bottle. The gulls whirled about, mindless yet distracted. Old ladies in their 70's and 80's sat on the benches and discussed selling real estate left behind by husbands long ago killed by the pace and stupidity of survival. For it all, there was peace in the air and we walked about and stretched on the lawns and didn't say much. It simply felt good being together. I bought a couple of sandwiches, some chips and drinks and we sat on the sand eating. Then I held Cass and we slept together about an hour. It was somehow better than love-making. There was a flowing together without tension. When we awakened we drove back to my place and I cooked a dinner. After dinner I suggested to Cass that we shack together. She waited a long time, looking at me, then she slowly said, "No." I drove her back to the bar, bought her a drink and walked out. I found a job as a packer in a factory the next day and the rest of the week went to working. I was too tired to get about much but that Friday night I did get to the West End Bar. I sat and waited for Cass. Hours went by. After I was fairly drunk the bartender said to me, "I'm sorry about your girl friend."

"What is it?" I asked.

"I'm sorry. Didn't you know?"

"No."

"Suicide. She was buried yesterday."

"Buried?" I asked. It seemed as if she would walk through the doorway at any moment. How could she be gone?

"Her sisters buried her."

"A suicide? Mind telling me how?"

"She cut her throat."

"I see. Give me another drink."

I drank until closing time. Cass the most beautiful of 5 sisters, the most beautiful in town. I managed to drive to my place and I kept thinking, I should have *insisted* she stay with me instead of accepting that "no." Everything about her had indicated that she had cared. I had simply been too offhand about it, lazy, too unconcerned. I deserved my death and hers. I was a dog. No, why blame the dogs? I got up and found a bottle of wine and drank from it heavily. Cass the most beautiful girl in town was dead at 20.

Outside somebody honked their automobile horn. They were very loud and persistent. I set the bottle down and screamed out: "GOD DAMN YOU, YOU SON OF A BITCH, SHUT UP!"

The night kept coming on in and there was nothing I could do.

KID STARDUST ON THE PORTERHOUSE

my luck was down again and I was too nervous at this time from excessive wine-drinking; wild-eyed, weak; too depressed to find my usual stop-gap, rest-up job as shipping clerk or stock boy, so I went down to the meat packing plant and walked into the office.

haven't I seen you before? the man asked.

no, I lied.

I'd been there 2 or 3 years before, gone through all the paper work, the medical and so forth, and they had led me down steps, 4 floors down and it had gotten colder and colder and the floors had been covered with a sheen of blood, green floors, green walls. I had been explained my job – which was to push a button and then through this hole in the wall there was a noise like the crushing of fullbacks or elephants falling in lay, and here it came – something dead, a lot of it, bloody, and he showed me, you take it and throw it on the truck and then push the button and another one comes along, then he walked away. when he did I took off my smock, my tin hat, my boots (issued 3 sizes too small) and walked up the stairway and out of there. now I was back, struck down again.

you look a little old for the job.

I want to toughen up. I need hard work, good hard work, I lied.

can you handle it?

I'm nothing but guts. I used to be in the ring. I've fought the best.

oh, yes?

yeah.

umm, I can see by your face. you must have been in some fierce ones.

never mind my face. I had fast hands. still have. I had to take some dives, had to make it look good.

I follow boxing. I don't recall your name.

I fought under another name, Kid Stardust.

Kid Stardust? I don't recall a Kid Stardust.

I fought in South America, Africa, Europe, the islands. I fought in the tank towns. that's why there's all these gaps in my employment records – I don't like to put down boxer because people think I am kidding or lying. I just leave the blanks and to hell with it.

all right, show up for your med. at 9:30 a.m. tomorrow and we'll put you to work. you say you want hard work?

well, if you have something else . . .

no, not right now. you know, you look close to 50 years old. I wonder if I'm doing the right thing? we don't like you people to waste our time.

I'm not people – I'm Kid Stardust.

o.k., kid, he laughed, we'll put you to WORK!

I didn't like the way he said it.

2 days later I walked through the passgate into the wooden shack where I showed an old man my slip with my name on it: Henry Charles Bukowski, Jr., and he sent me on to the loading dock – I was to see Thurman. I walked on over. there were a row of men sitting on a wooden bench and they looked at me as if I were a homosexual or a basket case.

I looked at them with what I imagined to be easy disdain and drawled in my best back-alley fashion:

where's Thurman? I'm supposed to see tha guy.

somebody pointed.

Thurman?

yeah?

I'm workin' for ya.

yeah?

yeah.

he looked at me.

where's yor boots?

boots?

got none, I said.

he reached under the bench and handed me a pair. an old hardened stiff pair. I put them on. same old story: 3 sizes too small. my toes were crushed and bending under.

then he gave me a bloody smock and a tin helmet. I stood there while he lit a cigarette, or as the English might say: while he lighted his cigarette. he threw away the match with a calm and manly flourish.

come on.

they were all Negroes and when I walked up they looked at me as if they were Black Muslims. I was nearly six feet but they were all taller than I, and if not taller then 2 or 3 times as wide.

Charley! Thurman hollered.

Charley, I thought. Charley, just like me. that's nice.

I was already sweating under the tin helmet.

put 'im to WORK!!

jesus christ o jesus christ. what ever happened to the sweet and easy nights? why doesn't this happen to Walter Winchell who believes in the American Way? wasn't I one of the most brilliant students in Anthropology? what happened?

Charley took me over and stood me in front of an empty truck a half block long that stood in the dock.

wait here.

then several of the Black Muslims came running up with wheel-barrows painted a scabby and lumpy white, like white was mixed in with henshit. and each wheel-barrow was loaded with mounds of hams that floated in a thin and watery blood. no, they didn't float in the blood, they sat in it, like lead, like cannonballs, like death.

one of the boys jumped into the truck behind me and the other began throwing the hams at me and I caught them and threw them to the guy behind me who turned and threw the ham into the back of the truck. the hams came fast FAST and they were heavy and they got heavier. as soon as I threw one ham and turned another was already on the way to me through the air. I knew that they were trying to break me. I was soon sweating sweating as if faucets had been turned loose, and my back ached, my wrists ached, my arms hurt, everything hurt and was down to the last impossible ounce of limp energy. I could barely see, barely summon myself to catch one more ham and throw it, one more ham and throw it. I was splashed in blood and kept getting the soft dead heavy FLUMP in my hands, the ham giving a little like a woman's butt, and I'm too weak to talk and say, hey, what the HELL'S the matter with you guys? the hams are coming and I am spinning, nailed, like a man on a cross under a tin helmet, and they keep running up barrows full of hams hams hams and at last they are all empty, and I stand there swaying and breathing the yellow electric light. it was night in hell. well, I always liked night work.

come on!

they took me into another room. up in the air through a large entrance high in the far wall one half a steer, or it might have been a whole one, yes, they were whole steers, thinking of it, all four legs, and one of them came out of the hole on a hook, having just been murdered, and the steer stopped right over me, it hung right over me there on that hook.

they've just killed it, I thought, they've killed the damn thing. how can they tell a man from a steer? how do they know that I am not a steer?

ALL RIGHT – SWING IT!

swing it?

that's right – DANCE WITH IT!

what?

o for christ's sake! GEORGE come here!

George got under the dead steer. he grabbed it. ONE. he ran forward. TWO. he ran backwards. THREE. he ran far forward. the steer was almost parallel to the ground. somebody hit a button and he had it. he had it for the meatmarkets of the world. he had it for the gossiping cranky well-rested stupid housewives of the world at 2 o'clock in the afternoon in their housesmocks, dragging red-stained cigarettes and feeling almost nothing.

they put me under the next steer.

ONE.

TWO.

THREE.

I had it. its dead bones against my living bones, its dead flesh against my living flesh, and the bone and the weight cut in, I thought of operas by Wagner, I thought of cold beer, I thought of sexy cunt sitting across from me on a couch with her legs crossed high and I have a drink in my hand and am slowly and surely talking my way toward and into the blank mind of her body, and Charley hollered HANG HER IN THE TRUCK!

I walked toward the truck. out of the shame of defeat taught me in American schoolyards as a boy I knew that I must not drop the steer to the ground because this would show that I was a coward and not a man and that I didn't therefore deserve much, just sneers and laughs and beatings, you had to be a winner in America, there wasn't any way out, and you had to learn to fight for nothing, don't question, and besides if I dropped the steer I might have to pick it up. besides it will get dirty. I don't want it to get dirty, or rather – they don't want it to get dirty.

I walked it into the truck.

HANG IT!

the hook which hung from the roof was dull as a man's thumb without a fingernail. you let the bottom of the steer slide back and went for the top, you poked the top part against the hook again and again but the hook would not go through. MOTHER ASS!!! it was all gristle and fat, tough, tough.

COME ON! COME ON!

I gave it my last reserve and the hook came through, it was a beautiful sight, a miracle, that hook coming through, that steer hanging there by itself completely off my shoulder, hanging for the housedresses and butchershop gossip.

MOVE ON!

a 285 pound Negro, insolent, sharp, cool, murderous, walked in, hung his meat with a snap, looked down at me.

we stays in line here!

o.k., ace.

I walked on in front of him. another steer was waiting for me. each time I loaded one I was sure that was the last one I could handle but I kept saying

one more
    just one more
    then I
    quit.
    fuck
    it.

they were waiting for me to quit, I could see the eyes, the smiles when they thought I wasn't looking. I didn't want to give them victory. I went for another steer. the player one last lunge of the big-time washed-up player I went for the meat.

2 hours went on then somebody hollered BREAK.

I had made it. a ten minute rest, some coffee, and they'd never make me quit. I walked out behind them toward a lunch-wagon that had drawn up. I could see the steam rising in the night from the coffee; I could see the doughnuts and cigarettes and coffee-cakes and sandwiches under the electric lights.

HEY, YOU!

it was Charley. Charley like me.

yeah, Charley?

before you take your break, get in that truck and move it out and over to stall 18.

it was the truck we had just loaded, the one half a block long. stall 18 was across the yard.

I managed to open the door and get up inside the cab. it had a soft leather seat and the seat felt so good that I knew if I didn't fight it I would soon be asleep. I wasn't a truck driver. I looked down and it looked like a half-dozen gear shifts, brakes, pedals and so forth. I turned the key and managed to start the engine. I played with pedals and gear shifts until the truck started to roll and then I drove it across the yard to stall 18, thinking all the while – by the time I get back the lunch-wagon will be gone. this was tragedy to me, real tragedy. I parked the truck, cut the engine and sat there a minute feeling the soft goodness of that leather seat. then I opened the door and got out. I missed the step or whatever was supposed to be there and I fell to the ground in my bloody smock and christ tin helmet like a man shot. It didn't hurt, I didn't feel it. I got up just in time to see the lunch-wagon driving off through the gate and on down the street. I saw them walking back in toward the dock laughing and lighting cigarettes.

I took off my boots, I took off my smock, I took off my tin helmet and walked to the shack at the yard entrance. I threw the smock, helmet and boots across the counter. the old man looked at me:

what? you quittin' this GOOD job?

tell 'em to mail me my check for 2 hours or tell 'em to stick it up their ass, I don't give a damn!

I walked out. I walked across the street to a Mexican bar and drank a beer and then got a bus to my place. the American schoolyard had beat me again.

LIFE IN A TEXAS WHOREHOUSE

I got off the bus in this place in Texas and it was cold and I was constipated, and you never can tell, it was a very large room, clean, for only $5 a week, and there was a fireplace, and I'd just gotten off my clothes when this old black guy ran into the room and started poking at the fireplace with this long poker. There wasn't any wood in the fireplace and I wondered what he was doing there poking in the fireplace with the poker. Then he'd look at me, grab his pecker and make a sound like, "isssssss, isssssss!" And I thought, well, for some reason he thought I was a punk but since I wasn't, I couldn't help him. Well, I thought, it's the world, that's the way the world works. He circled around a few times with the poker, then left the room.

Then, I climbed into bed. Riding busses always constipated me and also gave me insomnia, which I always had anyhow.

So anyhow the black guy with the poker ran out the door and I stretched out in bed and thought, well, maybe I'll be able to shit in a few days.

The door opened again and here came in a rather well-enjoined creature, female, and she got down on her knees and began scrubbing the woodwork, and her ass just moved and moved and moved as she scrubbed the woodwork.

"How about a nice girl?" she asked me.

"No. Too damned tired. Just got off the bus. All I want to do is sleep."

"A good piece of ass would really help you sleep. Only $5 too."

"I'm too tired."

"It's a nice clean girl."

"Where is she?"

"I'm the girl."

She stood up and faced me.

"Sorry, I'm just too tired, really."

"Only $2."

"No, I'm sorry."

She walked out. Then a few minutes later I heard this man's voice.

"Listen, you mean you couldn't sell him any ass? We gave him our best room for only $5. You mean to say you couldn't sell him any ass?"

"Bruno, I tried! Honesta christ, Bruno, I tried!"

"You filthy bitch!"

I knew the sound. It wasn't a slap. Most good pimps are worried about puffing up the face. They'll slap on the cheek, down by the jaw, stay away from eye and mouth. Bruno must have had a large stable. It was definitely the sound of fists upon head. She screamed and hit the wall and brother Bruno got her another one coming off the wall. Between fists and wall she bounced and screamed and I stretched in bed and thought, well, sometimes life does get interesting, but I don't *quite* want to hear all that. If I had known that was going to happen I would have let her have a little.

Then I slept.

In the morning I got up, dressed. Naturally I dressed. But I still couldn't shit. So I walked out on the street and began looking for photography studios. I walked into the first one.

"Yes, sir? Care to have your photo taken?"

She was a fine-looking redhead and smiled up at me.

"With a face like mine, what would I want my photo taken for? I'm looking for Gloria Westhaven."

"I'm Gloria Westhaven," she said, then crossed her legs and pulled her skirt back. I thought a man had to die to get to heaven.

"What's the matter with you?" I asked her. "You're not Gloria Westhaven. I met Gloria Westhaven on a bus from Los Angeles."

"What's *she* got?"

"Well, I heard that her mother owned a photography studio. I'm trying to find her. Something happened on the bus."

"You mean that nothing happened on the bus."

"I met her. When she got off, she had tears in her eyes. I rode all the way into New Orleans, then got a bus back. No woman ever cried over me before."

"Maybe she was crying about something else."

"I thought so too until all the other passengers began cussing me."

"And all you know is that her mother owns a photography studio?"

"That's all I know."

"All right, listen, I know the editor of the leading newspaper in this town."

"That doesn't surprise me," I said, looking down at her legs.

"O.k., leave me your name and where you're staying. I'll phone him the story only we'll have to change it. You met on an airplane, you see? Love in the air. Now you're separated and lost, you see? And you've flown all the way back from New Orleans and all you know is that her mother owns a photography studio. Got it? We'll have it in M—— K——'s column in tomorrow morning's newspaper. O.k.?"

"O.k.," I said. I took one last look at those legs and walked out as she dialed the phone. Here I was in the 2nd or 3rd largest city in Texas and I owned the town. I walked down to the nearest bar . . .

The place was quite full for that time of day. I sat down on the only empty stool. Well, no, there were two empty stools and one of them was on each side of this big guy. He was around 25, 6-4, a neat 270 pounds. I took one of the stools and ordered a beer. Drained the beer and ordered another one.

"That's the kind of drinking I like to see," said the big guy. "These punks in here, they just come sit around and nurse a beer for hours. I like the way you handle yourself, stranger. Whatta ya do and where ya from?"

"I don't do nothin'," I said, "and I'm from California."

"Got any ideas?"

"No, none. Just floatin' around."

I drank half of my second beer.

"I like you stranger," said the big guy, "so I'm going to confide in you. But I wanna say it real quiet, because even though I'm a big guy, I'm afraid we're a bit outnumbered."

"Shoot," I said, finishing my second beer.

The big guy leaned close to my ear: "Texans stink," he whispered.

I looked around, then quietly nodded my head, Yes.

When he had finished his swing I was under one of the tables the barmaid served at night. I crawled from under, wiped my mouth with a hanky, looked at the whole bar laughing, and walked out . . .

Back at the hotel I couldn't gain entrance. There was a newspaper under the door and the door was open just a slit.

"Hey, lemme in," I said.

"Who are you?" the guy asked.

"I'm in 102. I paid a week's rent here. Bukowski's my name."

"You're not wearin' boots, are ya?"

"Boots? What's that?"

"Rangers."

"Rangers? What's that?"

"Come on in," he said . . .

I hadn't been in my room about ten minutes and I was in bed with all this netting pulled around me. The whole of the bed – and it was a large one with a kind of roof – had all this netting around it. I pulled it all around the outsides and laid down in there with all this netting around me. It made me feel rather queer to do a thing like that, but the way things were going I felt I might as well feel like a queer as anything else. As if that weren't bad enough, there was a key in the door and the door opened. This time it was a short and wide negress with a rather kind-looking face and a tremendously wide ass.

And here was this big kind black girl pulling back my queer-netting and saying, "Honey, it's time for a change of sheets."

And I said, "But I just checked in yesterday."

"Honey, we don't run our sheet-changing on your schedule. Now get your little pink ass out of there and lemme get my job done."

"Uh huh," I said, and leaped out of bed, strictly naked. It didn't seem to affect her.

"You got a nice big bed here, honey," she told me. "You got the best room and bed in this hotel."

"Guess I'm lucky."

She spread those sheets and showed me all that ass. She showed me all that ass and then turned and said, "O.k., honey, your sheets is done. Anything else?"

"Well, I could use 12 or 15 quarts of beer."

"I'll get them for you. Gotta have the money first."

I gave her the money and figured, well, there goes that. I pulled the netting queerly about me and decided to sleep it off. But the big black maid came back and I pulled the netting back and we sat there and talked and drank the beer.

"Tell me about yourself," I said.

She laughed and did. Of course, she had not had an easy life. I don't know how long we drank. Finally she climbed upon that bed and gave me one of the best fucks I ever had . . .

I got up the next day and walked down the street and got the paper and there it was in the popular columnist's column. My name was mentioned. Charles Bukowski, novelist, journalist, traveler. We had met in the air, the lovely lady and I. And she had landed in Texas and I had gone on to New Orleans to cover an assignment. But had flown back, the lovely lady imbedded in my mind. Only knowing her mother owned a photography studio.

I went back to the hotel, got hold of a pint of whiskey and 5 or 6 quarts of beer, and I finally *shit* – what a joyful act! It might have been the column.

I climbed back into the netting. Then the phone rang. It was the extension phone. I reached out and picked it up.

"You have a call, Mr. Bukowski, from the editor of the ——
——. Would you care to answer?"

"All right," I said, "hello."

"Are you Charles Bukowski?"

"Yes."

"What are you doing in a place like that?"

"What do you mean? I've found the people here quite nice."

"That's the worst whorehouse in town. We've been trying to run that place out of town for 15 years. What made you go there?"

"It was cold. I just got into the first place I could. I came in by bus and it was cold."

"You came by air. Remember?"

"I remember."

"All right, I have the lady's place of residence. Do you want it?"

"All right, if it will be all right with you. If you're reluctant, forget it."

"I just don't understand what you're doing living at a place like that."

"All right, you're the editor of the biggest paper in town and you're talking to me over a telephone and I'm in a Texas whorehouse. Now, look, just forget it. The lady was crying or something; it worked on my mind. I'll just take the next bus out of town."

"Wait!"

"Wait, what?"

"I'll give you her address. She read the column. She read between the lines. She phoned me. She wants to see you. I didn't tell her where you were living. We are hospitable people here in Texas."

"Yes, I was in one of your bars the other night. I found out."

"You drink too?"

"I not only drink, I am a drunkard."

"I don't think I ought to give you the lady's address."

"Forget the whole fucking thing then," I said and hung up . . .

The phone rang again.

"You have a call, Mr. Bukowski, from the editor of the ——
——.

"Put him on."

"Look, Mr. Bukowski, we need a follow-up on the story. A lot of people are interested."

"Tell your columnist to use his imagination."

"Look, do you mind me asking what you do for a living?"

"I don't do anything."

"Just travel around on busses and make young ladies cry?"

"Not everybody can do that."

"Look, I'm going to take a chance. I'm going to give you her address. You run over and see her."

"Maybe I'm the one who's taking a chance."

He gave me the address. "Do you want me to tell you how to get there?"

"Never mind. If I can find a whorehouse, I can find hers."

"There's something I don't quite like about you," he said.

"Forget it. If she's a good piece of ass, I'll phone you back."

I hung up . . .

It was a small brown house. An old woman came to the door.

"I'm looking for Charles Bukowski," I told her. "No, pardon me," I said, "I'm looking for one Gloria Westhaven."

"I'm her mother," she said. "Are you the fellow from the airplane?"

"I'm the fellow from the bus."

"Gloria read the column. She knew it was you right away."

"Fine. What do we do now?"

"Oh, come on in."

I came on in.

"Gloria," the old woman hollered.

Gloria walked out. She looked all right, still. Just another one of those healthy Texas redheads.

"Please come in here," she said. "Excuse us, mother."

She walked me into her bedroom but left the door open. We both sat down, far away from each other.

"What do you do?" she asked.

"I'm a writer."

"Oh, how nice! Where've you been published?"

"I haven't been published."

"Then, in a way, you're really not a writer."

"That's right. And I'm living in a whorehouse."

"What?"

"I said, you're right, I'm really not a writer."

"No, I mean the other part."

"I'm living in a whorehouse."

"Do you always live in whorehouses?"

"No."

"How come you're not in the army?"

"I couldn't get past the shrink."

"You're joking."

"I'm glad I'm not."

"You don't want to fight?"

"No."

"They bombed Pearl Harbor."

"I heard."

"You don't want to fight against Adolph Hitler?"

"Not really. I'd rather somebody else do it."

"You're a coward."

"Yes, I am, and it's not that I mind killing a man so much, it's just that I don't like to sleep in barracks with a bunch of guys snoring and then being awakened by some horny damned fool with a bugle, and I don't like to wear that itchy olive drab shit; my skin is very sensitive."

"I'm glad something about you is."

"I am too, but I wish it weren't my skin."

"Maybe you ought to write with your skin."

"Maybe you ought to write with your pussy."

"You're vile. And cowardly. Somebody has to turn back the fascist hordes. I'm engaged to a Lt. in the U.S. Navy and if he were here right now, he'd thrash you good."

"He probably would, and that would only make me more vile."

"At least it would teach you to be a gentleman around ladies."

"I suppose you're right. If I killed Mussolini, would I be a gentleman?"

"Of course."

"I'll sign right up."

"They didn't want you. Remember?"

"I remember."

We both sat there a long time, not saying anything. Then I said, "Look, do you mind if I ask you something?"

"Go ahead," she said.

"Why did you ask me to get off the bus with you? And why did you cry when I didn't?"

"Well, it's your face. You're a little bit ugly, you know."

"Yes, I know."

"Well, it's ugly and tragic too. I just didn't want to let that 'tragic' go. I felt sorry for you, so I cried. How did your face ever get so tragic?"

"O jesus christ," I said, then I got up and walked out.

I walked all the way back to the whorehouse. The guy at the door knew me.

"Hey, champ, where'd you get the lip?"

"Something about Texas."

"Texas? Were you for or against Texas?"

"For Texas, of course."

"You're learnin', champ."

"Yeah, I know."

I walked upstairs and got on the phone and got the guy to dial me the editor of the newspaper.

"This is Bukowski, my friend."

"You met the lady?"

"I met the lady."

"How'd it work out?"

"Fine. Just fine. I must have creamed an hour. Tell your columnist."

I hung up.

I walked downstairs and outside and found the same bar. Nothing had changed. The big guy was still there, an empty barstool on either side of him. I sat down and ordered 2 beers. I drank the first one straight down. Then drank half the other.

"I remember you," said the big guy, "what was it about you?"

"Skin. Sensitive."

"You remember me?" he asked.

"I remember you."

"I thought you'd never be back."

"I'm back. Let's play the little game."

"We don't play games here in Texas, stranger."

"Yeah?"

"You still think Texans stink?"

"Some of them do."

There I was back under the table. I got out from under, stood up and walked out. I walked back to the whorehouse.

The next day in the paper it said that the Romance had failed. I had flown out of town to New Orleans. I got my stuff together and walked down to the bus station. I got to New Orleans, got a legitimate room and sat around. I saved the newspaper clippings for a couple of weeks, then threw them away. Wouldn't you have?

SIX INCHES

The first three months of my marriage to Sarah were acceptable but I'd say a little after that our troubles began. She was a good cook, and for the first time in years I was eating well. I began to put on weight. And Sarah began to make remarks.

"Ah, Henry, you're beginning to look like a turkey they're plumping up for Thanksgiving."

"Ats right, baby," I told her.

I was a shipping clerk in an auto parts warehouse and the pay was hardly sufficient. My only joys were eating, drinking beer and going to bed with Sarah. Not exactly a rounded life but a man had to take what he could get. Sarah was plenty. Everything about her spelled S–E–X. I had really gotten to know her at a Christmas party for the employees at the warehouse. Sarah was a secretary there. I noticed none of the fellows got near her at the party and I couldn't understand it. I had never seen a sexier woman and she didn't act the fool either. I got close to her and we drank and talked. She was beautiful. There was something odd about her eyes, though. They just kept looking into you and the eyelids didn't seem to blink. When she went to the restroom I walked over to Harry the truckdriver.

"Listen, Harry," I asked, "how come none of the boys make a play for Sarah?"

"She's a witch, man, a real witch. Stay away."

"There's no such thing as witches, Harry. All that has been disproven. All those women they burned at the stake in the old days, it was a cruel and a horrible mistake. There's no such thing as a witch."

"Well, maybe they did burn a lot of women wrongly, I can't say. But this bitch is a witch, take it from me."

"All she needs, Harry, is understanding."

"All she needs," said Harry, "is a victim."

"How do you know?"

"Facts," said Harry. "Two guys here. Manny, a salesman. And Lincoln, a clerk."

"What happened?"

"They just kind of disappeared in front of our eyes, only so slowly – you could see them going, vanishing . . ."

"What do you mean?"

"I don't want to talk about it. You'd think I was crazy."

Harry walked off. Then Sarah came out of the lady's room. She looked beautiful.

"What did Harry tell you about me?" she asked.

"How did you know I was talking to Harry?"

"I know," she said.

"He didn't say much."

"Whatever he said, forget it. It's bullshit. I won't let him have any and he's jealous. He likes to badmouth people."

"I'm not concerned with Harry's opinions," I told her.

"You and I are going to make it, Henry," she said.

She went to my apartment with me after the party and I'm telling you I've never been laid like that. She was the woman of all women. It was a month or so later that we were married. She quit her job right off, but I didn't say anything because I was so glad to have her. Sarah made her own clothes, did her own hair. She was a remarkable woman. Very remarkable.

But as I said, it was after about 3 months that she began making these remarks about my weight. At first they were just genial little remarks, then she began to get scornful about it. I came home one night and she said, "Take off your damned clothes!"

"What, my darling?"

"You heard me, bastard! Strip!"

Sarah was a little different then than I had ever seen her. I took off my clothes and underwear and threw them on the couch. She stared at me.

"Awful," she said, "what a lot of shit!"

"What, dear?"

"I said you look just like a big tub of shit!"

"Listen, honey, what's wrong? You got the rag on tonight?"

"Shut up! Look at that stuff hanging at your sides!"

She was right. There seemed to be a little pouch of fat on each side, hanging just above the hips. Then she doubled up her fists and hit me hard several times on each of the pouches.

"We've got to punch that shit! Break up the fat tissues, the cells . . ."

She punched me again, several times.

"Ow! Baby, that hurts!!"

"Good! Now, hit yourself!"

"Hit myself?"

"Go ahead, damn you!"

I hit myself several times, quite hard. When I was finished the things were still there, though now they looked quite red.

"We're going to get that shit off of you," she told me.

I figured that it was love and decided to cooperate . . .

Sarah began counting my calories. She took away my fried foods, bread and potatoes, salad dressing, but I kept my beer. I had to show her who was wearing the pants in our family.

"No, damn it," I said, "I won't give up my beer. I love you very much but the beer stays!"

"All right," said Sarah, "we'll make it work anyway."

"Make what work?"

"I mean, get that shit off of you, get you down to a desirable size."

"And what's a desirable size?" I asked.

"You'll see."

Each night when I got home she'd ask me the same question.

"Did you punch your sides today?"

"Oh, hell yes!"

"How many times?"

"400 punches on both sides, hard."

I would walk down the streets punching at my sides. People looked at me but it didn't matter after a while because I knew that I was accomplishing something and they weren't . . .

* * *

Things were working, marvelously. I came down from 225 to 197. Then from 197 to 184. I felt ten years younger. People remarked about how good I looked. Everybody except Harry the truck driver. Of course, he was just jealous because he never got into Sarah's panties. *His* tough shit.

One night on the scales I was down to 179.

I said to Sarah, "Don't you think we've come down enough? Look at me!"

The things on my sides were long gone. My belly hung in. My cheeks looked as if I were sucking them in.

"According to the charts," said Sarah, "according to my charts, you've not yet reached a desirable size."

"Look," I told her, "I'm six feet tall. What is the desirable weight?"

And then Sarah answered me quite strangely:

"I didn't say 'desirable weight,' I said, 'desirable size.' This is the New Age, the Atomic Age, the Space Age, and most important the Age of Overpopulation. I am the Savior of the World. I have the answer to the Overpopulation Explosion. Let others work on Pollution. Solving Overpopulation is the root; it will solve Pollution and many other things too."

"What the hell are you talking about?" I asked, ripping the cap off a bottle of beer.

"Don't worry about it," she answered, "you'll find out."

Then I began to notice, as I stepped on the scales, that although I was still losing weight I didn't seem to be getting any thinner. It was strange. And then I noticed that my pantscuffs were hanging down over my shoes – ever so slightly, and that my shirtcuffs were hanging down a bit over my wrists. When I drove to work I noticed that the steering wheel seemed further away. I had to pull the car seat up a notch.

One night I got on the scales.

155.

"Look here, Sarah."

"Yes, darling?"

"There's something I don't understand."

"What?"

"I seem to be *shrinking*."

"Shrinking?"

"Yes, shrinking."

"Oh, you fool! That's incredible! How can a man shrink? Do you really think that your diet is shrinking your bones? Bones don't melt! Reduction of calories only reduces fat. Don't be an idiot! Shrinking? Impossible!"

Then she laughed.

"All right," I said, "come here. Here's a pencil. Now I'm gonna stand against this wall. My mother used to do this with me as a kid when I was growing. Now put a line right there on the wall where the pencil hits after you place it straight across the top of my head."

"All right, silly," she said.

She drew the line.

A week later I was down to 131. It was happening faster and faster.

"Come here, Sarah."

"Yes, silly boy."

"Now, draw the line."

She drew the line. I turned around.

"Now see here, I've lost 24 pounds and 8 inches in the last week. I'm melting away! I'm now five feet two. This is madness! Madness! I've had enough. I've caught you cutting off my pants legs, my shirt sleeves. It won't work. I'm going to begin eating again. I think that you *are* some kind of witch!"

"Silly boy . . ."

It was soon after that the boss called me into the office.

I climbed into the chair across from his desk.

"Henry Markson Jones II?"

"Yes, sir?"

"You *are* Henry Markson Jones II?"

"Of course, sir."

"Well, Jones, we've been watching you carefully. I'm afraid you just don't fit this job anymore. We hate to see you go like this . . . I mean, we hate to let you go like this, but . . .

"Look, sir, I always do my best."

"We know you do, Jones, but you're just not doing a man's job back there anymore."

He let me go. Of course, I knew that I would get my unemployment compensation. But I thought it was small of him to let me go like that . . .

* * *

I stayed home with Sarah. Which made it worse – she fed me. It got so I couldn't reach the refrigerator door anymore. And then she put me on a small silver chain.

Soon I was two feet tall. I had to use a potty chair to shit. But she still let me have my beer, as promised.

"Ah, my little pet," she said, "you're so small and cute!"

Even our love life was ended. Everything had melted in proportion. I mounted her but after a while she'd just pick me off and laugh.

"Ah, you tried, my little duck!"

"I'm *not* a duck, I'm a man!"

"Oh my little sweet man-y man!"

She picked me up and kissed me with her red lips . . .

Sarah got me down to being 6 inches tall. She carried me to the store in her purse. I could look out at the people through the little air holes she had poked in her purse. I will say one thing for the woman. She still allowed me to have my beer. I drank it by the thimble. A quart would last me a month. In the old days it was gone in 45 minutes. I was resigned. I knew that if she wished to do so she could make me vanish entirely. Better 6 inches than nothing. Even a little life becomes very dear when you near the end of life. So, I amused Sarah. It was all I could do. She made me little clothes and shoes and put me on top of the radio and turned on the music and said, "Dance, little one! Dance, my dunce! Dance, my fool!"

Well, I couldn't collect my unemployment compensation so I danced on top of the radio while she clapped her hands and laughed.

You know, spiders frightened me terribly and flies were the size of giant eagles, and if a cat ever caught me it would torture me like a small mouse. But life was still dear to me. I danced and sang and hung on. No matter how little a man has he will find that he will always settle for less. When I shit on the rug I would get spanked. Sarah put little pieces of paper around and I shit on them. And I ripped off little pieces of that paper to wipe my butt with. It felt like cardboard. I got hemorrhoids. Couldn't sleep nights. Feelings of inferiority, of being trapped. Paranoia? Anyhow, I felt good when I sang and danced and Sarah let me have my beer. She kept me at an exact six inches for some reason. What the reason was, it was beyond me. As almost everything else was beyond me.

I made up songs for Sarah, that's what I called them: Songs for Sarah:

"o, I'm just a little snot,
that's all right until I get hot,
then there's nothing to stick it in
except the fucking head of a pin!"

Sarah would clap her hands and laugh.

"if ya wanna be an admir in the queen's navy
just be a clark for the fuckin' nark,
grow 6 inches tall and when the Queen goes to pee
you can peek up inter drippin' pussy . . ."

And Sarah would clap her hands and laugh. Well, that was all right. It had to be . . .

But one night something very disgusting happened. I was singing and dancing and Sarah was on the bed, naked, clapping her hands, drinking wine and laughing. I was putting on a good show. One of my best. But, as always, the top of the radio got hot and started burning my feet. I couldn't stand it anymore.

"Look, baby," I said, "I've had it. Take me down. Gimme a beer. No wine. You drink that cheapass wine. Gimme a thimble of that good beer."

"Sure, sweetie," she said, "you put on a wonderful show tonight. If Manny and Lincoln had acted as nice as you, they'd be here tonight. But they didn't sing or dance, they brooded. And worst of all, they objected to the Final Act."

"And what was the Final Act?" I asked.

"Now, sweetie, just drink your beer and relax. I want you to enjoy the Final Act. You are evidently a much more talented person than Manny or Lincoln. I do believe that we can have the Culmination of the Opposites."

"O, hell yes," I said, draining my beer. "Now give me a refill. And just what is the Culmination of the Opposites?"

"Enjoy your beer, little sweetie, you'll know soon enough."

I finished my beer and then the disgusting thing happened, a most disgusting thing. Sarah picked me up and placed me down between her legs, which she spread open just a bit. Then I was facing a forest of hair. I hardened my back and neck muscles, sensing what was to come. I was jammed into darkness and stench. I heard Sarah moan. Then Sarah began to move me slowly back and forth. As I said, the stench was unbearable, and it was difficult to breathe, but somehow there was air in there – various side-pockets and drafts of oxygen. Now and then my head, the top of my head bumped The Man in the Boat and then Sarah would let out an extra-illuminated moan.

Sarah began moving me faster and faster. My skin began to burn, it became harder to breathe; the stench became worse. I could hear her panting. It occurred to me that the sooner I ended the thing the less I would suffer. Each time I was rammed forward I would arch my back and neck, tilt everything of me into this hooking curve of a thing, bumping The Man in the Boat.

Suddenly I was ripped out of that terrible tunnel. Sarah held me up to her face.

"Come, you damned fiend of a thing! Come!" she demanded.

Sarah was totally drunk on wine and passion. I felt myself being rushed back into the tunnel. She worked me rapidly back and forth. Then suddenly I sucked air into my lungs to increase my size and then I gathered saliva into my jaws and spit it out – once, twice, 3 times, 4, 5, six times, then I stopped ... The stench increased beyond all imagination and then, at last, I was lifted out into the air.

Sarah lifted me into the lamplight and began kissing me all over my head and shoulders.

"O, my darling! o, my precious little cock! I love you!"

Then she kissed me with those horrible red and painted lips. I vomited. Then, spent in a swoon of wine and passion, she placed me between her breasts. I rested there and listened to her heart beat. She had taken me off of her damned leash, that silver chain, but it didn't matter. I was hardly free. One of her massive breasts had fallen to one side and I seemed to be right over the heart. The heart of the witch. If I were the answer to the Population Explosion then why hadn't she used me as more than a thing of entertainment, a sexual toy? I stretched out there and listened to that heart. I decided that she was a witch. Then I glanced up. Do you know what I saw? A most amazing thing. Up in that little crevice below the headboard. A hat pin. Yes, a hat pin, long, with one of those round purple glass things at the end of it. I walked up between her breasts, climbed her throat, got up on her chin (after much trouble), then walked quietly across her lips, and then she stirred a bit as I almost fell and had to grab to a nostril for support. Very slowly I got up by the right eye – her head was tilted slightly to the left – and then I was up on the forehead, having gone past the temple, and I was up into the hair – very difficult, wading through. Then I stood and stretched – reached up and just managed to grab the hat pin. Coming down was faster but more treacherous. I almost lost my balance several times, carrying that hat pin. One fall and it was over. I laughed several times because it was so ridiculous. The outcome of an office party for the gang, Merry Christmas.

Then I was down under that massive breast again. I laid the hat pin down and listened again. I listened for the exact sound of the heart. I determined it to be at a spot exactly below a small brown birthmark. Then I stood up. I picked up the hat pin with its purple glass end, beautiful in the lamplight. And I thought, will it work? I was 6 inches tall and I judged the hat pin to be half again longer than I. 9 inches. The heart seemed closer than that.

I lifted the pin and plunged it in. Just below the birthmark.

Sarah rolled and convulsed. I held to the hat pin. She almost threw me to the floor – which by comparative size seemed a thousand feet or more and would have killed me. I hung on. Her lips formed an odd sound.

Then she seemed to quiver all over like a woman freezing.

I reached up and jammed the remaining 3 inches of the pin down into her chest until the beautiful purple glass head of the pin was up against her skin.

Then Sarah was still. I listened.

I heard the heart, one two, one two, one two, one two, one two, one . . .

It stopped.

And then with my little killer's hands, I clutched and gripped the bedsheet and made my way to the floor. I was 6 inches tall and real and frightened and hungry. I found a hole in one of the bedroom screens which faced east and ran from ceiling to floor. I grabbed at the branch of a bush, climbed on, clambered along the branch to the inside of the bush. Nobody knew that Sarah was dead but I. But that had no realistic good. If I were to go on, I would have to have something to eat. But I couldn't help wondering how my case would be evolved in a court of law? Was I guilty? I ripped off a leaf and tried to eat it. No good. Hardly.

Then I saw the lady in the court to the south set out a plate of catfood for her cat. I crawled out of the bush and worked my way toward the catfood, watching for animals and movements. It tasted worse than anything I had ever eaten but I had no choice. I ate all the catfood I could – death tasted worse. Then I walked over to the bush and climbed back into it.

There I was, 6 inches tall, the answer to The Population Explosion, hanging in a bush with a bellyful of catfood.

There are details I don't want to bore you with. Escapes from cats and dogs and rats. Feeling myself growing bit by bit. Watching them carry Sarah's body out of there. Going in there and finding myself too small, still, to open the refrigerator door.

The day the cat almost caught me as I ate at his bowl. I had to break away.

I was then 8 or ten inches tall. I was growing. I even scared pigeons. When you scare pigeons you know that you are getting there. I simply ran down the street one day, hiding along the shadows of buildings and down beneath hedges and the like. I kept running and hiding until I got outside a supermarket and I hid under a newspaper stand just outside the entrance to the store. Then, as a big woman walked up and the electric door opened, I walked in behind her. One of the clerks at a checkstand looked up as I walked in behind the woman:

"Hey, what the hell's that?"

"What?" a customer asked him.

"I thought I saw something," said the clerk, "maybe not. I hope not."

I somehow sneaked back to the storeroom without being seen. I hid behind some cartons of baked beans. That night I came out and had a fine feed. Potato salad, pickles, ham on rye, potato chips and beer, plenty of beer. It became about the same routine. Each day, all day, I hid in the storeroom and at night I'd come out and have a party. But I was growing and hiding was becoming more difficult. I got to watching the manager put the money in the safe each night. He was the last to leave. I counted the pauses as he put the money away each night. It seemed to be – 7 right, 6 left, 4 right, 6 left, 3 right, open. I went over to the safe each night and tried the numbers. I had to make a kind of stairway out of empty cartons in order to get up to the dial. It didn't seem to work but I kept trying. Each night, I mean. Meanwhile I was growing fast. Perhaps I was 3 feet tall. The store had a small clothing section and I had to keep going into the larger sizes. The population problem was returning. Then one night the safe opened. I had 23 thousand dollars in cash. I must have hit them the night before banking time. I took the key the manager used in order to get out without the burglar alarm ringing. Then I walked down the street and got a week's worth of lodging at the Sunset Motel. I told the lady I worked as a midget in the movies. It just seemed to bore her.

"No television or loud noises after ten p.m. That's our rule here."

She took my money, gave me a receipt and closed her door.

The key said room 103. I hadn't even looked at the room. The doors said 98, 99, 100, 101, I was walking north toward the Hollywood Hills, toward those mountains behind them, with the great and golden light of the Lord shining upon me, growing.

THE FUCK MACHINE

it was a hot night in Tony's. you didn't even think of fucking. just drink cool beer. Tony coasted a couple down to me and Indian Mike, and Mike had the money out. I let him buy the first round. Tony rang it up, bored, looked around – 5 or six others staring into their beers. dolts. so Tony walked down to us.

"what's new, Tony?" I asked.

"ah, shit," said Tony.

"at ain't new."

"shit," said Tony.

"ah shit," said Indian Mike.

we drank at our beers.

"what do you think of the moon?" I asked Tony.

"shit," said Tony.

"yeah," said Indian Mike, "guy's an asshole on earth he's an asshole on the moon. makes no difference."

"they say there's probably no life on Mars," I said.

"so what?" asked Tony.

"oh shit," I said. "2 more beers."

Tony coasted them down, then walked down for his money. rang it up. walked back. "shit it's hot. I wish I were deader than yesterday's Kotex."

"where do men go when they die, Tony?"

"shit. who cares?"

"don't you believe in the Human Spirit?"

"a bagga bullshit!"

"how about Che? Joan of Arc? Billy the Kid? all those?"

"a bagga bullshit!"

we drank our beers, thinking about it.

"look," I said, "I gotta take a piss."

I walked back to the urinal and there, as usual, was Petey the Owl.

I took it out and began to piss.

"you sure got a little dick," he told me.

"when I'm pissing or meditating, yeh. but I'm what you call the super-stretch type. when I'm ready to go, each inch I got now equals six."

"that's good then, if you ain't lying. cause I see two inches showing."

"I just show the head."

"I'll give you a dollar to suck your cock."

"that ain't much."

"you're showing more than head. you're showing every bit of string you got."

"fuck you, Pete."

"you'll be back when you run out of beer money."

I walked back on out.

"2 more beers," I ordered.

Tony went through his routine. came back.

"it's so hot, I think I'm going crazy," he said.

"the heat just makes you realize your true self," I told Tony.

"wait a minute! you calling me a nut?"

"most of us are. but it's kept a secret."

"all right, saying your bullshit is straight, how many sane men are there on earth? are there any?"

"a few."

"how many?"

"out of the billions?"

"yeh. yeh."

"well, I'd say 5 or 6."

"5 or 6?" said Indian Mike. "well, suck my cock!"

"look," said Tony. "how do you *know* I'm nuts? how do we get away with it?"

"well, since we are all insane there are only a few to control us, far too few, so they just let us run around insane. that's all they can do at this moment. for a while I thought they might find some place to live in outer space while they destroyed us. but now I know that the insane control space also."

"how do you know?"

"because they planted an American flag on the moon."

"suppose the Russians had planted a Russian flag on the moon?"

"same thing," I said.

"then you're impartial?" Tony asked.

"I am impartial to all degrees of madness."

we became quiet. kept drinking. and Tony too, began pouring himself scotch and waters. he *could*. he owned the place.

"jesus, it's hot," said Tony.

"shit, yeh," said Indian Mike.

then Tony began talking. "insanity," said Tony, "ya know, there's something very insane going on at this *very* minute!"

"sure," I said.

"no, no, no . . . I mean right HERE at my place!"

"yeh?"

"yeh. it's so crazy, sometimes I get scared."

"tell me all about it, Tony," I said, always ready for somebody else's bullshit.

Tony leaned real close. "I know a guy's got a fuckmachine. no crazy sex magazine shit. like you see in the ads. hot water bottles with replaceable cornbeef pussies, all that nonsense. this guy has really put it together. a German scientist, we got to him, I mean our govt. did before the Russians could grab him. now keep it quiet."

"sure, Tony, sure . . ."

"Von Brashlitz. our govt. tried to get him interested in SPACE. no go. a brilliant old guy, but he just has this FUCK MACHINE in mind. at the same time he thinks he's some kind of an artist, calls himself Michelangelo at times . . . they pensioned him off at $500.00 a month to kind of keep him alive enough to stay outa the nuthouses. they watched him a while, then got a little bored or forgot, but they kept the checks coming, and now and then an agent would talk to him ten or twenty minutes a month, write a report that he was still crazy, then leave. so he just drifted around from town to town, dragging this big red trunk behind him. finally one night he come in here and begins drinking. tells me that he is just a tired old man, needs a real quiet place to do his research. I kept putting him off. lotta nuts come in here, ya know."

"yeh," I said.

"then, man, he kept getting drunker and drunker, and he laid it down to me. he had designed a mechanical woman who could give a man a better fuck than any woman created throughout the centuries! plus no kotex, no shit, no arguments!"

"I been looking," I said, "for a woman like that all my life."

Tony laughed. "every man has. I thought he was crazy, of course, until one night after closing I went down to his rooming house with him and he took the FUCK MACHINE out of the red trunk."

"and?"

"it was like going to heaven before you died."

"let me guess the rest," I asked Tony.

"guess."

"Von Brashlitz and his FUCK MACHINE are upstairs at your place right now."

"uh huh," said Tony.

"how much?"

"twenty bucks a piece."

"20 bucks to fuck a machine?"

"he's outdone whatever Created us. you'll see."

"Petey the Owl will blow me for a buck."

"Petey the Owl is o.k. but he ain't no invention that beats the gods."

I shoved over my 20.

"so help me, Tony, if this is some crazy kind of hot-weather gag, you've lost your best customer!"

"like you said earlier, we're all crazy anyhow. it's up to you."

"right," I said.

"right," said Indian Mike, "and here's my 20."

"I only get 50 percent, ya gotta understand. the rest goes to Von Brashlitz. 500 buck pension ain't much with inflation and taxes, and Von B. drinks schnapps like crazy."

"let's make it," I said, "you've got 40 bucks. where's this immortal FUCK MACHINE?"

Tony lifted a partition of the bar, said, "come through here. take the stairway to the back rear. just go up there, knock, say, 'Tony sent us'."

"any door #?"

"door #69."

"oh, hell yes," I said, "what else?"

"oh hell yes," said Tony. "get your balls."

we found the stairway. walked up. "Tony will do anything for a gag," I said.

we walked along. there it was: door #69.

I knocked: "Tony sent us."

"ah, do come in, gentlemen!"

here was this old horny-looking freak, glass of schnapps in his hand, double-lensed glasses. just like the old-time movies. he appeared to be having a visitor, a young thing, almost too young, looking flimsy and strong at the same time.

she crossed her legs, flashing all the bit: nylon knees, nylon thighs, and just that tiny part there where the long stockings ended and just that touch of flesh began. she was *all* ass and breast, nylon legs, cleanblue laughing eyes. . . .

"gentlemen, – my daughter, Tanya . . ."

"what?"

"ah, yes, I know, I am so . . . old . . . but like the myth of the black man with the ever-huge cock, there is also the myth of dirty old Germans who never stop fucking. you may believe what you wish to. this is my daughter, Tanya, anyhow . . ."

"hello, boys," she laughed.

then we all looked toward the door which was labeled: FUCK MACHINE STORAGE ROOM.

he finished off his schnapps.

"and so . . . you boys came over for the best FUCK ever, ya?"

"Daddy!" said Tanya, "must you always be so *crude*?"

Tanya recrossed her legs, higher this time, and I almost came.

then the professor finished another schnapps, then got up and walked over to the door labeled FUCK MACHINE STORAGE ROOM. he turned and smiled at us, then very slowly opened the door. he walked on in and came out rolling this thing on what looked like a hospital bed on wheels.

it was NAKED, a clod of metal.

the prof rolled the damn thing right out in front of us, then began humming some rotten song, probably something from the German.

a clod of metal with this hole in the center. the professor had an oil can in his hand, poked it into the hole and began punching in quite a quantity of this oil. meanwhile humming this insane German song.

he kept punching the oil in, then looked back over his shoulder and said, "nice, ya?" then he went back to work, pumping in the oil.

Indian Mike looked at me, tried to laugh, said, "god damn . . . we've been taken again!"

"yeah," I said, "it seems like it's been 5 years since I been laid, but I'll be damned if I'll stick my cock into that mound of hard lead!"

Von Brashlitz laughed. walked over to his liquor cabinet, found another 5th. of schnapps, poured a goody, sat down facing us.

"as we in Germany began knowing that the war was lost, and the net began to tighten – down to the final battle of Berlin – we knew that the war had taken on a new essence – the real war then became who was to grab the most German scientists. if Russia got the most German scientists or America – *those* were the ones who were going to get to the moon first, Mars first . . . *anything* first. well, I don't know how it really came out . . . numerically or in terms of scientific brain-power. I only know that the Americans got to me first, snapped me up, took me away in a car, gave me a drink, put pistols to my head, made promises, talked madly. I signed everything . . ."

"all right," I said, "so much for history. but I'm still not going to stick my dick, my poor little dick into that hunk of sheetmetal or whatever it is! Hitler must have really been a madman to nursemaid you. I wish the Russians had gotten to your ass first! I want my 20 bucks back!"

Von Brashlitz laughed, "heeeheeeheeehe . . . it is just my little joke, nein? heeheeeheeeheeee!"

he shoved that mound of lead back into the closet. slammed the door. "oh, heheeehe!" had a bit more schnapps.

Von B. poured another schnapps. he really put them down. "gentlemen, I am an *artist* and an inventor! my FUCK MACHINE is really my daughter, Tanya . . ."

"more little jokes, Von?" I asked.

"joke nothing! Tanya! go over and sit in the gentleman's lap!"

Tanya laughed, got up, walked over and sat in my lap. a FUCK MACHINE? I couldn't believe it! her skin was skin, or so it seemed, and her tongue as it worked into my mouth as we kissed, it was not mechanical – each movement was different, responding to my own.

I was busy at it, ripping her blouse from her breasts, working at her panties, hotter than I had been in years, and then we were tangled; we somehow got to standing – and I took her standing up, my hands ripping at her long blonde hair, bending her head back, then reaching down, spreading her asshole as I pumped, she came – I could feel the throbbing, and I joined.

it was the best fuck I had *ever* had!

Tanya went to the bathroom, cleaned-up and showered, dressed-up again for Indian Mike. I guess.

"man's greatest invention," Von Brashlitz said quite seriously.

he was quite right.

then Tanya came out and sat on MY lap.

"NO! NO! TANYA! IT'S THE OTHER MAN'S TURN! YOU JUST FINISHED FUCKING THAT ONE!"

she didn't seem to hear. and it was strange, even for a FUCK MACHINE, because, really, I had never been a very good lover.

"do you love me?" she asked.

"yes."

"I love you. and I am so happy. and . . . I'm not supposed to be alive. you know that, don't you?"

"I love you, Tanya. that's all that I know."

"god damn it!" screamed the old man, "this FUCKING MACHINE!" he walked over to this varnished box with the word TANYA printed on the side. there were these little wires sprouting out of it; there were dials, and needles that quivered, and many colors, lights that blinked on and off, things that ticked . . . Von B. was the craziest pimp I had ever met. he kept playing with the dials, then he looked at Tanya:

"25 YEARS! damn near a lifetime to build you! I even had to hide you from HITLER! and now . . . you try to turn into a mere and ordinary bitch!"

"I'm not 25," said Tanya, "I'm 24."

"you see? you see? just like a common bitch!"

he went back to his dials.

"you've put on a different shade of lipstick," I said to Tanya.

"you like it?"

"oh, yes!"

she leaned over and kissed me.

Von B. kept playing with his dials. I felt that he would win.

Von Brashlitz turned to Indian Mike. "it's just a minor kink in the machine. trust me. I'll get it straight in a minute, ya?"

"I hope so," said Indian Mike, "I've got 14 inches waiting and am twenty bucks down.

"I love you," Tanya told me, "I will never fuck any other man. if I can't have you, I won't have anybody."

"I'll forgive you, Tanya, for anything that you do."

the prof was getting pissed. he kept turning the dials but nothing was happening. "TANYA! it is time for you to FUCK the OTHER man! I am ... getting tired ... must have a bit of schnapps ... be off to sleep ... Tanya ..."

"ah," said Tanya, "you rotten old fuck! you and your schnapps, and then nibbling at my tits all night, so I can't even sleep! while you can't even raise a decent hard! you're disgusting!"

"VAS?"

"I SAID, 'YOU CAN'T EVEN RAISE A DECENT HARD!'"

"you, Tanya, will pay for this! you are *my* creation, I am not yours!"

he kept turning his magic knobs. I mean, on the machine. he was quite angry, and you could see that, somehow, the anger gave him a vital brilliance beyond himself. "just wait, Mike. all I have to do is to adjust the electronics! wait! *A short! I see it!*"

then he leaped up. this guy they had saved from the Russians.

he looked at Indian Mike. "it's straight now! the machine is in order! have fun!"

then he walked over to his schnapps bottle, poured another goody, sat down to watch.

Tanya got off of my lap and walked over to Indian Mike. I watched Tanya and Indian Mike embrace.

Tanya worked Indian Mike's zipper down, got his cock out, and man he had plenty of cock! he'd said 14 inches but it looked more like 20.

then Tanya put both her hands around Mike's cock.

he moaned in glory.

then she ripped the whole cock right out of and off of his body. threw it to the side.

I saw the thing roll along the rug like an insane sausage, dribbling little sad trailets of blood. it rolled up against a wall, then stayed there like something with a head but no legs and no place to go ... which was true enough.

next, here came the BALLS flying through the air. a heavy, looping sight. they simply landed upon the center of the rug and didn't know what to do but bleed.

so, they bled.

Von Brashlitz, the hero of the America-Russ invasion took a hard look at what was left of Indian Mike, my old beer-drinking buddy, very red on the floor, flowing from the center – Von B. took the highroad, down the stairway . . .

room 69 had done everything but that.

and then I asked her: "Tanya, the heat will be here very quickly. shall we dedicate the room number to our love?"

"of course, my love!"

we made it, just in time, and the stupid heat ran in.

one of the learned then pronounced Indian Mike dead.

and since Von B. was a kind of U.S. Govt. product, there was a hell of a lot of people around – various chickenshit officials – firemen, reporters, the cops, the inventor, the C.I.A., the F.B.I. and various other forms of human shit.

Tanya came over and sat in my lap. "they will kill me now. please try not to be sad."

I didn't answer.

then Von Brashlitz was screaming, pointing to Tanya – "I TELL YOU, GENTLEMEN, SHE HAS NO FEELING! I SAVED THE DAMN THING FROM HITLER! I tell you, it is nothing but a MACHINE!"

they all just stood there. nobody believed Von B.

it was simply the most beautiful machine, and so-called woman, they had ever seen.

"Oh shit! you idiots! every woman is a fucking machine, can't you see that? they play for the highest bidder! THERE IS NO SUCH THING AS LOVE! THAT IS A FAIRY-TALE MIRAGE LIKE CHRISTMAS!"

they still wouldn't believe.

"THIS is only a machine! have no FEAR! WATCH!"

Von Brashlitz grabbed one of Tanya's arms.

ripped it completely off of her body.

and inside – inside the hole of her shoulder – you could see it – there was nothing but wire and tubes – coiled and running things – plus some minor substance that faintly resembled blood.

I saw Tanya standing there with this coil of wire hanging from her shoulder, where the arm used to be. she looked at me:

"please, for *me* too! I asked you to try not to be too sad."

I watched as they ganged her, and ripped and raped and tore.

I couldn't help it. I put my head down between my legs and cried . . .

also, Indian Mike never got his 20 bucks worth.

* * *

some months went by. I never went back to the bar. there was a trial but the govt. exonerated Von B. and his machine. I moved to another town. far away. and one day sitting in a barbershop, I picked up this sex mag. here was an ad: "Blow up your own little dolly! $29.95. Resistant rubber material, *very* durable. Chains and whips included in package. A bikini, bras. panties. 2 wigs, lipstick and small jar of love-potion included. Von Brashlitz Co."

I sent him a money order. some box number in Mass. he had moved too.

the package arrived in about 3 weeks. very embarrassing. I didn't have a bicycle pump, and then I got the hots when I took the thing out of the package. I had to go down to the corner gas station and use their air hose.

it looked better as it blew up. big tits. big ass.

"whatcha got there, pal?" the gas station man asked me.

"look, man, I'm just borrowing a little air. don't I buy a lot of gas here, huh?"

"o.k., that's o.k., you can have the air. I just damn well can't help wondering whatcha got there . . ."

"just forget it!" I said.

"JESUS! look at those TITS!"

"I AM looking, asshole!"

I left him there with his tongue hanging out, then threw her over my shoulder and made it back to my place. I carried her into the bedroom.

the big question was yet to come?

I spread the legs and looked for some kind of opening.

Von B. hadn't completely slipped.

I climbed on top and began kissing that rubber mouth. now and then I reached for one of the giant rubber tits and sucked upon it. I had put a yellow wig on her and rubbed the love-potion all over my cock. it didn't take much love-potion. maybe he'd sent a year's worth.

I kissed her passionately behind the ears, stuck my finger up her ass, kept pumping. then I leaped off, chained her arms behind her back, there was this little lock and key and then I whipped her ass good with the leather thongs.

god, I gotta be nuts! I thought.

then I flipped her over and put it back in. humped and humped. frankly, it was rather boring. I imagined male dogs screwing female cats; I imagined 2 people fucking through the air as they jumped from the Empire State Building. I imagined a pussy as large as an octopus, crawling toward me, wet and stinking and aching for an orgasm. I remembered all the panties, knees, legs, tits, pussies I had ever seen, the rubber was sweating; I was sweating.

"I love you, darling!" I whispered into one of her rubber ears.

I hate to admit it, but I forced myself to come into that lousy hunk of rubber. it was hardly a Tanya at all.

I took a razor blade and cut the thing all to shit. dumped it out with the beercans.

how many men in America bought those stupid things?

or then you can pass half a hundred fuck machines in a 10 minute walk on almost any main sidewalk of America – the only difference *being* that they *pretended* that they were human.

poor Indian Mike. with that 20 inch dead cock.

all the poor Indian Mikes. all the climbers into Space. all the whores of Vietnam and Washington.

poor Tanya, her belly had been a hog's belly. veins the veins of a dog. she rarely shatted or pissed, she had just fucked – heart, voice and tongue borrowed from others – there were only supposed to be 17 possible organ transplants at that time. Von B. was far ahead of them.

poor Tanya, who had only eaten a little – mostly cheap cheese and raisins. she had had no desire for money or property or large new cars or overexpensive homes. she had never read the evening paper. had no desire for colored television, new hats, rain boots, backfence conversations with idiot wives; nor had she desired a husband who was a doctor, a stockbroker, a congressman or a cop.

and the guy at the gas station keeps asking me, "hey, what happened to that thing you brought down here one day and blew up with the air hose?"

but he doesn't ask anymore. I buy my gas at a new place. I don't even get my hair cut anymore where I saw that magazine with the Von Brashlitz rubber dolly sex ad. I am trying to forget everything.

what would you do?

THE GUT-WRINGING MACHINE

Danforth hung the bodies up one by one after they had been
wrung through the wringer. Bagley sat by the phones. "how many
we got?"

"19. looks like a good day."

"shit, yeah yeah. that sounds like a good day. how many did
we place yesterday?"

"14."

"fair. fair. we'll make it good if the way keeps up. I keep
worrying they might quit the thing in Viet," said Bagley of the
phones.

"don't be foolish – too many people profit and depend on that
war."

"but the Paris Peace Conference . . ."

"you just ain't yourself today, Bag. you know they just sit
around and laugh all day, draw their pay and then make the Paree
nightclubs each night. those boys are living good. they don't want
the Peace Conference to end anymore than we want the war to
end. we're all getting fat, and not a scratch. it's sweet. and if they
settle the thing somehow by accident, there'll be others. they keep
hot points glowing all over the globe."

"yeah, I guess I worry too much." one of the three phones on
the desk rang. Bagley picked it up. "SATISFACTORY HELP
AGENCY. Bagley speaking."

he listened. "yeh. yeh. we got a good cost accountant. salary? $300 the first two weeks, I mean 300 a week. we get the first two weeks' pay. then cut him to 50 a week or fire him. if you fire him after the first two weeks, we give YOU one hundred dollars. why? well, hell, don't you see, the whole idea is to keep things moving. it's all psychological, like Santa Claus. when? yeah, we'll send him right over. what's the address? fine, fine, he'll be there pronto. remember all the terms. we send him with a contract. bye."

Bagley hung up. hummed to himself, underlined the address. "get one down, Danforth. a tired, thin one. no use shipping out the best on first shot."

Danforth walked over to the wire clothesline and took the clamps off the fingers of a tired, thin one.

"walk him over here. what's his name?"

"Herman. Herman Telleman."

"shit, he don't look so good. looks like he still got a little blood in him, and I can see some color in his eye ... I think. listen, Danforth, you got those wringers running good and tight? I want all the guts squeezed out, no resistance at all, you understand? you do your job and I'll do mine."

"some of these guys came in pretty tough. some men have more guts than others, you know that. you can't always tell by looking."

"all right, let's try him. Herman. hey, sonny!"

"what's up, pops?"

"how'd you like a nice little job?"

"ah, hell no!"

"what? you don't want a nice little job?"

"what the fuck for? my old man, he was from Jersey, he worked all his damn life and after we buried him with his own money, ya know what he had left?"

"what?"

"15 cents and the end of a drab dull life."

"but don't you want a wife, a family, a home, respectability? a new car every 3 years?"

"I don't want no grind, daddy-o. don't put me in no flip-out cage. I just want to laze around. what the shit."

"Danforth, run this bastard through the wringer and make those screws tight!"

Danforth grabbed the subject but not before Telleman yelled "up your old mother's bunghole . . ."

"and squeeze ALL THE GUTS OUT OF HIM, ALL OF THE GUTS! do you hear me?"

"aw right, aw right!" answered Danforth. "shit. sometimes I think you got the easy end of the stick!"

"forget sticks! squeeze the guts out of him. Nixon might end the war . . ."

"there you go talking that nonsense again! I don't think you been sleeping good, Bagley. something wrong with you."

"yeah, yeah, you're right, insomnia. I keep thinking we should be making soldiers! I toss all night! what a business that would be!"

"Bag, we do the best with what we can, that's all."

"aw right, aw right, you run him through the wringer yet?"

"TWICE yet! I got *all* the guts out. you'll see."

"aw right, trot him over. let's try him."

Danforth brought Herman Telleman back. he did look a bit different. all the color was gone from his eyes and he had on this utterly false smile. it was beautiful.

"Herman?" asked Bagley.

"yes, sir?"

"what do you feel? or how do you feel?"

"I don't feel anything, sir."

"you like cops?"

"not cops, sir – policemen. they are the victims of our viciousness even though they at times protect us by shooting us, jailing us, beating us and fining us. There is no such thing as a bad cop. Policeman, pardon me. do you realize that if there were no policemen, we'd have to take the law into our own hands?"

"and then what would happen?"

"I never thought of that, sir."

"excellent. do you believe in God?"

"oh, yes sir, in God and Family and State and Country and honest labor."

"jesus christ!"

"what, sir?"

"sorry. now, here, do you like overtime on a job?"

"oh, yes sir! I would like to work 7 days a week if possible, and 2 jobs if possible."

"why?"

"money, sir. money for color tv, new autos, down payment on a home, silk pajamas, 2 dogs, an electric shave, life insurance, medical insurance, oh all kinds of insurance and college educations for my children if I have children and automatic doors on the garage and fine clothes and 45 dollar shoes, and cameras, wrist watches, rings, washers, refrigerators, new chairs, new beds, wall-to-wall carpeting, donations to the church, thermostat heating and . . ."

"all right. stop. now when are you going to use all this stuff?"

"I don't understand, sir."

"I mean, when you are working night and day and overtime, when are you going to enjoy these luxuries?"

"oh, there'll be a day, there'll be a day, sir!"

"and you don't think your kids will grow up some day and just think of you as an asshole?"

"after I've worked my fingers to the bone for them, sir! of course not!"

"excellent. now just a few more questions."

"yes, sir."

"don't you think that all this constant drudgery is harmful to the health and the spirit, the soul, if you will . . .?"

"oh hell, if I weren't working all the time I'd just be sitting around drinking or making oil paintings or fucking or going to the circus or sitting in the park watching the ducks. things like that."

"don't you think sitting around in the park watching the ducks is nice?"

"I can't make any money that way, sir."

"o.k., fuck-off.

"sir?"

"I mean, I'm through talking to you."

"o.k., this one's ready, Dan. fine job. give him the contract, make him sign it, he won't read the fine print. he thinks we're nice. trot him down to the address. they'll take him. I ain't sent out a better cost accountant in months."

Danforth had Herman sign the contract, checked his eyes again to make sure that they were dead, put the contract and the address in his hand, led him to the door and gave him a gentle push down the stairway.

Bagley just leaned back with an easy smile of success and watched Danforth run the other 18 through the wringer. where their guts went it was hard to see but almost every man lost his guts somewhere along the line. the ones labeled "married with family" or "over 40" lost their guts easiest. Bagley leaned back as Danforth ran them through the wringer, he heard them talking:

"it's hard for a man as old as I am to get a job, oh, it's so hard!"

another one said:

"oh, baby, it's cold outside."

another:

"I get tired of booking and pimping, getting busted, busted, busted. I need something secure, secure, secure, secure, secure . . ."

another:

"all right, I've had my fun. now . . ."

another:

"I don't have a trade. every man should have a trade. I don't have a trade. what am I going to do?"

another:

"I've been all over the world – in the army – I know things."

another:

"if I had it to do all over again, I'd be a dentist or a barber."

another:

"all my novels and short stories and poems keep coming back. Shit, I can't go to New York and shake the hands of the publishers! I have more talent than anybody but you've got to have the inside! I'll take any kind of job but I am better than any kind of job that I take because I am a genius."

another:

"see how pretty I am? look at my nose? look at my ears? look at my hair? my skin? the way I act! see how pretty I am? see how pretty I am? see how pretty I am? why doesn't anybody like me? because I'm so pretty. they're jealous, jealous, jealous . . ."

the phone rang again.

"SATISFACTORY HELP AGENCY. Bagley speaking. you what? you need a deep-sea diver? motherfuck! what? oh, pardon. sure, sure, we got dozens of unemployed deep-sea divers. his first 2 weeks' pay is ours. 500 a week. dangerous, you know, really dangerous – barnacles, crabs, all that . . . seaweed, maidens on rocks. octupi. bends. head-colds. fuck, yes. first 2 weeks' pay is ours. if you fire him after 2 weeks we give *you* $200. why? *why?* if a robin laid an egg of gold in your front room chair would you ask WHY? would you? we'll send you a deep-sea diver in 45 minutes! the address? fine, fine, ah, yes, fine, that's near the Richfield Building. yes, I know. 45 minutes. thank you. goodbye."

Bagley hung up. he was tired already and the day was just beginning.

"Dan?"

"yeah, mother?"

"bring me a deep-sea diver type. bit fat around the belly. blue eyes, medium hair on chest, balding before his time, slightly stoical, slightly stooped, bad eyesight and the unknown beginning of the cancer of the throat. that's a deep-sea diver, anybody knows what a deep-sea diver is. now bring one, mother."

"o.k., shithead."

Bagley yawned. Danforth unclamped one. brought him forth, stood him before the desk. his tag said, "Barney Anderson."

"hello, Barney," said Bag.

"where am I?" asked Barney.

"SATISFACTORY HELP AGENCY."

"boy, if you two ain't a couple of greasy-looking motherfuckers, I ain't never ever seen none!"

"what the fuck, Dan!"

"I ran him through 4 times."

"I told you to tighten those screws!"

"and I told you some men have more guts than others!"

"it's all a myth, you damn fool!"

"who's a damn fool?"

"you're both damn fools," said Barney Anderson.

"I want you to run his ass through the wringer three times," said Bagley.

"o.k., o.k., but first let's you and me get straight."

"aw right, for instance . . . ask this Barney guy who his heroes are.

"Barney, hoose yr herows?"

"well, lemme see – Cleaver, Dillinger, Che, Malcolm X., Gandhi, Jersey Joe Walcott, Grandma Barker, Castro, Van Gogh, Villon, Hemingway."

"ya see, he i-dentifies with all LOSERS. that makes him feel good. he's getting ready to lose. we're going to help him. he's been conned on this soul-shit and that's how we get their asses. there ain't no soul. it's all con. there ain't no heroes. it's all con. there ain't no winners – it's all con and horseshit. there ain't no saints, there ain't no genius – that's all con and fairytale, it makes the game go. each man just tries to hang on and be lucky – if he can. all else is bullshit."

"aw right, aw right, I dig your losers! but what about Castro? he looked pretty fat, last photo I saw of him."

"he subsists because the U.S. and Russia have decided to leave him in the middle. but suppose they really put the pack on the deck? what can he draw to? man, he don't hold enough chips to get into a decaying Egyptian whorehouse."

"fuck you two guys! I like who I like!" said Barney Anderson.

"Barney, when a man gets old enough, trapped enough, hungry enough, weary enough – he'll suck dick, tit, eat shit to stay alive; either that or suicide. the human race ain't got it, man. it's a bad crowd."

"so we're gonna change it, man. that's the trick. if we can make it to the moon we can clean the shit out of the shitbowl. we just been concentrating on the wrong things."

"you're sick, kid. and a little fat around the belly. and balding. Dan, shape him up."

Danforth took Barney Anderson and wrang and wrung and screamed him through the wringer three times, then brought him back.

"Barney?" asked Bagley.

"yes sir!"

"who are your heroes?"

"George Washington, Bob Hope, Mae West. Richard Nixon, the bones of Clark Gable and all the nice people I've seen at Disneyland. Joe Louis, Dinah Shore, Frank Sinatra, Babe Ruth, the Green Berets, hell the whole United States Army and Navy and especially the Marine Corps, and even the Treasury Dept., the CIA, the FBI, United Fruit, the highway Patrol, the whole god damned L.A. Police Dept., and the County Cops too. and I don't mean 'cops,' I mean 'policemen.' then there's Marlene Dietrich, with this slit up the side of her dress, she must be near 70 now? – dancing up at Vegas, my dick got big, what a wonderful woman. the good American life and the good American money can keep us young forever, don't you see?"

"Dan?"

"yeah, Bag?"

"this one's really ready! I ain't got much feeling left, but he even makes me sick. make him sign his little contract and send him out. they'll love him. god, what a man's gotta do to just stay alive? sometimes I even hate my own job. that's bad, ain't it, Dan?"

"sure, Bag. and as soon as I send this asshole on his way, I got just the little thing for you – a touch of the good ol' tonic."

"ah, fine, fine . . . what is it?"

"just a little quarter-turn through the wringer."

"WHAT?"

"oh, it's fine for the blues or for extemporaneous thinking. stuff like that."

"will it work?"

"it beats aspirin."

"o.k., get rid of the asshole."

Barney Anderson was sent down the stairway. Bagley got up and walked toward the nearest wringer. "these old gals – West and Dietrich, still flashing tits and legs, hell it don't make sense, they were doing that when I was 6 years old. what makes it work?"

"nuttin'. stretchers, girdles, powder, lights, false flesh coverings, padding, pudding, straw, horseshit. they could make your grandmother look like a 16 year old."

"my grandmother's dead."

"they could still do it."

"yeah, yeah, I guess you're right." Bagley walked toward the wringer.

"just a quarter turn now. can I trust you?"

"you're my partner, ain't you, Bag?"

"sure, Dan."

"how long we been in business together?"

"25 years."

"so, o.k., when I say a QUARTER-TURN, I mean a QUARTER-TURN."

"whatta I do?"

"just slip your hands in the rollers, it's like a washing machine."

"in there?"

"yeah. here we go! whoopee!"

"hey, man, remember, just a quarter of a turn."

"sure, Bag, don't you trust me?"

"I gotta now."

"you know, I been fucking your wife on the sly."

"you rotten son of a bitch! I'll kill you!"

Danforth left the machine running, sat down behind Bagley's desk, lit a cigarette. he hummed a little tune, "lucky lucky me, I can live in luxury, because I've got a pocket full of dreams . . . I got an empty purse, but I own the universe, because I've got a pocketful of dreams . . ."

he got up and walked over to the machine and Bagley.

"you said a quarter-turn," said Bagley. "it's been a turn and a half."

"don't you trust me?"

"more than ever, somehow."

"still, I been fucking your wife on the sly."

"well, I guess it's all right. I get tired of fucking her. every man gets tired of fucking his own wife."

"but I want you to want me to fuck your wife."

"well, I don't care but I don't know if I exactly *want* you to."

"I'll be back in about 5 minutes."

Danforth went back, sat in Bagley's swivel chair, put his feet up on the desk and waited. he liked to sing. he sang songs: "I got plenty of nuthin' and nuthin's plenty for me. I got the stars, I got the sun, I got the shining sea . . ."

Danforth smoked two cigarettes and went back to the machine.

"Bag, I been fucking your wife on the sly."

"oh, I want you to, man! I want you to! and ya know what?"

"what?"

"I'd kinda like ta watch."

"sure, that'd be o.k."

Danforth went to the phone, dialed a number.

"Minnie? yeah, Dan. I'm comin' over ta fuck ya again. Bag? oh, he's comin' too. he wants ta watch. no, we're not drunk. I just decided to close shop for the day. we've made it already. with the Israel-Arab thing and all the African wars, there's nothing to worry about. Biafra is a beautiful word. anyhow, we're coming over. I want to bunghole you. you got those big cheeks, jesus. I might even bunghole Bag. I think his cheeks are bigger than yours. keep tight, sweetie, we're on our way!"

Dan hung up. another phone rang. he picked it up. "jam it you rotten motherfucker, even the points of your tits smell like wet dogturds in a Westerly wind." he hung up and smiled. walked over and took Bagley out of the machine. they locked the office door and walked down the steps together. when they walked outside the sun was up and looking good. you could see through the thin skirts of the women. you could almost see their bones. death and rot was everywhere. it was Los Angeles, near 7th and Broadway, the intersection where the dead snubbed the dead and didn't even know why. it was a taught game like jumprope or dissecting frogs or pissing in the mailbox or jacking-off your pet dog.

"we got plenty a nuthin'," they sang, "and nuthin's plenty for we . . ."

arm and arm they made the underground garage, found Bag's 69 Caddy, got in, each lit a dollar cigar, Dan driving, got it out of there, almost hit a bum coming out of Pershing Square, turned West toward the freeway, toward freedom, Vietnam, the army, fucking, large areas of grass and nude statues and French wine, Beverly Hills . . .

Bagley leaned over and ran down Danforth's zipper as he drove.

I hope he leaves some for his wife, Danforth thought.

it was a warm Los Angeles morning, or maybe it was afternoon, he checked the dashboard clock – it read 11:37 a.m. just as he came. he ran the Caddy up to 80. the asphalt slipped underneath like the graves of the dead. he turned on the dash t.v., then reached for the telephone, then remembered to zip up. "Minnie, I love you."

"I love you too, Dan," she answered. "is that slob with you?"

"right beside me. he just caught a mouthful."

"oh, Dan, don't *waste* it!"

he laughed and hung up. they almost hit a nigger in a pickup truck. he wasn't black at all, he was a nigger, that's all he was. there wasn't a nicer city in the world when you had it made, and only one worse when you didn't have it made – the Big A. Danforth hit it up to 85. a motorcop smiled at him as he drove by. maybe he'd call Bob later that night. Bob was always so funny. his 12 writers always gave him those good lines. and Bob was just as natural as horseshit. it was wonderful.

he threw out the dollar cigar, lit another, ran the Caddy up to 90, straight at the sun like an arrow, business was good and life, and the tires whirled over the dead and the dying and the dying-to-be.

ZYAAAAAUUUUM!

3 WOMEN

we lived right across from McArthur park, Linda and I, and one
night while drinking we saw a man's body fall past our window.
It was an odd sight, something like a joke, but it wasn't any joke
when his body hit the pavement. "jesus christ," I told Linda, "he
plopped right apart like an old tomato! we are just made of guts
and shit and slimy stuff! come 'ere! come 'ere! look at 'im!" Linda
came to the window, then ran to the bathroom and vomited. she
came out. I turned and looked at her. "honest ta christ, baby, he's
just like a big spilled bowl of rotten meat and spaghetti, dressed
in a ripped suit and shirt!" Linda ran back in and heaved again.

I sat and drank the wine. soon I heard the siren, what they
really needed was the Sanitation Dept. well, what the fuck, we all
had our troubles. I never knew where our rent was coming from
and we were too sick from drinking to look for work. everytime
we worried, all we could do about our worries was to fuck. that
made us forget for a while. we fucked a lot, and lucky for me,
Linda was a good lay. that whole hotel was full of people like us,
drinking wine and fucking and not knowing what next. now and
then one of them jumped out of the window. but the money
always seemed to arrive for us from somewhere, just when all
seemed like we'd have to eat our own shit. once $300 from a dead
uncle, another time, a delayed income tax refund. another time I
was riding on a bus and on the seat in front of me were these 50

cent pieces. what it meant or who had done it, I didn't know, still don't understand. I moved one seat up and began stuffing the half bucks into my pockets. when the pockets got full, I pulled the cord and got off at the next stop. nobody said anything or tried to stop me. I mean, when you're drunk, you've got to be lucky, even if you're not one, you've got to be lucky.

part of each day we would spend in the park looking at the ducks. you've got to believe me, that when your health is down from continual drinking and lack of decent food, and you're tired of fucking while trying to forget, you can't beat the ducks. I mean, you've got to get out of your place, because you can get the deep blue blues and it soon might be you out the window. it is easier to do than you might imagine. so Linda and I would sit on a bench and watch the ducks. the ducks didn't worry worth a damn – no rent, no clothes, plenty of food – just float around shitting and quacking. nobbling, nibbling, eating all the time. once in a while one of those from the hotel would catch a duck at night, kill the thing, take it to their room, clean it and cook it. we thought about it but never did it. besides they were very hard to catch; you just get so close and SLUUUSH!!! a spray of water and the motherfucker would be gone! most of the time we ate small pancakes made of flour and water, or now and then we would steal some corn from somebody's garden – one guy specialized in a corn garden – I don't believe he got to eat a one of them, then there was always a bit of stealing from an outdoor market – I mean there was a vegetable stand in front of a grocery store – this meant an occasional tomato or two or a small cucumber, but we were petty thieves, small time, and we needed mostly luck. the cigarettes were easiest – a walk at night – somebody always left a car window down and a pack or half-pack of smokes on the dashboard. of course, the wine and the rent were the real problems and we fucked and worried about it.

and like all the days of final desperation, ours arrived. no more wine, no more luck, no more anything. no more credit with the landlady *or* the liquor store. I decided to set the alarm clock for 5:30 a.m. and walk down to the Farm Labor Market, but even the clock didn't work right. it had broken and I had opened it to repair it. it was a broken spring and the only way I could get the spring to work again was to break a portion of it off, hook it up again, lock up the works and wind it up. now if you want to know what a short spring does to an alarm clock or I guess any kind of clock, I'll tell you. the shorter the spring is, the faster the minute and hour hands go around. it was some crazy clock, I'll tell you, and when we were worn out with fucking to stop from worrying we used to watch that clock and try to tell what time it *really* was. you could see that minute hand moving – we used to laugh at it.

then one day – it took us a week to figure it – we found that the clock moved *thirty* hours for each *actual* twelve hours of time. also it had to be wound every 7 or 8 hours or it would stop. sometimes we'd wake up and look at the clock and wonder what time it was. "well, shit, baby," I'd say, "can't you figure out the thing? the clock moves 2 and one half times as fast as it should, it's simple."

"yeah, but what time did it say when we last set the clock?" she'd ask.

"damned if I know, baby, I was drunk."

"well, you better wind it or it'll stop."

"o.k."

I'd wind it, then we'd fuck.

so the morning I decided to go to the Farm Labor Market I couldn't set the clock. we got hold of a bottle of wine from somewhere and drank it slowly. I watched that clock, not knowing what it meant, and being afraid of missing the early morning, I just lay in bed and didn't sleep all night. then I got up, dressed and walked down to San Pedro street. everybody seemed to be just standing around waiting. there were quite a few tomatoes lying in the windows and I picked up two or 3 of them and ate them. there was a large blackboard: COTTONPICKERS NEEDED FOR BAKERSFIELD. FOOD AND LODGING. what the hell was that? *cotton* in Bakersfield, Calif? I thought Eli Whitney and the cotton gin had put all that out of the way. then a big truck drove up and it turned out they needed tomato-pickers. well, shit, I hated to leave Linda in that bed all alone like that. she could never stay in bed too long alone by herself like that. but I decided to try it. everybody started climbing into the truck. I waited and made sure that all the ladies were on board, and there were some big ones. everybody was in, and then I started to crawl up. a large Mexican, evidently the foreman, started putting in the tailgates – "sorry, senor, full up!" they drove off without me.

it was almost 9 a.m. by then and the walk back to the hotel took an hour. I passed all the well-dressed stupid-looking people.

and was almost run over once by an angry man in a black Caddy. I don't know what he was angry about. maybe the weather. it was a hot day. when I got back to the hotel I had to walk up the stairway because the elevator was right by the landlady's door and she was always fucking with the elevator, shining the brass, or just plain-ass snooping.

it was 6 floors up and when I got there I heard laughing from my room. that bitch Linda hadn't waited too long to get started. well, I'd whip her ass and his too. I opened the door.

it was Linda and Jeanie and Eve. "Sweetie!" said Linda. she came up to me. she was all dressed in highheels. she gave me a lot of tongue when she kissed. "Jeanie just got her first unemployment check and Eve is on the dole! we're celebrating!"

there was plenty of port wine. I went in and took a bath and then came out in my shorts. I always like to show off my legs. I had the biggest most powerful legs I had ever seen on any man. the rest of me wasn't too much. I sat in my torn shorts and put my legs up on the coffee table.

"shit! look at those legs!" said Jeanie.

"yeah, yeah," said Eve.

Linda smiled. I was poured a wine.

you know how such things go. we drank and talked, talked and drank. the girls went out for more bottles. more talk. the clock went round and round. soon it was dark. I was drinking alone, still in my torn shorts. Jeanie had gone to the bedroom and passed out in the bed. Eve had passed out on the couch and Linda had passed out on a smaller leather couch in the hall that led to the bathroom. I still couldn't understand that Mexican closing those tailgates on me. I was unhappy.

I went into the bedroom and got into bed with Jeanie. she was a large woman, and naked. I began kissing on her breasts, sucking at them. "hey, what you doing?"

"doin? I'm going to fuck you!"

I put my finger into her cunt and moved it back and forth. "I'm going to fuck you!"

"no! Linda would kill me!"

"she'll never know!"

I mounted and then very SLOWLY SLOWLY QUIETLY so the springs would not rattle, so there would not be a sound, I slid it in and out in and out EVER SO SLOWLY and when I came I thought I would never stop. it was one of the best fucks of my life, as I wiped off on the sheets the thought occurred to me – it could be that Man has been fucking improperly for centuries.

then I went, sat down in the dark, drank some more. I don't remember how long I sat there. I drank quite a bit. then I went over to Eve. Eve of the dole. she was a fat thing, a little wrinkled, but had very sexy lips, obscene sexy ugly lips. I began kissing that terrible and beautiful mouth. she didn't protest at all. she opened her legs and I entered. she was a little female pig, farting and grunting and sniffling, wiggling. when I came it wasn't like with Jeanie – long and trembling – it was just splot splot and then over. I got off. and before I could get back to my chair I could hear her snoring again. amazing – she fucked like she breathed – nothing to it. each woman fucked just a bit differently, and that's what kept a man going, that's what kept a man trapped.

I sat and drank some more thinking of what that dirty son of a bitch in control of the tailgate had done to me. it didn't pay to be polite. then I began to think about the dole. could an unmarried man and woman get on the dole? of course not. they were supposed to starve to death. and love was a kind of dirty word. but that was something of what it was between Linda and I – love. that's why we starved together, drank together, lived together. what did marriage mean? marriage meant a sanctified FUCK and a sanctified FUCK always and finally, without fail, got BORING, got to be a JOB. but that's what the world wanted: some poor son of a bitch, trapped and unhappy, with a job to do. well, shit, I'd move down to skidrow and move Linda in with Big Eddie. Big Eddie was an idiot but at least he'd buy her some clothes and put some steaks in her belly which was more than I was able to do.

Elephant Legs Bukowski, the social failure.

I finished off the bottle and decided I needed some sleep. I wound up the alarm clock and crawled in with Linda. she awakened and began rubbing up against me. "oh shit, oh shit," she said, "I don't know what's the matter with me!"

"whatza matta, baby? you sick? you want me to call the General Hospital?"

"oh no, shit, I'm just HOT! HOT! I'M SO HOT!"

"what?"

"I said, I'm burning up hot! FUCK ME!"

"Linda . . .

"what? what?"

"I'm so tired. no sleep for two nights. that long walk to the Labor Market and back, 32 blocks in the hot sun . . . useless. no job. fucking-ass tired."

"I'll HELP you!"

"whatcha mean?"

she crawled halfway down the couch and began licking at my penis. I groaned in weariness. "honey, 32 blocks in the hot sun . . . I'm burned out."

she kept working. she had a sandpaper tongue and knew what to do with it.

"honey," I told her, "I'm a social zero! I don't deserve you! please relent!"

like I say, she was good. some can, some can't. most just know the old-time headbob. Linda began with the penis, left off, went to the balls, then off the balls, back to the penis again, barberpole, a wonderful amount of energy, ALWAYS LEAVING THE HEAD OF THE COCK, ITSELF. UNTOUCHED. Finally she had me moaning to the ceiling telling her all various sorts of lies about what I would do for her when I finally got my ass straightened out and stopped being a bum.

then she came and took the head, put her mouth about a third of the way down, gave this little nip-suck of tooth pressure on, the wolf-nip and I came AGAIN – which made four times that night and I was completely done. some women know more than medical science.

when I awakened they were all up and dressed – looking good – Linda, Jeanie and Eve. they poked at me under the covers, laughing. "hey, Hank, we're going down to look for a live one! and we need an eye opener! we'll be down at Tommi-Hi's!"

"o.k., o.k., goodbye!"

they all left, wiggling ass out the door.

all Mankind was doomed forever.

I was just about asleep when the extension phone rang.

"Yeah?"

"Mr. Bukowski?"

"yeah?"

"I saw those women! they came from your room!"

"how do you know? you have 8 floors and about ten or twelve rooms to a floor."

"I know all my roomers, Mr. Bukowski! we have all respectable working people here!"

"yeah?"

"yes, Mr. Bukowski, I've been running this place for twenty years and never, never have I seen such goings on as at your place! we've always had respectable people here, Mr. Bukowski."

"yes, they're so respectable that every two weeks some son of a bitch climbs up onto the roof and takes a header straight into your cement entranceway between those phony potted plants."

"you've got until noon to get out, Mr. Bukowski!"

"what time is it now?"

"8 a.m.

"thank you."

I hung up. found an alka-seltzer. drank it out of a dirty glass. then found a touch of wine. I opened the curtains and looked out at the sun. it was a hard world, no news there, but I hated skidrow. I like little rooms, little places to make some kind of fight from. a woman. a drink. but no day by day job. I couldn't put it together. I was not clever enough. I thought of jumping out the window but couldn't do it. I got dressed and went down to Tommi-Hi's. the girls were laughing down at the end of the bar with two guys. Marty the bartender knew me. I waved him off. no money. I sat there.

a scotch and water arrived in front of me. a note.

"meet me at the Roach Hotel, room 12, at midnight. I'll have the room for us.

love, Linda."

I drank the drink, got out of the way, tried the Roach Hotel at midnight the desk clerk said, "nothing doing. no room 12 reserved for a Bukowski." I came at one a.m. I'd been in the park all day, all night, sitting. same thing. "no room 12 reserved for you, sir."

"any room reserved for me under that name or under the name of Linda Bryan?"

he checked his books.

"nothing sir."

"do you mind if I look into room 12?"

"there's nobody there, sir. I told you, sir."

"I'm in love, man. I'm sorry. please let me have a look!"

he gave me one of those looks reserved for 4th class idiots, tossed me the doorkey.

"be back within 5 minutes or you're in trouble."

I opened the door, switched on the lights – "Linda!" – the roaches, seeing the light, all ran back under the wallpaper.

there were thousands of them. when I put out the light you could hear them all crawling back out. the wallpaper, itself, seemed to be just a large roachskin.

I took the elevator back down to the desk clerk.

"thanks," I said, "you were right. nobody in room 12."

for the first time his voice seemed to take on some kind of kindness.

"I'm sorry, man."

"thanks," I said.

when I got outside the hotel I turned left, which is east, which was skidrow, and as my feet moved me slowly toward there I wondered, why do people lie? now I no longer wonder but I still remember, and now when they lie I almost know about it while they are doing it, but I'm still not as wise as that desk clerk in the roach hotel who knew that the lie was everywhere, or the people who dove past my window while I was drinking port on warm afternoons in Los Angeles across from McArthur park, where they still catch, kill, eat the ducks, and, the people.

the hotel is still there and the room we stayed in and if you care to come by some day I will show it to you. but there's hardly sense in that, is there? let's just say that one night I fucked or got fucked by 3 women. and let that be story enough.

3 CHICKENS

Vicki was all right. but we had our troubles. we were on the wine. port. that woman would get drunk and get to talking and she would make up some of the vilest imaginable stuff about me. and that tone of voice: shoddy and lisping and grating and insane. it would get to any man. it got to me.

once she was screaming these insanities from the fold-down bed in our apartment. I begged her to stop. but she wouldn't. finally, I just walked over, lifted up the bed with her in it and folded everything into the wall.

then I went over and sat down and listened to her scream.

but she kept screaming so I walked over and pulled the bed out of the wall again there she lay, holding her arm, claiming it was broken.

"your arm can't be broken," I said.

"it is, it is. oh, you slimy jackoff bastard, you've broken my arm!"

I had some more drinks but she just kept holding her arm and whining. I finally had enough and telling her I'd be right back I went downstairs and outside and found some old wooden boxes behind a grocery store. I found good sturdy slats, ripped them off, pulled out the nails, got back on the elevator and rode back to our apartment.

it took about 4 slats. I bound them around her arm with rippings from one of her dresses. she quieted down for a couple of hours. then she started in again. I couldn't take it anymore. so I called a taxi. we went to the General Hospital. as soon as the taxi left I took the boards off and threw them into the street. then they x-rayed her CHEST and put her arm in a cast, can you imagine that? I suppose if she broke her head they'd x-ray her ass.

anyhow, she used to sit in the bars after that and say, "I am the only woman who has been folded into a wall in a wall bed."

and I wasn't so sure of THAT either, but I let her go on saying it.

now, another time she angered me and I slapped her but it was across the mouth and it broke her false teeth.

I was surprised that it broke her false teeth. and I went out and got this super cement glue and I glued her teeth together for her. it worked for a while and then one night as she sat there drinking her wine she suddenly had a mouthful of broken teeth.

that wine was so strong it undid the glue. it was disgusting. we had to get her some new teeth. how we did it, I don't quite remember, but she claimed they made her look like a horse.

we'd usually always have these arguments after we drank awhile, and Vicki claimed I'd get very mean when I was drunk but I think that she was the one who was mean. anyhow, sometime during the argument she'd get up, slam the door and run outside to some bar. "looking for a live one," as the girls would say.

it always made me feel bad when she left. I've got to admit it. sometimes she wouldn't come back for 2 or 3 days. and nights. it wasn't a very nice thing to do.

one time she ran out and I sat there drinking the wine, thinking about it. then I got up and found the elevator and rode on down to the streets too. I found her in her favorite bar. she sat there holding a kind of purple scarf. I'd never seen the purple scarf before. holding out on me. I walked up to her and said quite loudly:

"I've tried to make a woman out of you but you're nothing but a god damned whore!"

the bar was full. every seat taken. I lifted my hand. I swung. I backhanded her off that god damned stool. she fell to the floor and screamed.

this was at the back end of the bar. I didn't even turn to look at her. I walked the length of the bar to the exit. then I turned and faced the crowd. it was very quiet.

"now," I said to them, "if there's anybody here who doesn't LIKE what I just did, just SAY something . . ."

it was quieter than quiet.

I turned around and walked out the doorway. the moment I hit the street I could hear them babbling and buzzing in there, buzzing and babbling.

the SHITS! not a man in the boatload!

– but, of course, she came back. and, well, anyhow to get on, this one night lately we are sitting around drinking the wine and the same old arguments started. this time I decided to go.

"I'M GONNA GET THE FUCK OUTA THIS HOLE!" I yelled at Vicki. "I CAN'T STAND NO MORE OF YOUR GOD DAMNED ABUSE!"

she jumped in front of the door.

"over my dead body, that's the only way you are getting out of here!"

"o.k., if that's the way it's gotta be."

I slammed her a good one and she fell down in front of the doorway. I had to move her body to get out.

I took the elevator down. feeling rather good. a good jaunty 4-floor ride down. the elevator was kind of a cage-like contraption and smelled like old stockings, old gloves, old dustmops, but it gave me a feeling of security and power – somehow – and the wine rode all through me.

but then I got outside and had a change of mind. I went to the liquor store. bought 4 more bottles of wine and went back to my place and rode the elevator back up. the same feeling of security and power. I walked into my place. Vicki was sitting in a chair crying.

"I've come back to you, you lucky darling," I told her.

"you bastard, you hit me. YOU HIT ME!"

"umm," I said, opening a new bottle. "and you give me any more shit and I'll hit you again."

"YEAH!" she screamed, "YOU'D HIT ME BUT YOU WOULDN'T HAVE ENOUGH GUTS TO HIT A MAN!"

"HELL NO!" I screamed back, "I WOULDN'T HIT A MAN! YOU THINK I'M CRAZY? WHAT'S THAT GOT TO DO WITH IT?"

that settled her for a bit and we sat for a bit and we sat drinking down the waterglassfuls of wine, port.

then she started in on her abusive stuff again, mostly claiming I jacked off while she was asleep.

well, even if it were true I figured that was my business and if it wasn't, then she was REALLY crazy. she claimed I jacked off in the bathtub, in the closet, in the elevator, everywhere.

everytime I got out of the tub she'd run into the bathroom, like: "there! I SEE IT! LOOK AT IT!"

"you crazy bat, that's just a dirt-ring."

"no, that's COME! that's COME!"

or she'd run in while I was bathing under the arms or between the legs and say, "see, see, SEE! you're DOING IT!"

"doing WHAT? can't a man wash his BALLS? those are MY balls, god damn you! can't a man wash his own balls?"

"what's that thing sticking up there?"

"my left index finger. now get the HELL OUT OF HERE!!!"

or in bed, I'd be sound asleep and all of a sudden this hand grabbing my string and nuggets, man, sound asleep in the middle of the night, these FINGERNAILS!

"AH HA! I CAUGHT YOU! I CAUGHT YOU!"

"you crazy bat, the next time you do that I SWEAR I AM GOING TO KILL YOU!"

"I CAUGHT YOU, I CAUGHT YOU, I CAUGHT YOU!"

"for christ's sake, go to sleep . . ."

so this night she just sat there screaming her jackoff accusations. I just sat there and drank my wine and didn't deny anything. this made her angry, angrier.

and angrier.

finally she couldn't stand it, all her talk about jackingoff, I mean ME supposedly jackingoff and me just sitting there smiling at her, and she jumped up and ran out the door.

I let her go. I sat there and drank my wine. port.

same old stuff.

I thought it over. umm, umm, well.

then very leisurely I got up and took the elevator down. same old feeling of power. I was not angry. I was very calm. it was just the same old war.

I walked on down the street but I didn't go to her favorite bar. why repeat the same play? you are a whore; I tried to make a woman out of you. balls. after a while a man could get to sounding pretty silly. so I went to another bar and sat down on a stool near the door. I ordered a drink and took a slug, set the thing down, and then I saw her. Vicki. she was at the other end of the bar. for some reason she looked scared shitless.

but I didn't go on down. I just stared at her as if I didn't know her.

then I noticed something next to me in one of those old-fashioned fox furs. the dead fox's head hung down over her breast looking at me. the breast looked at me.

"your fox looks like it needs a drink, sweetie," I told her.

"it's dead; it don't need a drink. I need a drink or I'm gonna die."

well, a nice guy like me. who am I to spread death? I bought her a drink. her name, she told me, was Margy. I told her that I was Thomas Nightengale, shoesalesman. Margy. all these women with names, drinking, crapping, having monthlies. fucking men. getting folded into walls. it was too much.

we had a couple more, and already she was in her purse, flashing the photo of her children, an ugly demented boy and a girl without any hair. they were some dull place in Ohio, the father had them, the father was a beast, a money-maker; no sense of humor, no understanding. oh, one of THOSE? and he brought these women in the house and screwed them in front of her with all the lights on.

"ah, I see, I see," I said. "yes, of course, most men are beasts, they simply do not understand. and you're SUCH a sweetie, what the hell, it ain't right."

I suggested we go to another bar. Vicki's ass was twitching and she was half Indian.

we left her there. we went around the corner. we had one around the corner.

then I suggested we go to my place. do a little eating. I mean, get something to cook, bake, fry.

I didn't tell her about Vicki, of course. but Vicki always prided herself on her god damned baked chickens. maybe it was because she looked like one. a baked chicken with horse teeth.

so I suggested we get a chicken, bake it, bathe it in whiskey. she did not demur.

so. liquor store. 5th of whiskey. 5 or 6 quarts of beer.

we found an all night market. the place even had a butcher.

"we wanta bake a chicken," I said.

"oh, christ," he said.

I dropped one of the quarts of beer. it really exploded.

"christ," he said.

I dropped another to see what he would say.

"oh, jesus," he said.

"I want THREE CHICKENS," I said.

"THREE CHICKENS?"

"jesus christ, yes," I said.

the butcher reached in and got three very white-yellow chickens with a few long black unplucked hairs that looked like human hairs on them and he wrapped them all up, a big big bundle, all in pink tough paper with this real gripping tape, and I paid him and we got out of there.

I dropped 2 more quarts of beer on the way.

I rode up the elevator, feeling my power rising. when we got inside my door I lifted Margy's dress to see what was holding her stockings up. then I gave her a big chummy whiskey-goose with long-finger right hand. she screamed and dropped the big pink bundle. it fell on the rug and the 3 chickens came out. those 3 chickens, all white-yellow with their 29 or 30 drooling dropping murdered human hairs sticking to them looked very strange gaping there on that worn rug of yellow and brown flowers and trees and Chinese dragons, under electric light in los angeles at the end of the world near 6th street and Union.

"oooh, the chickens."

"fuck the chickens."

her garter belt was dirty. it was perfect. I goosed her again.

well, shit, so I sat down and peeled the whiskey bottle, poured a couple of tall waterglasses full, took off my shoes stockings pants shirt, took one of her cigarettes. sat in my underwear. I always do that, right away. I like to be comfortable. if the broad don't like it, fuck her. she can go. but they always stay. I got a manner. some broads say I should have been a king. others say other things. fuck 'em.

she drank most of her drink and started for her purse. "I have some children in Ohio. they're lovely children . . ."

"forget that. we've been through that stage. tell me, do you suck dick?"

"what do you mean?"

"OH, BALLS!" I smashed my glass against the wall.

then I got another one, filled it up, and we drank some more.

I don't know how long we worked on the whiskey but it must have gotten to me because the next thing I know I was laying on the bed naked. staring up at the electric light and Margy was standing there naked and she was rubbing my penis quite rapidly with her fox fur. and while she was rubbing she was saying over and over, "I am going to fuck you, I am going to fuck you . . ."

"listen," I said. "I don't know if you can fuck me. I jacked-off in the elevator earlier this evening. I think it was about 8 o'clock."

"I will fuck you anyhow."

she really speeded up that fox fur. it was all right. maybe I could get one for myself. I once knew a guy who put raw liver in a long drinking glass and screwed that. me, I didn't like to stick my thing into anything that could break or slice. imagine going to a doctor with a bloody cock and saying it happened while screwing a water glass. once while I was bumming in a small town in Texas I saw this well-built wonderful fuck of a young broad married to this little shriveled up old dwarf with nasty disposition and some kind of malady that made him trembly all over. she supported him and pushed him around in a wheelchair, and I used to think of him pouncing on all that good meat. I'd get a picture of it, you know, and then finally I got the story. when she had been a younger girl she had gotten this coke bottle stuck all the way into her snatch and just couldn't get the thing out and had to go to a doctor. he got it out, and somehow the story got out. she was ruined in that town after that, and didn't have sense enough to get out. nobody wanted her except the nasty dwarf with the shakes. he didn't give a damn – he had the best piece of ass in town.

where was I? oh, yeah.

her fox fur went faster and faster and I finally got something going just as I heard a key go into the door. oh, shit, it was probably Vicki!

well, it's simple, I thought. I'll just boot her ass out and go about my business.

the door opened and there stood Vicki with 2 cops standing behind her.

"GET THAT WOMAN OUT OF MY HOUSE!" she screamed.

COPS! I couldn't believe it. I pulled the sheet over my pulsating and throbbing and giant sexual organ and pretended to be asleep. it looked like I had a cucumber under there.

Margy was screaming back: "I know you, Vicki, this ain't your god damned house! this guy EARNS his way by licking your asshole hairs! he gets you babbling to heaven in Morse code with that long sandpaper tongue of his, and you're nothing but a WHORE, a true blue turdy-gulping 2-dollar whore. and THAT went out with Franky D., and you were 48 THEN!"

hearing that, my cucumber went down. both of these broads must have been 80 years old. singly, that is, together they might have reached back to suck-off Abe Lincoln. something like that. suck-off General Robert E. Lee, Patrick Henry. Mozart. Dr. Samuel Johnson. Robespierre. Napoleon. Machiavelli? wine preserves. God endures. the whores blow on.

and Vicki screamed back: "WHO'S A WHORE? WHO'S A WHORE, HUH? YOU'RE A WHORE, THAT'S WHO! YOU'VE BEEN SELLING THAT CLAPPED HOLE OF YOURS UP AND DOWN ALVARADO STREET FOR 30 YEARS! A BLIND RAT WOULD BACK UP 4 TIMES IF HE RAN INTO THERE ONCE! AND YOU HOLLERING 'POW! POW!' WHEN YOU'RE LUCKY ENOUGH TO GET A GUY TO COME! AND *THAT* WENT OUT WHEN CONFUCIUS FUCKED HIS MOTHER!"

"WHY YOU CHEAP BITCH. YOU'VE GIVEN OUT MORE BLUE BALLS THAN A SILVER CHRISTMAS TREE IN DIS-NEYLAND. WHY YOU . . ."

"listen, ladies," said one of the cops. "I will have to ask you to watch your remarks and lower the volume. understanding and kindness are the keynotes of Democratic thought. oh, I just DO love the way Bobby Kennedy wears that tickling blobbing knot of raunchy hair over one side of his darling head don't you just?"

"why you fuckin' queer," said Margy, "is that why you wear them tight pants, to make your asshole sweeter? god, it DOES look NICE! I'd kinda like to do you in myself. I see you shits bending over into car windows giving out tickets on the freeways and I always feel like pinching your tight little asses."

the cop suddenly got a brilliant flare in his dead eyes, he unhitched his club and tapped Margy along the side of the neck with it. she fell to the floor.

then he slipped the bracelets on her. I could hear those clicks, and the bastards ALWAYS snapped them too tight. but they felt almost GOOD once you got them on, kind of forceful and heavy and you felt like Christ or something dramatic.

I kept my eyes closed so I couldn't see whether they threw a robe or something over her.

then the cop who snapped the bracelets said to the other cop, "I'll take her on the elevator. we'll go on the elevator."

and I couldn't hear very well, but I listened as they went down, and I heard Margy screaming, "oooooh, oooooooh, you bastard. let go of me, let go of me!"

and he kept saying, "shut up, shut up, shut up! you're only getting what you deserve! and you haven't seen ANYTHING yet! this . . . is just the . . . beginning!"

then she really screamed.

then the other cop walked over to me. through one narrowed eye I could see him put his big black shiny shoe up on the mattress, up on the sheet.

he looked down at me.

"is this guy a fag? he looks like a fag, sure as hell."

"I don't THINK he is. he might be. he can sure ball a broad, though."

"you want me to run him in?" he asked Vicki.

I had my eyes closed. it was a long wait. god, it was a long wait. that big foot there on my sheets. the electric light shining down.

then she spoke. finally. "no, he's . . . o.k. leave him there."

the cop took his foot down. I heard him walk across the room, then wait at the door. he spoke to Vicki:

"I'm going to have to charge you 5 bucks more for your protection next month. you're getting a bit harder to watch out for."

then he was gone. I mean, out into the hall. I waited for him to get into the elevator. I heard it go down to the first floor. I counted to 64. then, I LEAPED OUT OF BED.

my nostrils were flaring like Gregory Peck in heat.

"YOU ROTTEN BITCH. YOU EVER DO THAT AGAIN AND I'M GOING TO KILL YOU!"

"NO, NO, NO!!!!"

I raised my hand to give her the old backhand.

"I TOLD HIM NOT TO TAKE YOU!" she screamed at me.

"ummm. that's right. I've got to consider that."

I lowered my hand.

then there was some whiskey left and some wine too. I got up and put the chain on the door.

we turned off the lights and sat there and drank and smoked and talked about things. this, and that. easy and casual. then, like old times, we looked at the same red horse that flew and flew in red neon on the side of a building just downtown to our east. it flew and flew on the side of this building all night. no matter what happened. you know what it was, a kind of red horse with red wings of neon. but I told you that. a winged horse. anyhow. like always, we counted: one, two, three, four, five, six, seven. the wings always flapped 7 times. then the horse, everything, stood still. then, it started again. our whole apartment would be in this red glow. then when the horse stopped flying, somehow things would get white for a flash. I don't know why. I think that it was caused by an advertisement beneath the red winged horse. it said, some kind of product, buy this or buy that, in this WHITE. anyhow.

we sat and talked and drank and smoked.

later we went to bed together. she kissed very nicely, her tongue was kind of an apologetic sadness.

then we fucked. we fucked as the red horse flew.

7 times the wings flapped. and in the center of the rug the 3 chickens were still there, watching. the chickens turned red, the chickens turned white, the chickens turned red. 7 times they turned red. then they turned white. 14 times they turned red. then they turned white. 21 times they turned red. then they turned white. 28 times . . .

it had ended a better night than most.

TEN JACK-OFFS

old Sanchez is a genius but I am the only one who knows it and it's always good to go see him. there are very few people I can stay in a room with more than 5 minutes without feeling gutted. Sanchez passes my tests, and I am very test, hehehehe, oh my god, anyhow, I go to see him now and then in his hand-built two story shack. he installed his own plumbing, has a free-feed line from a high-power voltage line, has connected himself up a telephone which feeds underground from a neighbor's installation, but he explains to me that he cannot call long distance or out of the city without exposing his sycophancy. he even lives with a young woman who says very little, paints, walks about looking sexy and makes love to him and him to her, of course. he bought the ground for very little and although the place is some distance from Los Angeles, you might call this an advantage. he sits among wires, popular mechanics magazines, tape recording sets, shelves and shelves of books on all subjects. he is concise, never rude; he is humourous and magic, he writes very well but is not interested in fame. once in a great while he will out from his cave and read his poetry at some university, and it is said that the walls and the ivy tremble and shake for weeks afterwards along with the co-eds. he has taped 10,000 tapes of conversation, sounds, music . . . dull and undull, usual and otherwise. the walls are covered with photos, advertisements, drawings, hunks of rock, snake skins, skulls, dried rubbers, soot, silver and spots of golddust.

"I'm afraid I'm cracking," I tell him, "eleven years on the same job, the hours dragging over me like wet shit, wow, and all the faces melted down to zeros, yapping, laughing at nothing. I'm no snob, Sanchez, but sometimes it gets to be a real horror show and the only end is death or madness."

"sanity is an imperfection," he says, dropping a couple of pills into his mouth.

"jesus, I mean, I'm taught at several universities, some prof is writing a book on me ... I've been translated into several languages ..."

"we all have. you're getting old, Bukowski, you're weakening. keep your moxie. Victory or Death."

"Adolph."

"Adolph."

"large gamble, large loss."

"right, or invert it for the common man."

"well, fuck."

"yeah."

it gets quiet for a while, then he says, "you can come live with us."

"thanks, sure, man. but I think I'll try a little more moxie first."

"your game."

Over his head is a black sign upon which he has pasted in white type:

> "*A BOY HAS NEVER WEPT, NOR DASHED A THOU-SAND KIM.*"
> — *Dutch Schultz, on his deathbed.*
> "*WITH ME, GRAND OPERA IS THE BERRIES.*"
> — *Al Capone*
> "*NE CRAIGNEZ POINT, MONSIEUR, LE TORTUE.*"
> — *Leibnetz.*
> "*THERE IS NO MORE.*"
> — *Motto of Sitting Bull.*
> "*THE POLICEMAN'S CLIENT IS THE ELECTRIC CHAIR.*"
> — *George Jessel.*
> "*FAST AND LOOSE IN ONE THING, FAST AND LOOSE IN EVERYTHING.*

*I NEVER KNEW IT FAIR. NO MORE
WILL YOU. NOR NO ONE."*
> – *Detective Bucket.*

"AMEN IS THE INFLUENCE OF NUMBERS."
> – *Pico Della Mirandola,*
> *in his kabbalistic conclusions.*

*"SUCCESS AS THE RESULT OF INDUSTRY IS A
PEASANT IDEAL."*
> – *Wallace Stevens.*

*"TO ME, MY SHIT STINKS BETTER EXCEPT THAN
A DOG'S."*
> – *Charles Bukowski.*

*"NOW THE PORNOGRAPHERS WERE ASSEMBLED
WITHIN THE CREMATORIUM."*
> – *Anthony Bloomfield.*

*"ADAGE OF SPONTANEITY – THE BACHELOR
GRINDS HIS CHOCOLATE HIMSELF."*
> – *Marcel Duchamp.*

"KISS THE HAND YOU CANNOT SEVER."
> – *Taureg saying.*

"WE ALL, IN OUR DAY, WERE SMART FELLOWS."
> – *Admiral St. Vincent.*

"MY DREAM IS TO SAVE THEM FROM NATURE."
> – *Christian Dior.*

"OPEN SESAME – I WANT OUT."
> – *Stanislas Jerzy Lec.*

*"A YARDSTICK DOES NOT SAY THAT
THE OBJECT TO BE MEASURED
IS ONE YARD LONG."*
> – *Ludwig Wittgenstein.*

I am a bit gone on beer. "Say, I like that last one: 'the object to
be murdered does not have to be a yard long.'"

"I think that's even better but it's not what is said."

"all right. how's Kaakaa? that's baby-language for shit. and a
more sexy woman I've never seen."

"I know. and it started with Kafka. she used to like Kafka and
I called her that. then she changed it herself." he gets up and
walks to a photo. "come 'ere, Bukowski." I flip my beercan into
the trashcan and walk on over. "what's this?" asks Sanchez.

I look at the photo. it is a very good photo.

"well, it looks like a cock."

"what kinda cock?"

"a stiff cock. a big one."

"it's mine."

"so?"

"don't you notice?"

"what?"

"the sperm."

"yes, I see it. I didn't want to say . . ."

"why not? what the hell's wrong with you?"

"I don't understand."

"I mean, do you see the sperm or don't you?"

"what do you mean?"

"I mean, I'm JACKING OFF, can't you understand how hard that is to do?"

"it's not hard, Sanchez, I do it all the time . . ."

"oh, you ox! I mean I had the camera rigged-up with a string. Do you realize what an enactment it was to remain quietly in focus, ejaculate and trigger the camera at the same time?"

"I don't use a camera."

"how many men do? you miss the point, as usual. who the hell you are translated into the German, the Spanish, the French and so forth, I'll never know! look, do you realize that it took me THREE DAYS to make this SIMPLE photograph? do you know how many times I had to JACKOFF?"

"4 times?"

"TEN TIMES!"

"oh, Lord! how about Kaakaa?"

"she *liked* the photo."

"I mean . . ."

"good god, boy, I don't have the tongue to answer your simplicity."

He goes on around back there and plops himself in his chair again among his wires and pliers and translations and his huge BITTER-LEAP notebook, Adolph's nose glued to the black front with edgeworks of the Berlin bunker in the background.

"I'm working on something now," I tell him, "story about me walking in to interview the great composer. he's drunk. I get drunk, there's a maid. we're on the wine. he leans forward and tells me, 'The Meek Shall Inherit the Earth,' –"

"yeah?"

"and then he says, 'translated that means that the stupid have the greatest persistency.'"

"kind of lousy," he says, "but it's all right for you."

"but I don't know what to do with the story. I've got this maid walking around in a very short thing and I don't know what to do with her. the composer gets drunk, I get drunk and she walks around flashing her ass, hot as hell, and I don't know what to do with it. I thought I might save the story by whiplashing the maid with my belt buckle and then sucking the composer's dick. but I've never sucked dick, never felt like it, I'm square, so I left the story in the center and never finished it."

"every man is a homo, a dick-sucker; every woman is a dyke, why do you worry so much?"

"because if I'm not happy I'm no good and I don't want to be no good."

We sit there a while and then she comes from upstairs, this flaxen straight string hair.

it's the first woman I could eat, I think.

but she walks past Sanchez and his tongue licks his lips just a bit, she walks past me like separate ball-bearings of magic wavering crazy flesh, may the heavens kiss my balls if it is not so, and she waves through it all glorious as avalanche smashed by sun . . .

"hello, Hank," she says.

"Kaakaa," I laugh.

she goes behind her table and begins her bits of painting and he sits there, Sanchez, beard blacker than black power, but calm calm, no claims. I begin to get drunk, say nasty things, say anything. then I begin to get dull. I mumble, I murmur. "Oh, sorry . . . ta spoil yr evening . . . so sorry, fuckers . . . ya . . . I'm a killer but I won't kill anybody. I got class. I'm Bukowski! translated into SEVEN LANGUAGES! I AM the ONE! BUKOWSKI!"

I fall forward trying to look at the jack-off picture again, pitch over something. it is one of my own shoes. I have this god damn bad habit of taking off my own shoes.

"Hank," she says, "be careful."

"Bukowski?" he asks, "you all right?"

he lifts me up. "man, I think you better stay here tonight."

"NO GOD DAMN IT, I'M GOING TO THE WOOD-CHOPPERS BALL!"

next thing I know he's got me over his shoulder, Sanchez has and he's carrying me to his upstairs pad, you know, where he and his woman do the thing, and then I'm down on the bed, he's gone, door closed, and then I hear some kind of music downstairs, and laughter, the both of them, but kind laughter, no malice, and I did not know what to do, one did not expect the best, luck or people, everybody failed you finally, well, and then the door opened, a pop of light, and there was Sanchez –

"hey, Bubu, a bottle of good French wine . . . sip it slowly, do you most good. you'll sleep. be happy. I won't say we love you, that's too easy. and if you want to come downstairs, dance and sing, talk, o.k. do what you want. here's the wine."

he hands me the bottle. I lift it like some crazy cornet, again and again. through a ripped curtain a part of the worn moon leaps. it is a perfectly good night; it is not jail; it is far from that . . .

in the morning when I awaken, go down to piss, come out from pissing, I find them both asleep on that narrow couch hardly enough for one body, but they are not one body and their faces together and asleep their bodies together and asleep, why be corny??? I only feel the tiny clutch at the throat, the automatic transmission blues of loveliness, that somebody has it, that they don't even hate me . . . that they even wish me what? . . .

I walk out staunching and griefing and feeling and sick and blue and bukowski, old, starlit sun, my god, reaching into the final corner, the last midnight blast, cold Mr. C., big H, Mary Mary, clean as a bug on the wall, the heat of December a brainweb across my everlasting spine, Mercy like Kerouac's dead baby sprawled across Mexican railroad tracks in the everlasting July of suck-off tombs, I leave them in their there thar, the genius and his love, both better than I, but Meaning, itself, shitting, shifting, sanding down, until, I maybe writing this down by myself, leaving a few things out (I have been threatened by various powerful forces for doing things that are only normal and gaga gladful to do)

and I get into my eleven year old car
and now I have driven away
find myself here
and write you here a little illegal story of
love
beyond myself

but, perhaps, understandable to
you.

yours truly,

Sanchez and Bukowski

p.s. – this time the Heat missed. don't keep more than you can
swallow: love, heat or hate.

TWELVE FLYING MONKEYS WHO WON'T COPULATE PROPERLY

The bell rings and I open the side window by the door. It is night.
"Who is it?" I ask.

Somebody walks up to the window but I can't see the face. I
have two lights over the typewriter. I slam the window but there
is talking out there. I sit down to the typewriter but there is still
talking out there. I leap up and rip open the door and scream:

"I TOLD YOU COCKSUCKERS NOT TO BOTHER ME!"

I look around and there is one guy standing on the bottom of
the steps and another guy standing on the porch, pissing. He is
pissing into a bush to the left of the porch, standing on the edge
of the porch, his piss arcing in a heavy swath, upward and then
down into the bush.

"Hey, this guy is pissing into my bush," I say.

The guy laughs and keeps pissing. I grab him by the pants, pick
him up and throw him, still pissing, over the top of the bush and
into the night. He doesn't return. The other guy says, "What did
you do that for?"

"I felt like it."

"You're drunk."

"Drunk?" I ask.

He walks around the corner and is gone. I close the door and
sit down to the typer again. All right, I have this mad scientist,

he's taught monkeys to fly, he's got eleven monkeys with these wings. The monkeys are very good. The scientist has even taught them to race. Race around these pylons, yes. Now let's see. Gotta make it good. To get rid of a story you gotta have fucking, lots of it, if possible. Better make it twelve monkeys, six male and six of the other kind. All right now. Here they go. The race is on. There they go around the first pylon. How am I going to get them to fucking? I haven't sold a story in two months. I should have stayed in the goddamned post office. All right. There they go. Around the first pylon. Maybe they just fly off. Suddenly. How about that? They fly to Washington, D.C. and hang around the Capitol dropping turds on the public, pissing on them, smearing their turds across the White House. Can I have one drop a turd on the President? No, that's asking too much. Okay, make it a turd on the Secretary of State. Orders are given to shoot them out of the sky. That's tragic, isn't it? But what about the fucking? All right. All right. Work it in. Let's see. Okay, ten of them are shot out of the sky, poor little things. There are only two others. A male and one other kind. They can't seem to be found. Then a cop is walking though the park one night, and there they are, the last two of them, wings strapped on, fucking like the devil. The cop walks up. The male hears, turns his head, looks up, gives a silly little monkey-grin, never missing a stroke, then turns his head and goes back to banging. The cop blows his head off. The monkey's head, that is. The female flips the male off in disgust and stands up. For a monkey, she is a pretty little thing. For a moment the cop thinks of, thinks of – But no, it would be too tight, maybe, and she might bite, maybe. While he's thinking this, she turns and begins to fly off. The cop aims as she rises, hits her with a bullet, she falls. He runs up. She is wounded but not dead. The cop looks around, lifts her up, takes it out, tries to work it in. No good. Just room for the head. Shit. He drops her to the ground, puts the gun to her brain and B A M! it's over.

The bell rings again.

I open the door.

Three guys walk in. Always these guys. A woman never pisses on my porch, a woman hardly ever comes by. How am I going to get any sex ideas? I have almost forgotten how to do it. But they say it's like riding a bicycle, you never forget. It's better than riding a bicycle.

It's Crazy Jack and two guys I don't know.

"Look, Jack," I say, "I thought I was rid of you."

Jack just sits down. The other two guys sit down. Jack has promised me never to come by again but he is on the wine most of the time, so promises don't mean much. He lives with his mother and pretends to be a painter. I know four or five guys living with or supported by their mother, and the guys pretend to genius. And all the mothers are alike: "Oh, Nelson has never had any work accepted. He's too far ahead of his time." But say Nelson is a painter and gets something hung: "Oh, Nelson has a painting hanging at the Warner-Finch Galleries this week. His genius is being recognized at last! He's asking $4,000 for the work. Do you think that's too much?" Nelson, Jack, Biddy, Norman, Jimmy and Ketya. Fuck.

Jack has on blue jeans, is barefooted, no shirt, undershirt, just a brown shawl thrown over him. One guy has a beard and grins and blushes continually. The other guy is just fat. Some kind of leech.

"Have you seen Borst lately?" Jack asks.

"No."

"Let me have one of your beers."

"No. You guys come around, drink all my shit, split and leave me on a dry shore."

"All right."

He leaps up, runs out and gets his wine bottle which he has hidden under the cushion on the porch chair. He comes back, takes off the lid, takes a suck.

"I was down at Venice with this chick and one hundred rainbows. I thought I spotted the heat and I ran up to Borst's place with this chick and the hundred rainbows. I knocked on the door and told him, 'Quick, let me in! I've got one hundred rainbows and the heat is right behind me!' Borst closed the door. I kicked it in and ran in with the chick. Borst was on the floor, jacking off some guy. I ran into the bathroom with the chick and locked the door. Borst knocked. I said, 'Don't you dare come in here!' I stayed in there with the chick for about an hour. We knocked off two pieces of ass to amuse ourselves. Then we came out."

"Did you dump the rainbows?"

"Hell no, it was a false alarm. But Borst was very angry."

"Shit," I say, "Borst hasn't written a decent poem since 1955. His mother supports him. Pardon me. But I mean, all he does is look at TV, eat these delicate little celeries and greens and jog along the beach in his dirty underwear. He used to be a fine poet when he was living with those young boys in Arabia. But I can't sympathize. A winner goes wire to wire. It's like Huxley said, Aldous, that is, 'Any man can be a . . .' "

"How you doing?" Jack asks.

"Nothing but rejects," I say.

The one guy begins playing his flute. The leech just sits there. Jack lifts his wine bottle. It is a beautiful night in Hollywood, California. Then the guy who lives in the court behind me falls out of bed, drunk. It makes quite a sound. I'm used to it. I'm used to the whole court. All of them sit in their places, shades drawn. They get up at noon. Their cars sit out front dust-covered, tires going down, batteries weakening. They mix drink with dope and have no visible means of support. I like them. They don't bother me.

The guy gets into bed again, falls out.

"You silly damn fool," you hear him say, "get back into that bed."

"What's all that noise?" Jack asks.

"Guy behind me. He's very lonely. Drinks a beer now and then. His mother died last year and left him twenty grand. He sits around and masturbates and looks at baseball games and cowboy shootums on TV. Used to be a gas station attendant."

"We've got to split." says Jack, "want to come with us?"

"No," I say.

They explain that it is something to do with the House of Seven Gables. They are going to see somebody who had something to do with the House of Seven Gables. It isn't the writer, the producer, the actors, it is somebody else.

"Well, no," I say, and they all run out. It is a beautiful sight.

Then I sit down to the monkeys again. Maybe I can juggle those monkeys up. If I can get all twelve of them fucking at once! That's it! But how? And why? Check the Royal Ballet of London. But why? I'm going crazy. Okay, the Royal Ballet of London has this idea. Twelve monkeys flying while they ballet. Only before the performance somebody gives them all the Spanish Fly. Not the ballet. The monkeys. But the Spanish Fly is a myth, isn't it? Okay, enter another mad scientist with a real Spanish Fly! No, no, oh my God, I just can't get it right!

The phone rings. I pick it up. It's Borst:

"Hello, Hank?"

"Yeah?"

"I have to keep it short. I'm broke."

"Yes, Jerry."

"Well, I lost my two sponsors. The stock market and the tight dollar."

"Uh huh."

"Well, I always knew it was going to happen. So I'm getting out of Venice. I can't make it here. I'm going to New York City."

"What?"

"New York City."

"I thought that's what you said."

"Well, I'm broke you see, and I think I can really make it there."

"Sure, Jerry."

"Losing my sponsors is the best thing that ever happened to me."

"Really?"

"Now I feel like fighting again. You've heard about people rotting along the beach. Well, that's what I've been doing down here: rotting. I've got to get out of here. And I'm not worried. Except for the trunks."

"What trunks?"

"I can't seem to get them packed. So my mother's coming back from Arizona to live here while I'm gone, and eventually I'll be back here."

"All right, Jerry."

"But before I go to New York I'm going to stop off at Switzerland and perhaps Greece. Then I'm coming back to New York."

"All right, Jerry, keep in touch. Always good to hear."

Then I am back to the monkeys again. Twelve monkeys who can fly, fucking. How can it be done? Twelve bottles of beer are gone. I find my reserve half-pint of scotch in the refrigerator. I mix one-third glass scotch with two-thirds water. I should have stayed in the goddamned post office. But even here, like this, you have a minor chance. Just get those twelve monkeys fucking. If you'd been born a camel boy in Arabia you wouldn't even have this chance. So get your back up and get those monkeys at it. You've been blessed with a minor talent and you're not in India where probably two dozen boys could write you under if they knew how to write. Well, maybe not two dozen, maybe just a round dozen.

I finish the half-pint, drink half a bottle of wine, go to bed, forget it.

The next morning at nine a.m. the doorbell rings. There is a young black girl standing there with a stupid-looking white guy in rimless glasses. They tell me that I have made a promise to go boating with them at a party three nights ago. I get dressed, get into the car with them. They drive to an apartment and a black-haired kid walks out. "Hello, Hank," he says. I don't know him. It appears I met him at the party. He passes out little orange life-belts. Next I know we're down at the pier. I can't tell the pier from the water. They help me down a swinging wooden contraption that leads to a floating dock. The bottom of the contraption and the dock are about three feet apart. They help me down.

"What the fuck is this?" I ask. "Does anybody have a drink?" I am with the wrong people. Nobody has a drink. Then I am in a small rowboat, rented, and somebody has attached a half-horsepower motor. The bottom of the boat is filled with water and two dead fish. I don't know who the people are. They know me. Fine, fine. We head out to sea. I vomit. We pass a suckerfish floating near the top of the water. A suckerfish, I think, a suckerfish wrapped around a flying monkey. No, that's terrible. I vomit again.

"How's the great writer?" asks the stupid-looking guy in the prow of the boat, the guy with the rimless glasses.

"What great writer?" I ask, thinking he is talking about Rimbaud, although I never thought Rimbaud a great writer.

"You," he says.

"Me?" I say, "Oh, fine. Think I'm going to Greece next year."

"Grease?" he says. "You mean up your ass?"

"No," I answer, "up yours."

We head out to sea where Conrad made it. To hell with Conrad. I'll take coke with bourbon in a dark bedroom in Hollywood in 1970, or whatever year you read this. The year of the monkey-orgy that never happened. The motor flits and gnashes at the sea; we plunge on toward Ireland. No, it's the Pacific. We plunge on toward Japan. To hell with it.

25 BUMS IN RAGS

you know how it is with horseplayers. you hit it hot and you think it's all over. I had this place in back, even had my own garden, planted all kinds of tulips, which grew, beautifully and amazingly. I had the green hand. I had the green money. what system I had devised I can no longer remember, but it was working and I wasn't and that's a pleasant enough way to live. and there was Kathy. Kathy had it. the old guy next door would actually slobber at the mouth when he saw her. he was always knocking at the door. "Kathy! oooh, Kathy! Kathy!"

I'd answer the door, just dressed in my shorts.

"ooooh, I thought . . ."

"what do you want, mother?"

"I thought Kathy . . ."

"Kathy's taking a shit. any message?"

"I . . . bought these bones for your dog."

he had a big bag of dry chicken bones.

"feeding a dog chicken bones is like putting broken razor-blades in a child's cereal. you trying to kill my dog, fucker?"

"oh, no!"

"then jam the bones and split."

"I don't understand."

"stick that bag of chicken bones up your ass and get the hell out of here!"

"I just thought Kathy . . ."

"*I told* you, Kathy's taking a SHIT!"

I slammed the back door on him.

"you shouldn't be so hard on the old fart, Hank, he says I remind him of his daughter when she was young."

"all right, so he made it with his daughter. let him screw swiss cheese. I don't want him at the door."

"I suppose you think I let him in after you go to the track?"

"I don't even wonder about that."

"what do you wonder about?"

"all I wonder is which one of you rides topside."

"you son of a bitch, you can leave now!"

I was getting on my shirt and pants, then socks and shoes.

"I won't be 4 blocks away before you're locked in embrace."

she threw a book at me. I wasn't looking and the edge of the book hit me over the right eye. a cut started and a spot of blood hit my hand as I tied my right shoe.

"I'm sorry, Hank."

"don't get NEAR me!"

I went out and got into the car, backed out the drive at 35 miles an hour, taking part of the hedge with me, then some of the stucco from the front house with my left rear fender. there was blood on my shirt then and I took out my handkerchief and held it over the eye. it was going to be a bad Saturday at the track. I was mad.

I bet like the atomic bomb was on the way. I wanted to make ten grand. I bet longshots. I didn't cash a ticket. I lost $500. all I had taken out. I just had a dollar in my wallet. I drove in slowly. it was going to be a terrible Saturday night. I parked the car and went in the back door.

"Hank . . ."

"what?"

"you look like death. what happened?"

"I blew it. I blew the roll. 500."

"jesus. I'm sorry," she said, "it's my fault." she came up to me, put her arms around me. "god damn, I'm sorry, daddy. it was my fault, I know it."

"forget it. you didn't make the bets."

"are you still mad?"

"no, no, I know you're not fucking that old turkey."

"can I make you something to eat?"

"no, no, just get us a fifth of whiskey and the paper."

I got up and went to the hidden money cache. we were down to $180. well, it had been worse, many times, but I felt that I was on my way back to the factories and the warehouses, *if* I could get that. I came out with a ten. the dog still liked me. I pulled his ears. he didn't care how much money I had or how little. a real ace dog. yeah. I walked out of the bedroom. Kathy was putting on lipstick in front of the mirror. I pinched her on the ass and kissed her behind the ear.

"get me some beer and cigars too. I need to forget."

she left and I listened to her heels clicking on the drive. she was as good a woman as I had found and I had found her in a bar. I leaned back in the chair and stared at the ceiling. a bum. I was a bum. always this distaste for work, always trying to live off my luck. when Kathy came back I told her to pour a big one. she knew. she even peeled the cellophane off my cigar and lit it for me. she looked funny, and fine. we'd make love. we'd make love through the sadness. I just hated to see it go: car, house, dog, woman. it had been gentle and easy living.

I guess I was shaken because I opened the paper and looked at the WANT ADS.

"hey, Kathy, here's something. men wanted, Sunday. pay same day."

"oh, Hank, rest up tomorrow. you'll get those horses Tuesday. everything will look better then."

"but shit, baby, every buck counts! they don't run on Sunday. Caliente, yeah, but you can't beat that 25 percent Caliente take and the distance. I can get good and drunk tonight and then pick up this shit tomorrow. those extra bucks might make the difference."

Kathy looked at me funny. she'd never heard me talk like that before. I always acted like the money would be there. that 500 dollar loss had left me in shock. she poured me another tall one. I drank it right off. shock, shock, lord, lord, the factories. the wasted days, the days without meaning, the days of bosses and idiots, and the slow and brutal clock.

we drank until two a.m., just like at the bar, then went to bed, made love, slept. I set the alarm for four a.m., was up and in the car and downtown skidrow at 4:30 a.m. I stood on the corner with about 25 bums in rags. they stood there rolling cigarettes and drinking wine.

well, it's money, I thought. I'll get back ... some day I'll vacation in Paris or Rome. shit on these guys. I don't belong here.

then something said to me, that's what they're ALL thinking: I don't belong here. each one of THEM is thinking that about HIMSELF. and they're right. so?

the truck came along about 5:10 a.m. and we climbed in.

god, I could be sleeping along behind Kathy's fine ass about now. but it's money, money.

guys were talking about just getting off the boxcar. they stank, poor fellows. but they didn't seem miserable. I was the only one who was miserable.

I would be getting up about now, taking a piss. I would be having a beer in the kitchen, looking for the sun, seeing it get lighter, peeking at my tulips. then going back to bed with Kathy.

the guy next to me said, "hey, buddy!"

"yeah," I said.

"I'm a Frenchman," he said.

I didn't answer.

"can you use a blowjob?"

"no," I said.

"I saw one guy blowing another in the alley this morning. this one guy had this LONG THIN white dick and the other guy was still sucking and the come was dripping out of his mouth. I watched and watched and god I'm hot as hell. let me suck your dick, buddy!"

"no," I told him, "I don't feel like it right now."

"well, if I can't do that, maybe you can suck mine."

"get the hell out of here!" I told him.

the Frenchman moved further back into the truck. by the time we'd gone another mile his head was bobbing. he was doing it right in front of everybody, to some old guy who looked like an Indian.

"GO, BABY, GET IT ALL!!!" somebody shouted.

some of the bums laughed but most of them were just silent, drinking their wine and rolling their cigarettes. the old Indian acted like it wasn't even happening. by the time we got to Vermont the Frenchman had got it all and we all climbed out, the Frenchman, the Indian, myself and the other bums. they gave us each a little tab of paper and we walked into a cafe. the little tab was good for a doughnut and a coffee. the waitress held her nose up. we stank. dirty cocksuckers.

then somebody finally hollered, "everybody out!"

I followed them out and we went into a big room and sat in these chairs like they used to have in school, or college rather, say like in Music Appreciation. with the big slab of wood for the right arm so you could open your notebook and write on it there. anyhow, so there we sat for another 45 minutes. then some snot kid with a can of beer in his hand, said, "o.k., get your SACKS!"

the bums all leaped up at ONCE and RAN to this large back room. what the hell? I thought. I slowly walked on back and looked in the other room, the bums were in there pushing and fighting for the best paper carriers. it was deadly and senseless battle. when the last man had left the back room I walked in and picked up the first sack I found on the floor. it was very dirty and full of rips and holes. when I walked out into the other room the bums all had their paper carriers on their backs, wearing them. I found a seat and just sat there with mine in my lap. somewhere along the line I think they had gotten our names; I think it was before you got your coffee and doughnut tab you gave your name. so we sat there and were called out in groups of 5 or 6 or 7. this took, it seemed, another hour. anyhow, by the time I got into the back of this smaller truck with a few others, the sun was well up. they gave us each a little map of the streets we were to deliver papers to. I opened my little map. I recognized the streets all right: GOD OH MIGHTY, OUT OF THE WHOLE TOWN OF LOS ANGELES THEY HAD GIVEN ME MY OWN NEIGHBOR-HOOD!

I had the rep as drinker, gambler, hustler, man of leisure, shack-job specialist. how could I be SEEN with that filthy dirty sack on my back? delivering newspapers full of ads?

they put me out on my corner. very familiar surroundings, indeed. there was the flowershop, there was the bar, the gas station, everything ... around the corner my little house with Kathy sleeping in her warm bed. even the dog was asleep. well, it's Sunday morning, I thought. nobody will see me. they sleep late. I'll run through the god damned route. and I did.

I ran up and down 2 streets very quickly and nobody saw the great man of class and soft white hands and great soulful eyes. I was going to get by with it.

then up the 3rd street. it was going well until I heard the voice of a little girl. she was in her yard. about 4 years old.

"hey, mister!"

"oh, yes? little girl? what is it?"

"where's your dog?"

"oh, haha, he's still asleep."

"oh."

I always walked the dog up that street. there was a vacant lot there he always shit in. that did it. I took all my remaining newspapers and dumped them into the back of an abandoned car near the freeway. the car had been there for months with all the wheels gone. I didn't know what it meant. but I put all the newspapers on the rear floor. then I walked around the corner and went into my house. Kathy was still asleep. I awakened her.

"Kathy! Kathy!"

"oh, Hank . . . everything all right?"

the dog ran on in and I petted him.

"you know what those sons of bitches DID?"

"what?"

"they gave me my *own* neighborhood to deliver papers in!"

"oh. well, it's not nice but I don't think the people will mind."

"don't you understand? I've built this REP! I'm the hustler! I can't be seen with a bag of shit on my back!"

"oh, I don't think you have all that REP! it's just in your head."

"listen, are you going to give me a lot of shit? you've had your ass in this warm bed while I've been out there with a lot of cocksuckers!"

"don't be angry. I've got to pee. wait a minute."

I waited out there while she took her sleepy female piss. god, they were SLOW! the cunt was a very inefficient pissing machine. dick had it all beat.

Kathy came out.

"please don't worry, Hank. I'll put on an old dress and help you deliver the papers. we'll finish fast. people sleep late on Sundays."

"but I've already been SEEN!"

"you've already been seen? who saw you?"

"that little girl in the brown house with the weeds on Westmoreland st."

"you mean Myra?"

"I don't know her name!"

"she's only 3."

"I don't know how old she is! she asked about the dog!"

"what about the dog?"

"she asked where it WAS!"

"come on, I'll help you get rid of the papers."

Kathy was climbing into an old ripped dress.

"I got rid of them. it's over. I dumped them into the back of that abandoned car."

"will they catch you?"

"FUCK! who cares?"

I went into the kitchen and got a beer. when I got back Kathy was in bed again. I sat in a chair.

"Kathy?"

"uh?"

"you just don't realize who you're living with! I'm class, real class! I'm 34 but I haven't worked 6 or 7 months since I was 18 years old. and no money. look at my hands! I've got hands like a pianist!"

"Class? you OUGHT to HEAR yourself when you're drunk! you're horrible, horrible!"

"are you trying to start some shit again, Kathy? I've kept you in furs and hundred proof since I dug you outa that gin mill on Alvarado st."

Kathy didn't answer.

"in fact," I told her, "I am a genius but nobody knows it but me."

"I'll buy that," she said. then she dug her head into the pillow and went back to sleep.

I finished the beer, had another, then went 3 blocks over and sat on the steps of a closed grocery store that the map said would be the meeting place where the man would pick me up. I sat there from 10 a.m. to 2:30 p.m. it was dull and dry and stupid and torturous and senseless. then the rotten truck came at 2:30 p.m.

"hey. buddy?"

"yum?"

"you finished already?"

"yum."

"you're fast!"

"yep."

"I want you to help this one guy finish his route."

oh, fuck.

I got into the truck and then he let me off. here was this guy. he was CREEPING. he threw each paper with great care upon each porch. each porch got special treatment. and he seemed to enjoy his work. he was on his last block. I finished the whole thing off in 5 minutes. then we sat and waited for the truck. for an hour.

they drove us back to the office and we sat in our school chairs again. then two snot-nosed kids came out with cans of beer in their hands. one called off names and the other gave each man his money.

on a blackboard written in chalk behind the heads of the snot-noses was a message:

"ANY MAN WHO WORKS FOR US 30 DAYS IN A ROW
WITHOUT MISSING A DAY
WILL BE GIVEN
A FREE
SECOND HAND SUIT."

I kept watching as each man was handed his money. it couldn't be true. it APPEARED that each man was given three one dollar bills. at the time, the lowest basic wage scale by law was one dollar an hour. I had been on that corner at 4:30 a.m. now it was 4:30 p.m. to me, that was 12 hours.

I was one of the last names called. I think I was 3rd from last. not a one of those bums raised hell. they just took the $3 and went out the door.

"Bukowski!" the snot-nosed kid hollered.

I walked up. the other snot-nosed kid counted out 3 very clean and crisp Washingtons.

"listen," I said, "don't you guys realize that there is a basic wage law? one buck an hour."

the snot-nose raised his beer. "we deduct for transportation, breakfast and so forth. we only pay for average working time which we figure to be about 3 hours or so."

"I see twelve hours out of my life. and I've got to take a bus downtown now to go get my car and drive it back in."

"you're lucky to have a car."

"and you're lucky I don't jam that can of beer up your ass!"

"I don't set company policy, sir, please don't blame me."

"I'm going to report you to the State Labor Board!"

"Robinson!" the other snot-nose hollered.

the next to last bum got up from his seat for his $3 as I walked out the door and on up to Beverly blvd. to wait for the bus. by the time I got home and got a drink in my hand it was 6 p.m. or so. I really got drunk then. I was so frustrated I banged Kathy 3 times. broke a window. cut my foot on broken glass. sang songs from Gilbert and Sullivan, which I once learned from an insane English teacher who taught an English class which began at 7 a.m. in the morning. L.A. City College. Richardson was his name, and maybe he wasn't insane. but he taught me Gilbert and Sullivan and gave me a "d" in English for showing up no sooner than 7:30 a.m. with hangover, WHEN I showed. but that's something else. Kathy and I had some laughs that night, and although I broke a few things I was not as nasty and stupid as usual.

and that Tuesday at Hollywood Park I won $140 at the races and I was once again the quite casual lover, hustler, gambler, reformed pimp and tulip grower. I drove slowly up the driveway, savoring the last of the evening sun. then I strolled in through the back door. Kathy had on some meat loaf with plenty of onions and crap and spices in it just the way I liked it. she was bent over at the stove and I grabbed her from the back.

"ooooo . . ."

"listen, baby . . ."

"yeah?"

she stood there with the large dripping spoon in her hand. I slipped a ten into the neck of her dress.

"I want you to get me a fifth of whiskey."

"sure, sure."

"and some beer and cigars. I'll watch the food."

she took off her apron and went into the bathroom for a moment. I could hear her humming. a moment later I sat in my chair and listened to her heels clicking down the drive. there was a tennis ball. I took the tennis ball and bounced it on the floor so it hit the wall and zoomed high into the air. the dog who was 5 feet long and 3 feet tall, ½ wolf, leaped into the air, there was the snap of teeth and he had that tennis ball, up near the ceiling. for a moment he seemed to hang up there. what a beautiful dog, what a beautiful life. when he hit the floor I got up to check the meatloaf. it was all right. everything was.

NON-HORSESHIT HORSE ADVICE

so, the Hollywood Park meet has begun, and naturally I have been
out a couple of times, and the scene is not very variable: the horses
look the same and the people a little worse, the horseplayer is a
combination of extreme conceit, madness and greed. one of
Freud's main pupils (I don't recall his name right now, only
remember reading the book) said that gambling is a substitute for
masturbation. of course, the problem with any direct statement is
that it can easily become an untruth, a part truth, a lie or a wilted
gardenia. yet, checking out the ladies (between races) I do find the
same oddity: before the first race they sit with their skirts down
as much as possible, and as each race proceeds the skirts climb
higher and higher, until just before the 9th race it takes all one's
facilities not to commit rape upon one of the darlings. whether it
is a sense of masturbation that causes this or whether the dear
little things need rent and bean money, I don't know. probably a
combo. I saw one lady leap over 2 or 3 rows of seats after getting
a winner, and screaming, screeching, divine as an iced-grapefruit
vodka across the top of a hangover. "she's getting hers now," said
my girlfriend.

"yeah," I said, "but I wish I had gotten there first."

for those of you unfamiliar with the basic principles of
horse-wagering, allow me to divert you with a few basics. the
difficulty in the average person leaving the track with any money

at all is easily propounded if you will follow this – the track and the state take roughly 15% out of each dollar bet, plus breakage. the 15% is divided about in half between the state and the track. in other words, 85 cents out of each dollar is returned to the holders of winning tickets. breakage is the penny difference on the ten cent breakdown of the payoff. in other words, say if the totalizer machine breaks the payoff down to a $16.84 payoff, then the winning player gets $16.80, the 4 cents on each winning bet going elsewhere. now I am not sure, because the thing is *not* publicized but I also believe that on, say, a $16.89 payoff, the payoff is still $16.80 and the 9 cents goes elsewhere, but I am not positive of this and "Open City" certainly can't afford a libel suit now or ever and neither can I, so I will not make this a positive presumption, but if any "Open City" reader has the facts on this, I do wish he would write O.C. and advise me. this penny breakage alone could make millionaires out of any of us.

now take the average goof who has worked all week and is looking for a little bit of luck, entertainment, masturbation. take 40 of them, give them each $100, and presuming that they are average bettors, the general medium based upon a 15% take, forgetting breakage, would have 40 of them leaving with $85. but it doesn't work that way – 35 of them will leave almost completely broke, one or two of them will win $85 or $150 by sheer fortune of falling upon the right horses and not knowing why. the 3 or 4 others will break even.

all right, then, who is getting all this money that the little bettor who works a turret lathe or drives a bus all week, loses? easy: the betting stables who send off bad-form horses in a spot that it is profitable for them to win in. stables cannot make it upon purse money alone, that is, most of them can't. give a stable a top handicap horse and they are in, but even they must resort to pulls and deliberately bad races in order to get weight off for a top money race. in other words, say a top-weighted horse gifted with 130 pounds by the track handicapper for an early $25,000 race will tend to lose this race and get weight off on that performance for a later $100,000 race. now these statements cannot be proven but if you will follow this conjecture you might make a little money or at least save a little. but it is the stables who must race in the lower class races with lower purses who must maneuver their horses for a price. in some cases, the owner of the horse or horses himself is not aware of the maneuvering; this is because trainers and grooms, hot-walkers, exercise jocks are grossly underpaid (in time and effort put in, compared to other industries) and their only way to get out is to put one over. the racetracks are aware of this and attempt to keep the game clean, to give it a holy sheen of honesty, but for all their efforts – barring tough guys, cons, syndicates, operators, from the track, there are still "goodies" put over on the crowd, a so-called pig who "wakes up" and wins by 3 to 10 lengths at odds of 5 to up to 50 to 1. but these are only animals, not machines. so there's an excuse, an excuse to haul away millions in wheelbarrows from the racetrack, tax-free. human greed will not relent, it will continue to feed itself. the communist party be damned.

all right, that's bad enough. let's take something else. besides the public being automatically wrong just by instinct (ask the stockbroker – when you want to know which way to move just move the opposite from the big crowd with the small, scared, tight money). but the something else is this: a possible mathematic. taking the dollar base – you invest the first dollar, you get back 85 cents. automatic take. second race, you have to *add* 15 cents, then another 15% take. now take 9 races and take a 15% take – on a break-even basis – upon your original dollar. is it just 9 times 15% or is it much more? it would take one of these Caltech cats to tell me and I don't know any Caltech cats. anyway, if you have followed me up to here, you must realize that it is very difficult to make a "living" at the racetrack as some starry-eyed dreamers would like to do.

I am a "hard-nose": that is, any given day at any track you just ain't gonna take much money from me; on the other hand, I ain't gonna make much. naturally, I have some good plays and I'd be a damn fool to reveal them to everybody because then they would not work. once the public gets onto something it is dead and it changes. the public is not allowed to win in any game ever invented and that includes the American Revolution. but for "Open City" readers I have a few basics that might save you a little money. take heed.

a/ watch your underlay shots. an underlay is a horse that closes in odds under the trackman's morning line. in other words, the trackman lists the horse at 10 to 1 and it is going off at 6 to 1. money is much more serious than anything else. check your underlays carefully, and if the line is just not a careless mistake by the trackman and the horse does not show any recent fast works or a switch to a "name" jockey, and if the horse is not dropping weight and is running against the same class, you will probably get a fairly good run for your money.

b/ lay off the closers. this is a horse, that say closed from 5 to 16 lengths from the beginning call to the last and still did not win and is coming back against the same or similar. the crowd loves the "closer," through fear & tight money and stupidity, but the closer is generally a lard-ass, lazy and only passes tired horses who have been running and fighting for the front end. not only does the crowd love this type of junk-horse but they will consistently bet him down to odds less than 1/3 of his worth. even though this type of horse continually runs out, the crowd out of fear will go to him because they are tight up against the rent money and feel that a closer possesses some kind of super strength. 90% of the races are won by horses on the front end or near the front end of all the running, at plausible and reasonable prices.

c/ if you must bet a "closer" bet him in shorter races, 6 or 7 furlongs, where the crowd believes he does not have time "to get up." here they go for the speed and are stuck again. 7 furlongs is the best closer's race in the business because of only *one* curve. a speed horse gets the advantage of being out in front and saving ground on the turns. 7 furlongs with one curve and the long backstretch is the perfect closer's race; much better than a mile and a quarter, even better than a mile and one half. I am giving you some good stuff here, I hope you heed it.

d/ watch your toteboard – money in American society is more serious than death and you hardly get anything for nothing. if a horse is listed at 6 to 1 on the morning line and he is going off at 14 to 25 to 1, forget it. either the trackman had a hangover when he made his morning line or the stable just isn't going that race. you don't get anything free in this world; if you don't know anything about racing, do bet horses *that go off close to their morning line.* large overlays are nil and almost impossible. all the little grandmamas go home to eat bitter toast with gummed teeth upon Papa's retirement death certificate.

e/ only bet when you can lose. I mean without ending up sleeping on a park bench or missing 3 or 4 meals. the main thing, get the rent down first. avoid pressures. you will be luckier. and remember what the pros say, "If you've got to lose, lose in front." in other words, make them beat *you.* if you're going to lose *anyhow*, then to hell with it, get you a dancer out of the gate, you've got it won until they beat you, until they pass you. the price is usually generous because the public hates what they call a "quitter" – a horse that opens daylight on the pack and still manages to lose. this looks bad to them. to me a "quitter" is *any* horse that does not win a race.

f/ any profit-loss venture is not based upon the number of winners you have but *upon the number of winners at the price.* empires have been built upon one quarter of one per cent. but back to basics, you can have three 6 to 5 winners in 9 races and wash out, but you can have one 9 to 1 and one 5 to 1 and get over. this does not always mean that a 6 to 5 is a bad bet, but if you know little or next to nothing about racing, it might be best to hold your bets between 7 to 2 and 9 to 1. or if you must indulge in wild fancies, keep your bets between 11 and 19 to 1. in fact, many 18 or 19 to 1's bounce in if you can find the right ones.

but, actually, a man can never know enough about horse racing or anything else. just when he thinks he knows he is just beginning. I remember one summer I won 4 grand at Hollypark and I went down to Del Mar in a new car, cocky, poetic, knowledgeable, I had the world by the nuts, and I rented myself a little motel by the sea and the ladies showed up as the ladies will when you are drinking and laughing and don't care and have some money (a fool and his money are soon parted) and I had a party every night and a new broad every other night, and it was a kind of joke I used to tell them, the place was right over the sea, and I'd say, after much drinking and talking, "Baby, I come with the WOOSH OF THE SEA!"

ANOTHER HORSE STORY

the harness racing season has been under way, as they say, for a
week or 2 now, and I have been out 5 or 6 times, perhaps
breaking even for the course, which is a hell of a waste of time –
anything is a waste of time unless you are fucking well or creating
well or getting well or looming toward a kind of phantom
love-happiness. we will all end up in the crud-pot of defeat – call
it death or error. I am not a word-man. I do suppose, tho, as one
keeps making adjustments to the tide, we can call it experience
even if we are not so sure that it is wisdom. then too, it is possible
for a man to live a whole life of constant error in a kind of numb
and terrorized state. you've seen the faces. I've seen my own.

so during all the heat wave they are still out there, the bettors,
having gotten a little money somewhere, the hard way, and trying
to beat the 15 percent take. I sometimes think of the crowd as
hypnotized, a crowd that has nowhere else to go. and after the
races they get into their old cars, drive to their lonely rooms and
look at the walls. wondering why they did it – heels run down,
bad teeth, ulcers, bad jobs, men without women, women without
men. nothing but shit.

there are some laughs. there have to be. walking into the men's
room between races the other day I came upon a young man
gagging, then shouting in fury: "god damn son of a bitch, some
god damn son of a bitch didn't flush his shit away! HE LEFT IT

THERE! the son of a bitch, I walked in and there it WAS! I'll bet he does that at home too!"

this boy was screaming. the rest of us were standing there pissing or washing our hands, thinking about the last race or the next one. I know some freaks that would be delighted to come upon a potful of fresh turds. but that's the way it works – the wrong guy gets it.

another day I am sweating, battling, scratching, praying, jacking to stay 10 or 12 bucks ahead, and it is a very difficult harness race, I don't even think the drivers know who is going to win, and this big fat woman, ponderous whale of healthy stinking blubber, walked up to me, put that stinking fat against my body front, and squeezed 2 little eyes, a mouth and the rest into my face and said, "what are the hands on the first horse?"

"the hands on the first horse?"

"yes, what are the hands on the first horse?"

"god damn you lady, get away from me, and don't bother me. get away! get away!"

she did. the whole track is full of crazy people. some of them come there when the gates open. they stretch out on the seats or on a bench and sleep all through the races. they never see a race. then they get up and go home. others walk around just vaguely aware that a race of some kind is going on. they buy coffee or just stand around looking as if life has been stunned and burned out of them. or sometimes you see one standing in a dark corner, jamming a whole hot dog down the throat, gagging, choking, delighted with the mess of themselves. and at the end of each day you see one or 2 with their heads down between their legs. sometimes they are crying. where do losers go? who wants a loser?

essentially, in one way or another, everybody thinks that he has the key to beating the thing, even if it is only such an unjustified assumption that their luck must change, some play stars, some play numbers, some play strictly time, others play drivers, or closers or speed or names or god knows what. almost all of them lose, continually. almost all their income goes directly into the mutuel machines. most of these people have unbearably fixed egos – they are tenaciously stupid.

I won a few dollars Sept. 1. let's go over the card. Andy's Dream won the first at 9/2 from a morning line of 10. good play. unwarranted action on beaten horse running from outside post.

2nd race – Jerry Perkins, 14 year old gelding nobody wants to claim because of age, drops into $15 claimer. a good horse, consistent within his class, but you had to take 8/5 under a morning line of four. won easy. third race won by Special Product, a horse that broke in his last four races at long odds. he broke stride again this time, pulled up, righted himself and still came on to beat the 3/5 favorite Golden Bill. a possible bet if you are in touch with God and God is interested. ten to one. in the fourth race, Hal Richard a consistent 4 year old gelding won at three to one, beating out two shorter choices that showed better times but no winning ability. a good bet. in the fifth, Eileen Colby wins after Tiny Star and Marsand break and the crowd sends off April Fool at 3/5. April Fool has only been able to win four races out of 32, and one local handicapper tabs him "better than these by five lengths." all this on time effort of last race in better class when April Fool finishes seven lengths out. the crowd is taken again.

then in the sixth race, Mister Honey is given a morning line of 10 but is sent off as second choice of 5/2 and wins easy, having won three out of nine in tougher class at short odds. Newport Buell, a cheaper horse is sent off at even money because he closed ground in last at nine to one. a bad bet. the crowd doesn't understand. in the seventh, Bills Snookums, a winner of seven out of nine in class and with the leading rider Farrington up is made the new 8/5 favorite and justifiably so.

the crowd bets Princess Sampson down to 7/2. this horse has won only 6 races out of 67. naturally, the crowd gets burned again.

Princess Sampson shows the best time in a tougher race but just does not want to win. the crowd is time-happy. they do not realize that time is caused by pace and pace is caused by the discretion – or lack of it – of the lead drivers. in the eighth, Abbemite Win gets up in a four or five horse scramble. it was an open race and one I should have stayed out of. in the ninth, they let the public have one. Luella Primrose. the horse had failed consistently at short odds and today got on its own pace without a challenger. 5/2. one for the ladies, and how they screamed. a pretty name. and they'd been losing their drawers on the thing all through the meet.

most of the cards are as reasonable as this, and it would seem possible to make a living at the track against the 15 percent take. but the outside factors beat you. the heat. tiredness. people spilling beer on your shirt. screaming. stepping on your feet.

women showing their legs. pickpockets. touts. madmen. I was $24 ahead going into the ninth race and there wasn't a play in the ninth.

being tired, I didn't have the resistance to stay out. before the race went off I had dropped in $16, shopping, feeling for a winner that didn't show. then they sent in the public play on me. I was not satisfied with a $24 day. I once worked for $16 a week at New Orleans. I was not strong enough to take a gentle profit, so I walked out $8 winner. not worth the struggle: I could have stayed home and written an immortal poem.

a man who can beat the races can do about anything he makes up his mind to do. he must have the character, the knowledge, the detachment. even with these qualities, the races are tough, especially with the rent waiting and your whore's tongue hanging out for beer. there are traps beyond traps beyond traps. there are days when everything impossible happens. the other day they ran in a 50 to one shot in the first race, a 100 to one in the second, and capped off the day with an 18 to one in the last race. when you are trying to scrape up pesos for the landlord and potato and egg money, this kind of day can very much make you feel like an imbecile.

but if you come back the next day they will give you six or seven reasonable winners at fair prices. it's there but most of them don't go back. it takes patience and it's hard work: you have to think. it's a battlefield and you can become shell-shocked. I saw a friend of mine out there the other day, glaze-eyed, punched-out. it was late in the day and it had been a reasonable card, but somehow they had gotten past him and I could tell that he had bet too much trying to get out. he walked past me, not knowing where he was. I watched him. he walked right into the women's crapper. they screamed and he came running out. it was what he needed. it pulled him out and he caught the winner of the next race. but I would not advise this system to all losers.

there are laughs and there is sadness. there is an old boy who walked up to me one time. "Bukowski," he said very seriously, "I want to beat the horses before I die."

his hair is white, totally white, teeth gone, and I could see myself there in 15 or 20 years, if I make it.

"I like the six horse," he told me.

"luck," I told him.

he'd picked a stiff, as usual. an odds-on favorite that had only won one race in 15 starts that year. the public handicappers had the horse on top too. the horse had won $88,000 LAST year. best time.

I bet ten win on Miss Lustytown, a winner of nine races this year. Miss Lustytown paid 4/1. the odds-on finished last.

the old man came by, raging. "how the hell! Glad Rags ran 2:01 and 1/5 last time and gets beat by a 2:02 and 1/5 mare! they oughta close this place up!"

he raps his program, snarling at me. his face is so red that he appears to have a sunburn. I walk away from him, go over to the cashier's window and cash in.

when I get home, there is one magazine in the mail, THE SMITH, parodying my prose style, and another magazine, THE SIXTIES, parodying my poetic style.

writing? what the hell's that? somebody is worried or pissed about my writing. I look over and sure enough there's a typewriter in the room. I am a writer of some kind, there's another world there of maneuvering and gouging and groups and methods.

I let the warm water run, get into the tub, open a beer, open the racing form. the phone rings. I let it ring. for me, maybe not for you, it's too hot to fuck or listen to some minor poet. Hemingway had his pulls. give me a horse's ass – that gets there first.

THE BIRTH, LIFE AND DEATH OF AN UNDERGROUND NEWSPAPER

There were quite a few meetings at Joe Hyans' house at first and I usually showed drunk, so I don't remember much about the inception of *Open Pussy*, the underground newspaper, and I was only told later what had happened. Or rather, what I had done.

Hyans: "You said you were going to clean out the whole place and that you were going to start with the guy in the wheelchair. Then he started to cry and people started leaving. You hit a guy over the head with a bottle."

Cherry (Hyans' wife): "You refused to leave and you drank a whole fifth of whiskey and kept telling me that you were going to fuck me up against the bookcase."

"Did I?"

"No."

"Ah, then next time."

Hyans: "Listen, Bukowski, we're trying to get organized and all you do is come around and bust things up. You're the nastiest damn drunk I've *ever* seen!"

"OK, I quit. Fuck it. Who cares about newspapers?"

"No, we want you to do a column. We think you're the best writer in Los Angeles."

I lifted my drink. "That's a motherfucking insult! I didn't come here to be insulted!"

"OK, maybe you're the best writer in California."

"There you go! *Still* insulting me!"

"Anyhow, we want you to do a column."

"I'm a poet."

"What's the difference between poetry and prose?"

"Poetry says too much in too short a time; prose says too little and takes too long."

"We want a column for *Open Pussy*."

"Pour me a drink and you're on."

Hyans did. I was on. I finished the drink and walked over to my skidrow court thinking about what a mistake I was making. I was almost fifty years old and fucking with these long-haired, bearded kids. Oh God, *groovy*, daddy, oh *groovy!* War is shit. War is hell. Fuck, don't fight. I'd known all that for fifty years. It wasn't quite as exciting to me. Oh, and don't forget the *pot*. the stash. *Groove*, baby!

I found a pint in my place, drank it, four cans of beer and wrote the first column. It was about a three-hundred-pound whore I had once fucked in Philadelphia. It was a good column. I corrected the typing errors, jacked off and went to sleep . . .

It started on the bottom floor of Hyans' two-story rented house. There were some half-assed volunteers and the thing was new and everybody was excited but me. I kept searching out the women for ass but they all *looked* and *acted* the same – they were all nineteen years old, dirty-blonde, small ass, small-breasted, busy, dizzy, and, in a sense, conceited without quite knowing why. Whenever I'd lay my drunken hands upon them they were always quite cool. Quite.

"Look, Gramps, the only thing we want to see *you* raise is a North Vietnamese flag!"

"Ah, your pussy probably stinks anyhow!"

"Oh, you *are* a filthy old man! You really are . . . so disgusting!"

And then they'd walk off shaking those little delicious apple buttocks at me, only carrying in their hand – instead of my lovely purple head – some juvenile copy about the cops shaking down the kids and taking away their Baby Ruth bars on the Sunset Strip. Here I was, the greatest living poet since Auden and I couldn't even fuck a dog in the ass . . .

The paper got too big. Or Cherry got worried about me lounging about on the couch drunk and leering at her five-year-old daughter. When it really got bad was when the daughter started sitting on my lap and looking up into my face while squirming, saying, "I like you, Bukowski. Talk to me. Let me get you another Beer, Bukowski."

"Hurry back, sweetie!"

Cherry: "Listen, Bukowski, you old letch . . ."

"Cherry, children love me. I can't help it."

The little girl, Zaza, ran back with the beer, got back into my lap. I opened the beer.

"I like you, Bukowski, tell me a story."

"OK, honey. Well, once upon a time there was this old man and this lovely little girl lost in the woods together . . ."

Cherry: "Listen, you old letch . . ."

"Ta, ta, Cherry, I *do* believe you have a dirty mind!"

Cherry ran upstairs looking for Hyans who was taking a crap. "Joe, Joe, we've just got to move this paper out of here! I mean it!". . .

They found a vacant building up front, two floors, and one midnight while drinking port wine, I held the flashlight for Joe while he broke open the phone box on the side of the house and rearranged the wires so he could have extension phones without charge. About this time the only other underground newspaper in L.A. accused Joe of stealing a duplicate copy of their mailing list. Of course, I knew Joe had morals and scruples and ideals – that's why he quit working for the large metro daily. That's why he quit working for the other underground newspaper. Joe was some kind of Christ. Sure.

"Hold that flashlight steady," he said . . .

In the morning, at my place, the phone rang. It was my friend Mongo the Giant of the Eternal High.

"Hank?"

"Yeh?"

"Cherry was over last night."

"Yeh?"

"She had this mailing list. Was very nervous. She wanted me to hide it. Said Jensen was on the prowl. I hid it in the cellar under a pile of India ink sketches Jimmy the Dwarf did before he died."

"Did you screw her?"

"What for? She's all bones. Those ribs would slice me to pieces while I fucked."

"You screwed Jimmy the Dwarf and he only weighed eighty-three pounds."

"He had soul."

"Yeh?"

"Yeh."

I hung up. . .

For the next four or five issues, *Open Pussy* came out with sayings like, "WE LOVE THE L.A. FREE PRESS," "OH, WE LOVE THE L.A. FREE PRESS," "LOVE, LOVE, LOVE THE L.A. FREE PRESS."

They should have. They had their mailing list.

One night Jensen and Joe had dinner together. Joe told me later that everything was now "all right." I don't know who screwed who or what went on under the table. And I didn't care . . .

And I soon found that I had other readers besides the beaded and the bearded . . .

In Los Angeles the new Federal Building rises glass-high, insane and modern, with the Kafka-series of rooms each indulged with their own personal frog jacking-off bit; everything feeding off of everything else and thriving with a kind of worm-in-the-apple warmth and clumsiness. I paid my forty-five cents per half hour parking, or rather I was given a time ticket for that amount and I walked into the Federal Building, which had downstairs murals like Diego Rivera would have done if nine tenths of his sensibilities had been cut away – American sailors and Indians and soldiers smiling away, trying to look noble in cheap yellows and retching rotting greens and pissy blues.

I was being called into personnel. I knew that it wasn't for a promotion. They took the letter and cooled me on the hard seat for forty-five minutes. It was part of the old you-got-shit-in-your-intestines and we-don't-have routine. Luckily, from past experience, I read the warty sign, and I cooled it myself, thinking about how each of the girls who walked by would go on a bed, legs high, or taking it in the mouth. Soon I had something huge between my legs – well, huge for me – and had to stare at the floor.

I was finally called in by a very black and slinky and well-dressed and pleasant Negress, very much class and even a spot of soul, whose smile said she knew that I was going to be fucked but who also hinted that she wouldn't mind throwing me a little pee-hole herself. It eased matters. Not that it mattered.

And I walked in.

"Have a seat."

Man behind desk. Same old shit. I sat.

"Mr. Bukowski?"

"Yeh."

He gave me his name. I wasn't interested.

He leaned back, stared at me from his swivel.

I'm sure he expected somebody younger and better-looking, more flamboyant, more intelligent-looking, more treacherous-looking . . . I was just old, tired, disinterested, hung-over. He was a bit gray and distinguished, if you know the type of distinguished I mean. Never pulled beets out of the ground with a bunch of wet-backs or been in the drunktank fifteen or twenty times. Or picked lemons at six a.m. without a shirt on because you knew that at noon it would be 110 degrees. Only the poor knew the meaning of life; the rich and the safe had to guess. Strangely then, I began thinking of the Chinese. Russia had softened; it could be that only the Chinese knew, digging up from the bottom, tired of soft shit. But then, I had no politics, that was more con: history screwed us all, finally. I was done ahead of time – baked, fucked, screwed-out, nothing left.

"Mr. Bukowski?"

"Yeh?"

"Well, ah . . . we've had an informant . . ."

"Yeh. Go ahead."

". . . who wrote us that you are not married to the mother of your child."

I imagined him, then, decorating a Christmas tree with a drink in his hand.

"That's true. I am not married to the mother of my child, aged four."

"Do you pay child support?"

"Yes."

"How much?"

"I'm not going to tell you."

He leaned back again. "You must understand that those of us in government service must maintain certain standards."

Not really feeling guilty of *anything*, I didn't answer.

I waited.

Oh, where are you, boys? Kafka, where are you? Lorca, shot in the dirty road, where are you? Hemingway, claiming he was being tailed by the C.I.A. and nobody believing him but me . . .

Then, old distinguished well-rested non-beetpicking gray turned around and reached into a small and well-varnished cabinet behind him and pulled out six or seven copies of *Open Pussy*.

He threw them upon his desk like stinking siffed and raped turds. He tapped them with one of his non-lemonpulling hands.

"We are led to believe that YOU are the writer of these columns – *Notes of a Dirty Old Man*."

"Yeh."

"What do you have to say about these columns?"

"Nothing."

"Do you call this *writing*?"

"It's the best that I can do."

"Well, I'm supporting two sons who are now taking journalism at the best of colleges, and I HOPE . . ."

He tapped the sheets, the stinking turd sheets, with the bottom of his ringed and un-factoried and un-jailed hand and said:

"I hope that my sons never turn out to write like YOU do!"

"They won't," I promised him.

"Mr. Bukowski, I think that the interview is finished."

"Yeah," I said. I lit a cig, stood up, scratched my beer-gut and walked out.

The second interview was sooner than I expected. I was hard at work – of course – at one of my important menial tasks when the speaker boomed: "*Henry Charles Bukowski, report to the Tour Superintendent's office!*"

I dropped my important task, got a travel form from the local screw and walked on over to the office. The Tour-Soup's male secretary, an old gray flab, looked me over.

"Are *you* Charles Bukowski?" he asked me, quite disappointed.

"Yeh, man."

"Please follow me."

I followed him. It was a large building. We went down several stairways and down around a long hall and then into a large dark room that entered into another large and very dark room. Two men were sitting there at the end of a table that must have been seventy-five feet long. They sat under a lone lamp. And at the end of the table sat this single chair – for me.

"You may enter," said the secretary. Then he shorted out.

I walked in. The two men stood up. Here we were under one lamp in the dark. For some reason, I thought of all the assassinations.

Then I thought, this is America, daddy, Hitler is dead. Or is he?

"Bukowski?"

"Yeh."

They both shook hands with me.

"Sit down."

Groovy, baby.

"This is Mr. —— from Washington," said the other guy who was one of the local topdogturds.

I didn't say anything. It was a nice lamp. Made of human skin?

Mr. Washington did the talking. He had a portfolio with quite a few papers within.

"Now, Mr. Bukowski . . ."

"Yeh?"

"Your age is forty-eight and you've been employed by the United States Government for eleven years."

"Yeh."

"You were married to your first wife two and a half years, were divorced, and you married your present wife when? We'd like the date."

"No date. No marriage."

"You have a child?"

"Yeh."

"How old?"

"Four."

"You're *not* married?"

"No."

"Do you pay child support?"

"Yes."

"How much?"

"About standard."

Then he leaned back and we sat there. The three of us said nothing for a good four or five minutes.

Then a stack of the underground newspaper *Open Pussy* appeared.

"Do you write these columns? *Notes of a Dirty Old Man?*" Mr. Washington asked.

"Yeh."

He handed a copy to Mr. Los Angeles.

"Have you seen this one?"

"No, no, I haven't."

Across the top of the column was a walking cock with legs, a huge HUGE walking cock with legs. The story was about a male friend of mine I had screwed in the ass by mistake, while drunk, believing that it was one of my girlfriends. It took me two weeks to finally force my friend to leave my place. It was a true story.

"Do you call this *writing*?" Mr. Washington asked.

"I don't know about the writing. But I thought it was a *very* funny story. Didn't you think it was humorous?"

"But this . . . this illustration across the top of the story?"

"The walking cock?"

"Yes."

"I didn't draw it."

"You have nothing to do with the selection of illustrations?"

"The paper is put together on Tuesday nights."

"And you are not there on Tuesday nights?"

"I am supposed to be here on Tuesday nights."

They waited some time, going through *Open Pussy*, looking at my columns.

"You know," said Mr. Washington, tapping the *Open Pussies* again with his hand, "you would have been all right if you had kept writing *poetry*, but when you began writing *this* stuff . . ."

He again tapped the *Open Pussies*.

I waited two minutes and thirty seconds. Then I asked: "Are we to consider the postal officials as the new critics of literature?"

"Oh, no no," said Mr. Washington, "we didn't mean *that*."

I sat and waited.

"There is a certain conduct expected of postal employees. You are in the Public Eye. You are to be an example of exemplary behavior."

"It appears to me," I said, "that you are threatening my freedom of expression with a resultant loss of employment. The A.C.L.U. might be interested."

"We'd still prefer you didn't write the column."

"Gentlemen, there comes a time in each man's life when he must choose to stand or run. I choose to stand."

Their silence.

Wait.

Wait.

The shuffling of *Open Pussies*.

Then Mr. Washington: "Mr. Bukowski?"

"Yeh?"

"Are you going to write any more columns about the Post Office?"

I had written one about them which I thought was more humorous than demeaning – but then, maybe *my* mind was twisted.

I let them wait this time. Then I answered: "Not unless you make it necessary for me to do so."

Then *they* waited. It was kind of an interrogation chess game where you hoped the other man would make the wrong move: blurt out his pawns, knights, bishops, king, his queen, his guts. (And meanwhile, as you read this, here goes my goddamned job. Groovy, baby. Send dollars for beer and wreaths to The Charles Bukowski Rehabilitation Fund at . . .)

Mr. Washington stood up.

Mr. Los Angeles stood up.

Mr. Charles Bukowski stood up.

Mr. Washington said: "I think that the interview is over."

We all shook hands like sun-maddened snakes.

Mr. Washington said: "Meanwhile, don't jump off of any bridges . . ."

(Strange: I hadn't even thought about it.)

". . . we haven't had a case like this in ten years."

(In ten years? Who was the last poor sucker?)

"So?" I asked.

"Mr. Bukowski," said Mr. Los Angeles, "report back to your position."

I really had an unquieting time (or is it disquieting?) trying to find my way back to the work floor from that underground Kafkaesqueish maze, and when I did, here all my subnormal fellow workers (good pricks all) started chirping at me:

"Hey, baby, where ya been?"

"What'd they want, daddieo?"

"You knocked up another black chick, big daddy?"

I gave them the Silence. One learns from dear old Uncle Sammy.

They kept chirping and flipping and fingering their mental assholes. They were really frightened. I was Old Kool and if they could break Old Kool they could break any of them.

"They wanted to make me Postmaster," I told them.

"And what happened, daddieo?"

"I told them to jam a hot turd up their siffed-up snatch."

The foreman of the aisle walked by and they all gave him the proper obeisance but me, but I, but Bukowski, I lit a cigar with an easy flourish, threw the match on the floor and stared at the ceiling as if I were having great and wonderful thoughts. It was con; my mind was blank; I only wanted a halfpint of Grandad and six or seven tall cool beers . . .

The fucking paper grew, or seemed to, and moved to a place on Melrose. I always hated to go there with copy, though, because everybody was so shitty, so truly shitty and snobby and not quite right, you know. Nothing changed. The history of the Man-beast was very slow. They were like the shits I'd faced when I first walked into the copy room of the L.A. City College newspaper in 1939 or 1940 – all these little hoity-toity dummies with little newspaper hats over their heads while writing stale, stupid copy. So very important – not even human enough to acknowledge your presence. Newspaper people were always the lowest of the breed; janitors who picked up women's cuntrags in the crappers had more soul – naturally.

I looked at those college freaks, walked out, never went back.

Now. *Open Pussy*. Twenty-eight years later.

Copy in my hand. There was Cherry at a desk. Cherry was on the telephone. Very important. Couldn't speak. Or Cherry not at the telephone. Writing something on a piece of paper. Couldn't speak. The same old con of always. Thirty years hadn't broken the dish. And Joe Hyans running around, doing big things, running up and down the stairs. He had a little place on top. Rather exclusive, of course. And some poor shit in a back room with him there where Joe could watch him getting copy ready for the printer on the IBM. He gave the poor shit thirty-five a week for a sixty-hour week and the poor shit was glad, grew a beard and lovely soulful eyes and the poor shit hacked out the third-rate piteous copy. With the Beatles playing full volume over the intercom and the phone ringing continually, Joe Hyans, editor, was always RUNNING OFF TO SOME-PLACE IMPORTANT SOMEWHERE. But when you read the paper the next week you'd wonder where he'd run. It wasn't in there.

Open Pussy went on, for a while. My columns continued to be good, but the paper itself was half-ass. I could smell the death-cunt of it . . .

There was a staff meeting every other Friday night. I busted up a few of them. And after hearing the results, I just didn't go anymore. If the paper wanted to live, let it live. I stayed away and just slid my stuff under the door in an envelope.

Then Hyans got me on the phone: "I've got an idea. I want you to get me together the best poets and prose writers that you know and we are going to put out a literary supplement."

I got it together for him. He printed it. And the cops busted him for "obscenity."

But I was a nice guy. I got him on the phone. "Hyans?"

"Yeh?"

"Since you done got busted for the thing, I'm a gonna let you have my column for free. That ten bucks you been paying me, it goes for the *Open Pussy* defense fund."

"Thanks very much," he said.

So there he was, getting the best writing in America for nothing . . .

Then Cherry phoned me one night.

"Why don't you come to our staff meetings anymore? We all miss you, terribly."

"What? What the hell you saying, Cherry? You on the stuff?"

"No, Hank, we all love you, really. Do come to our next staff meeting."

"I'll think about it."

"It's dead without you."

"And death with me."

"We want you, old man."

"I'll think about it, Cherry."

So, I showed. I had been given the idea by Hyans, himself, that since it was the first anniversary of *Open Pussy* the wine and the pussy and the life and the love would be flowing.

But coming in very high and expecting to see fucking on the floor and love galore, I only saw all these little love-creatures busily at work. They reminded me very much, so humped and dismal, of the little old ladies working on piecework I used to deliver cloth to, working my way up through rope hand-pulled elevators full of rats and stink, one hundred years old, piecework ladies, proud and dead and neurotic as all hell, working, working to make a millionaire out of somebody . . . in New York, in Philadelphia, in St. Louis.

And *these*, for *Open Pussy*, were working *without* wages, and there was Joe Hyans, looking a bit brutal and fat, walking up and down behind them, hands folded behind his back, seeing that *each* volunteer did his (her) duty properly and exactly.

"Hyans! *Hyans, you filthy cocksucker!*" I screamed as I walked in. "*You are running a slave-market, you are a lousy pewking Simon Legree! You cry for justice from the police and from Washington D.C. and you are the biggest lousiest swine of them all! You are Hitler multiplied by a hundred, you slave-labor bastard! You write of atrocities and then triple them yourself. Who the fuck you think you're fooling, mother? Who the fuck you think you are?*"

Luckily for Hyans, the rest of the staff was quite used to me and they thought that whatever I said was foolishness and that Hyans Himself stood for Truth.

Hyans Himself walked up and put a stapler in my hand.

"Sit down," he said, "we are trying to increase the circulation. Just sit down and clip one of these green ads to each of the newspapers. We are sending out leftover copies to potential subscribers . . ."

Dear old Freedom Loveboy Hyans, using big business methods to put over his crap. Brainwashed beyond himself.

He finally came up and took the stapler out of my hand. "You're not stapling fast enough."

"Fuck you, mother. There was supposed to be champagne all over this place. Now I'm eating staples . . ."

"Hey, Eddie!"

He called over another slave-labor member – thin-cheeked, wire-armed, penurious. Poor Eddie was starving. Everybody was starving for the Cause. Except Hyans and his wife, and they lived in a two-story house and sent one of their children to a private school, and there was old Poppa back in Cleveland, one of the head stiffs of the *Plain Dealer*, with more money than anything else.

So Hyans ran me out and also a guy with a little propeller on the top of a beanie cap, Lovable Doc Stanley I believe he was called, and also Lovable Doc's woman, and as the three of us left out the back door quite calmly, sharing a bottle of cheap wine, there came the voice of Joe Hyans: "And get out of here, and don't any of you *ever* come back, but I don't mean *you*, Bukowski!"

Poor fuck, he knew what kept the paper going . . .

Then there was another bust by the police. This time for printing the photo of a woman's cunt. Hyans, at this time, as always, was mixed up. He wanted to hype the circulation, by any means, or kill the paper and get out. It was a vise he couldn't seem to work properly and it drew tighter and tighter. Only the people working for nothing or for thirty-five dollars a week seemed to have any interest in the paper. But Hyans did manage to lay a couple of the younger female volunteers so he wasn't wasting his time.

"Why don't you quit your lousy job and come work for us?" Hyans asked me.

"How much?"

"Forty-five dollars a week. That includes your column. You will also distribute to the boxes on Wednesday night, your car, I'll pay the gas, and you write up special assignments. Eleven a.m. to 7:30 p.m., Fridays and Saturdays off."

"I'll think about it."

Hyans' old man came in from Cleveland. We got drunk together over at Hyans' house. Hyans and Cherry seemed very unhappy with Pops. And Pops could put away the whiskey. No grass for him. I could put away the whiskey too. We drank all night.

"Now the way to get rid of the *Free Press* is to bust up their stands, run the peddlers off the streets, bust a few heads. That's what we used to do in the old days. I've got money. I can hire some hoods, some mean sons of bitches. We can hire Bukowski."

"God damn it!" screamed young Hyans, "I don't want to *hear* your *shit*, you understand?"

Pops asked me, "What do you think of my idea, Bukowski?"

"I think it's a good idea. Pass the bottle over here."

"Bukowski is insane!" screamed Joe Hyans.

"You print his column," said Pops.

"He's the best writer in California," said young Hyans.

"The best insane writer in California," I corrected him.

"Son," Pops went on, "I have all this money. I want to put your paper over. All we gotta do is bust a few . . ."

"No. No. No!" Joe Hyans screamed. "I won't *have it!*" Then he ran out of the house. What a wonderful man Joe Hyans was. He ran out of the house. I reached for another drink and told Cherry that I was going to fuck her up against the bookcase.

Pops said he'd take seconds. Cherry cussed us while Joe Hyans ran off down the street with his soul . . .

The paper went on, coming out once a week somehow. Then the trial about the photo of the female cunt came up.

The prosecuting attorney asked Hyans: "Would you object to oral copulation on the steps of the City Hall?"

"No," said Joe, "but it would probably block traffic."

Oh, Joe, I thought, you *blew* that one! You shudda said, "I'd prefer for oral copulation to go on *inside* the City Hall where it usually does."

When the judge asked Hyans' lawyer what the meaning of the photo of the female sex organ was, Hyans' lawyer answered, "Well, that's just the way it is. That's the way it is, daddy."

They lost the trial, of course, and appealed for a new one.

"A roust," said Joe Hyans to the few and scattered news media about, "nothing but a police roust."

What a brilliant man Joe Hyans was . . .

Next I heard from Joe Hyans was over the phone: "Bukowski, I just bought a gun. One hundred and twelve dollars. A beautiful weapon. I'm going to kill a man!"

"Where are you now?"

"In the bar, down by the paper."

"I'll be right there."

When I got there he was walking up and down outside the bar.

"Come on," he said, "I'll buy you a beer."

We sat down. The place was full. Hyans was talking in a very loud voice. You could hear him all the way to Santa Monica.

*"I'm going to splatter his brains out against the wall –
I'm going to kill the son of a bitch!"*

"What guy, kid? Why do you want to kill this guy, kid?"

He kept staring straight ahead.

"Groove, baby. Why ya wanna kill this sunabitch, huh?"

"He's fucking my wife, that's why!"

"Oh."

He stared some more. It was like a movie. It wasn't even as good as a movie.

"It's a beautiful weapon," said Joe. "You put in this little clip. It fires ten shots. Rapid-fire. There'll be nothing left of the bastard!"

Joe Hyans.

That wonderful man with the big red beard.

Groovy, baby.

Anyhow I asked him, "How about all these anti-war articles you've printed? How about the love bit? What happened?"

"Oh come on *now* Bukowski, you've never believed in all that pacifism shit?"

"Well, I don't know . . . Well, I guess not exactly."

"I've warned this guy that I am going to kill him if he doesn't stay away, and I walk in and there he is sitting on the couch in my own house. Now what would *you* do?"

"You're making this a personal property thing, don't you understand? Just fuck it. Forget it. Walk away. Leave them there together."

"Is that what you've done?"

"After the age of thirty – always. And after the age of forty, it gets easier. But in my twenties I used to go insane. The first burns are the hardest."

"*Well, I am going to kill the son of a bitch! I'm going to blow his goddamned brains out!*"

The whole bar was listening. Love, baby, love.

I told him, "Let's get out of here."

Outside the bar door Hyans dropped to his knees and screamed, a long milk-curdling four-minute scream. You could hear him all the way to Detroit. Then I got him up and walked him to my car. As he got to the car door on his side, he grabbed the handle, dropped to his knees and let go another hog-caller to Detroit. He was hooked on Cherry, poor fellow. I got him up, put him in the seat, got in the other side, drove north to Sunset and then east along Sunset and at the signal, red, at Sunset and Vermont, he let go another one. I lit up a cigar. The other drivers stared at the red beard screaming.

I thought, he isn't going to stop. I'll have to knock him out.

But then as the signal turned green he ended it and I shifted it out of there. He sat there sobbing. I didn't know what to say. There wasn't anything to say.

I thought, I'll take him to see Mongo the Giant of the Eternal High. Mongo's full of shit. Maybe he can dump some shit on Hyans. Me, I hadn't lived with a woman for four years. I was too far out of it to see it anymore.

Next time he screams, I thought, I've got to knock him out. I can't stand another one of those.

"Hey! Where we going?"

"Mongo's."

"Oh no! Not Mongo's! I hate that guy! He'll only make fun of me! He's a cruel son of a bitch!"

It was true. Mongo had a good mind but a cruel one. It wasn't any good going over there. And I couldn't handle it either. We drove along.

"Listen," said Hyans, "I've got a girlfriend around here. Couple blocks north. Drop me off. She understands me."

I turned it north.

"Listen," I said, "don't shoot the guy."

"Why?"

"Because you are the only one who will print my column."

I drove to the place, let him out, waited until the door opened, then drove off. A good piece of ass might smooth him out. I needed one too . . .

Next I heard from Hyans, he had moved out of the house.

"I couldn't stand it anymore. Why, the other night I took a shower, I was getting ready to fuck her, I wanted to fuck some life into her bones, but you know what?"

"What?"

"When I walked in on her she ran out of the house. What a bitch!"

"Listen, Hyans, I know the game. I can't talk against Cherry because the next thing you know, you'll be back together again and then you'll remember all the dirty things I said about her."

"I'm never going back."

"Uh huh."

"I've decided not to shoot the bastard."

"Good."

"I'm going to challenge him to a boxing match. Full ring rules. Referee, ring, glove and all."

"OK," I said.

Two bulls fighting for the cow. And a bony one at that. But in America the loser oftentimes got the cow. Mother instinct? Better wallet? Longer dick? God knows what . . .

While Hyans was going crazy he hired a guy with a pipe and a necktie to keep the paper going. But it was obvious that *Open Pussy* was on its last fuck. And nobody cared but the twenty-five and thirty-dollar-a-week people and the free help. They enjoyed the paper. It wasn't all that good but it wasn't all that bad either. You see, there was my column: *Notes of a Dirty Old Man.*

And pipe and necktie got the paper out. It looked the same. And meanwhile I kept hearing: "Joe and Cherry are together again. Joe and Cherry split again. Joe and Cherry are back together again. Joe and Cherry . . ."

Then one chilly blue Wednesday night I went out to a stand to buy a copy of *Open Pussy*. I had written one of my best columns and wanted to see if they had had the guts to run it. The stand contained last week's *Open Pussy*. I smelled it in the deathblue air: the game was over. I bought two tall six-packs of Schlitz and went back to my place and drank down the requiem. Always being ready for the end I was not ready when it happened. I walked over and took the poster off the wall and threw it into the trash: "OPEN PUSSY. A WEEKLY REVIEW OF THE LOS ANGELES RENAISSANCE."

The government wouldn't have to worry anymore. I was a splendid citizen again.

Twenty thousand circulation. If we could have made sixty – without family troubles, without police rousts – we could have made it. We didn't make it.

I phoned the office the next day. The girl at the phone was in tears. "We tried to get you last night, Bukowski, but nobody knew where you lived. It's terrible. It's finished. It's over. The phone keeps ringing. I'm the only one here. We're going to hold a staff meeting next Tuesday night to try to keep the paper going. But Hyans took everything – all the copy, the mailing list and the IBM machine which didn't belong to him. We're cleaned out. There's nothing left."

Oh, you've got a sweet voice, baby, such a sad sad sweet voice, I'd like to fuck you, I thought.

"We are thinking of starting a hippie paper. The underground is dead. Please show at Lonny's house Tuesday night."

"I'll try," I said, knowing that I wouldn't be there. So there it was – almost two years. It was over. The cops had won, the city had won, government had won. Decency was in the streets again. Maybe the cops would stop giving me tickets every time they saw my car. And Cleaver wouldn't be sending us little notes from his hiding place anymore. And you could buy the *L.A. Times* anywhere. Jesus Christ and Mother in Heaven, Life was Sad.

But I gave the girl my address and phone number, thinking we might make it on the springs. (Harriet, you never arrived.)

But Barney Palmer, the political writer, did. I let him in and opened up the beers.

"Hyans," he said, "put the gun in his mouth and pulled the trigger."

"What happened?"

"It jammed. So he sold the gun."

"He could have tried for seconds."

"It takes a lot of guts just to try it once."

"You're right. Forgive me. Terrible hangover."

"You want to hear what happened?"

"Sure. It's my death, too."

"Well, it was Tuesday night, we were trying to get the paper ready. We had your column and thank Christ it was a long one because we were short of copy. It looked like we couldn't make the pages. Hyans showed, glassy-eyed, drunk on wine. He and Cherry had split again."

"Ugh."

"Yeh. Anyhow, we couldn't make the pages. And Hyans kept getting in the way. Finally he went upstairs and got on the couch and passed out. The minute he left, the paper began to get together. We made it and had forty-five minutes to get to the printer's. I said I'd drive it down to the printer's. Then you know what happened?"

"Hyans woke up."

"How did you know?"

"I'm that way."

"Well, he insisted on driving the copy to the printer's himself. He threw the stuff in the car but he never made the printer's. The next day we came in and found the note he left, and the place was cleaned out – the IBM machine, the mailing list, everything . . ."

"I've heard. Well, let's look at it this way: he started the goddamned thing, so he had a right to end it."

"But the IBM machine, he didn't own it. He might get into a jam over it."

"Hyans is used to jams. He thrives on them. He gets his nuts. You ought to hear him scream."

"But it's all the little people, Buk, the twenty-five-buck-a-week guys who gave up everything to keep the thing going. The guys with cardboard in their shoes. The guys who slept on the floor."

"The little guys always get it in the ass, Palmer. That's history."

"You sound like Mongo."

"Mongo is usually right, even though he is a son of a bitch."
We talked a little more, then it was over.

A big black kitty walked up to me at work that night. "Hey,
brother, I hear your paper folded."
"Right, brother, but where did you hear?"
"It's in the *L.A. Times*, first page of the second section. I guess
they are rejoicing."
"I guess they are."
"We liked your paper, man. And your column too. Real tough
stuff."
"Thank you, brother."
At lunchtime (10:24 p.m.) I went out and bought the *L.A.
Times*. I took it across the street to the bar over there, bought a
dollar pitcher of beer, lit a cigar and walked over to a table under
a light:

OPEN PUSSY DEEP IN RED

*Open Pussy, the second largest underground newspaper in
Los Angeles, has ceased publication, its editors said Thursday. The newspaper was 10 weeks short of its second
anniversary.*

*"Heavy debts, distribution problems and a $1,000 fine on
an obscenity conviction in October contributed to the demise
of the weekly newspaper," said Mike Engel, the managing
editor. He placed final circulation of the newspaper at about
20,000.*

*But Engel and other editorial staff members said they
believed that Open Pussy could have continued and that its
closing was the decision of Joe Hyans, its 35-year-old
owner-chief editor.*

*When the staff members arrived at the paper's office at
4369 Melrose Ave. Wednesday morning they found a note
from Hyans which declared, in part:*

*"The paper has already fulfilled its artistic purpose.
Politically, it was never too effective anyway. What's been
taking place in its pages recently is no improvement over
what we printed a year ago.*

*"As an artist, I must turn away from a work which does
not grow . . . even though it is a work of my own hand and
even though it is bringing in bread (money)."*

I finished the pitcher of beer and went into my governmental job . . .

A few days later I found a note in my mailbox:

10:45 a.m., Monday

Hank –

I found a note in my mailbox this morning from Cherry Hyans. (I was away all day Sunday and Sunday night.) She says she has the kids and is sick and in bad trouble at ——— Douglas Street. I can't find Douglas on the fucking map, but wanted to let you know about the note.

Barney

A couple of days later the phone rang. It wasn't a woman with a hot snatch. It was Barney.

"Hey, Joe Hyans is in town."

"So are you and I," I said.

"Joe's back with Cherry."

"Yeh?"

"They are going to move to San Francisco."

"They ought to."

"The hippie paper thing fell through."

"Yeh. Sorry I couldn't make it. Drunk."

"That's OK. But listen, I'm on a writing assignment now. But as soon as I finish, I want to contact you."

"What for?"

"I've got a backer with fifty grand."

"Fifty grand?"

"Yeh. Real money. He wants to do it. He wants to start another paper."

"Keep in touch, Barney. I've always liked you. Remember the time you and I started drinking at my place at four in the afternoon, talked all night and didn't finish until eleven a.m. the next morning?"

"Yeh. It was a hell of a night. For an old guy, you can drink anybody under."

"Yeh."

"So, when I clean this writing up, I'll let you know."

"Yeh. Keep in touch, Barney."

"I will. Meanwhile, hang in."

"Sure."

I went into the crapper and took myself a beautiful beershit. Then I went to bed, jacked off, and slept.

LIFE AND DEATH IN THE CHARITY WARD

The ambulance was full but they found me a place on top and away we went. I had been vomiting blood from the mouth in large quantities and I was worried that I might vomit upon the people below me. We rode along listening to the siren. It sounded far off, it sounded as if the sound weren't coming from our ambulance. We were on the way to the county hospital, all of us. The poor. The charity cases. There was something different wrong with all of us and many of us would not be coming back. The one thing we had in common was that we were all poor and didn't have much of a chance. We were packed in there. I never realized that an ambulance could hold so many people.

"Good Lord, oh good Lord," I heard the voice of a black woman below me, "I never thought this would happen to ME! I never thought nothing like this would Lord . . ."

I didn't feel that way about it. I had been playing with death for some time. I can't say we were the best of friends but we were well acquainted. He had moved a little close a little fast on me that night. There had been warnings: pains like swords stuck in my stomach but I had ignored them. I had thought I was a tough guy and pain to me was just like bad luck: I ignored it. I just poured whiskey on top of the pain and went about my business. My business was getting drunk. The whiskey had done it; I should have stayed on the wine.

Blood that comes from the inside is not the bright red color that comes, say, from a cut on the finger. The blood from inside is dark, a purple, almost black, and it stinks, it stinks worse than shit. All that life giving fluid, it smelled worse than a beer shit.

I felt another vomiting spasm coming on. It was the same feeling as throwing up food and when the blood came out, one felt better. But it was only an illusion ... each mouthful out brought one closer to Pappa Death.

"O good Lord God, I never thought ..."

The blood came up and I held it in my mouth. I didn't know what to do. Up there on the upper tier I would have wetted my friends down quite good. I held the blood in my mouth trying to think about what to do. The ambulance turned a corner and the blood began to dribble out the corners of my mouth. Well, a man had to maintain decencies even while he was dying. I got myself together, closed my eyes and swallowed my blood back down. I was sickened. But I had solved the problem. I only hoped we got someplace soon where I could let the next one go.

Really, there wasn't any thought of dying; the only thoughts I had were (was) one: this is a terrible inconvenience, I am no longer in control of what is happening. They narrowed down your choices and pushed you around.

The ambulance got there and then I was on a table and they were asking me questions: what was my religion? where was I born? did I owe the county any $$$ from earlier trips to their hospital? when was I born? parents alive? married? all that, you know. They talk to a man as if he had all his faculties; they don't even pretend that you are dying. And they are hardly in a hurry. It does have a calming effect but that's not their reason: they are simply bored and they don't care whether you die, fly or fart. No, they rather you didn't fart.

Then I was on an elevator and the door opened into what appeared to be a dark cellar. I was rolled out. They placed me on a bed and left. An orderly appeared out of nowhere and gave me a small white pill.

"Take this," he said. I swallowed the pill and he handed me a glass of water and then vanished. It was the kindest thing that had happened to me in some time. I leaned back and noticed my surroundings. There were 8 or ten beds, all occupied by male Americans. We each had a tin bucket of water and a glass on the night stand. The sheets seemed clean. It was very dark in there and cold, much the feeling of an apartment house cellar. There was one small light bulb, unshaded. Next to me was a huge man, he was old, in his mid fifties, but he was huge; although much of the hugeness was fat, he did give off the feeling of much strength. He was strapped down in his bed. He stared straight up and spoke to the ceiling.

". . . and he was such a nice boy, such a clean nice boy, he needed the job, he said he needed the job, and I said, 'I like your looks, boy, we need a good fry cook, a good honest fry cook, and I can tell an honest face, boy, I can tell character, you work with me and my wife and you got a job here for life, boy . . .' and he said, 'All right, sir,' just like that he said it and he looked happy about gettin' that job and I said, 'Martha, we got us a good boy here, a nice clean cut boy, he ain't gonna tap the till like the rest of those dirty sons of bitches.' Well, I went out and got a good buy on chickens, a real good buy on chickens. Martha can do more things with a chicken, she's got that magic touch with chicken. Col. Sanders can't touch her with a 90 foot pole. I went out and bought 20 chickens for that weekend. We were going to have a good weekend, a chicken special. 20 chickens I went out and got. We were going to put Col. Sanders out of business. A good weekend like that, you can pull 200 bucks clear profit. That boy even helped us pluck and cut those chickens, he did it on his own time. Martha and I didn't have no children. I was really taking a liking to that boy. Well, Martha fixed the chicken in the back, she got all that chicken ready . . . we had chicken 19 different ways, we had chicken coming out of our assholes. All the boy had to do was cook up the other stuff like burgers and steak and so forth. The chicken was set. And by god, we had a big weekend. Friday night, Saturday and Sunday. That boy was a good worker, and pleasant too. He was nice to be around. He made these funny jokes. He called me Col. Sanders and I called him son. Col. Sanders and Son, that's what we were. When we closed Saturday night we were all tired but happy. Every damned bit of chicken was gone. The place had been packed, people waitin' on seats, you never saw anything like it. I locked the door and got out a 5th of good whiskey and we sat there, tired and happy, having a few drinks. The boy washed all the dishes and swept the floor. He said, 'All right, Col. Sanders, when do I report tomorrow?' He smiled. I told him 6:30 a.m. and he got his cap and left. 'That's a hell of a nice boy, Martha,' I said and then I walked over to the till to count the profits. The till was EMPTY! That's right, I said, 'The till was EMPTY!' And the cigar box with the other 2 days profit, he found that too. Such a clean cut boy . . . I don't understand it . . . I said he could have a job for life, that's what I told him. 20 chickens . . . Martha really knows her chickens . . . And that boy, that dirty chickenshit, he ran off with all that damned money, that boy . . ."

Then he screamed. I've heard a great many people scream but I've never heard anybody scream like that. He rose up against his straps and screamed. It looked as if those straps were going to break. The whole bed rattled, the wall roared the scream back at us. The man was in total agony. It wasn't a short scream. It was a long one and it went on and on. Then he stopped. We 8 or ten male Americans, ill, stretched in our beds and enjoyed the silence.

Then he began talking again. "He was such a nice boy, I liked his looks. I told him he could have the job for life. He made these funny jokes, he was nice to be around. I went out and got those 20 chickens. 20 chickens. On a good weekend you can clear 200. We had 20 chickens. The boy called me Col. Sanders . . ."

I leaned out of bed and vomited out a mouthful of blood . . .

The next day a nurse came out and got me and helped me on a rolling platform. I was still vomiting up blood and was quite weak. She rolled me on the elevator.

The technician got behind his machine. They poked a point into my belly and told me to stand there. I felt very weak.

"I'm too weak to stand up," I said.

"Just stand there," said the technician.

"I don't think I can," I said.

"Hold still."

I felt myself slowly beginning to fall over backwards.

"I'm falling," I said.

"Don't fall," he said.

"Hold still," said the nurse.

I fell over backwards. I felt as if I were made of rubber. There was no feeling when I hit the floor. I felt very light. I probably was.

"Oh god damn it!" said the technician.

The nurse helped me up and stood me up against the machine with this point jamming into my stomach.

"I can't stand," I said, "I think I'm dying. I can't stand up. I'm sorry but I can't stand up."

"Stand still," said the technician, "just stand there."

"Stand still," said the nurse.

I could feel myself falling. I fell over backwards.

"I'm sorry," I said.

"God damn you!" the technician screamed, "you made me waste two films! Those god damned films cost money!"

"I'm sorry," I said.

"Take him out of here," said the technician.

The nurse helped me up and put me back on the roller. The humming nurse rolled me back to the elevator, humming.

They did take me out of that cellar and put me into a large room, a very large room. There were about 40 people dying in there. The wires to the buttons had been cut and large wooden doors, thick wooden doors coated with slabs of tin on both sides closed us away from the nurses and the doctors. They had put the sides up around my bed and I was asked to use the bedpan but I didn't like the bedpan, especially to vomit blood into and far less to shit into. If a man ever invents a comfortable and usable bedpan he will be hated by doctors and nurses for eternity and beyond.

I kept having a desire to shit but not much luck. Of course, all I was getting was milk and the stomach was ripped open so it couldn't very well send too much down to the asshole. One nurse had offered me some tough roast beef with half-cooked carrots and half-mashed potatoes. I refused. I knew they just wanted another empty bed. Anyhow, there was still this desire to shit. Strange. It was my second or third night in there. I was very weak. I managed to unattach one side and get out of bed. I made it to the crapper and sat there. I strained and sat there and strained. Then I got up. Nothing. Just a little whirlpool of blood. Then a merry-go-round started in my head and I leaned against the wall with one hand and vomited up a mouthful of blood. I flushed the toilet and walked out. I got halfway to my bed and another mouthful came up. I fell. Then on the floor I vomited up another mouthful of blood. I didn't know that there was so much blood inside of people. I let go another mouthful.

"You son of a bitch," an old man hollered at me from his bed, "shut up so we can get some sleep."

"Sorry, comrade," I said, and then I was unconscious . . .

The nurse was angry. "You bastard," she said, "I told you not to take down the sides of your bed. You fuckin' creeps sure make my night a drag!"

"Your pussy stinks," I told her, "you belong in a Tijuana whore house."

She lifted my head by the hair and slapped me hard across the left side of my face and then backhanded me across the right.

"Take that back!" she said. "Take that back!"

"Florence Nightingale," I said, "I love you."

She put my head back down and walked out of the room. She was a lady of true spirit and fire; I liked that. I rolled over into my own blood, getting my smock wet. That'd teach her.

Florence Nightingale came back with another female sadist and they put me in a chair and slid the chair across the room toward my bed.

"Too much god damned noise!" said the old man. He was right.

They got me back into bed and Florence put the bed side back up. "Son of a bitch," she said, "stay in there now or next time I'm gonna lay on you."

"Suck me off," I said, "suck me off before you leave."

She leaned over the railing and looked into my face. I have a very tragic face. It attracts some women. Her eyes were wide and passionate and looked into mine. I pulled the sheet down and pulled up my smock. She spit into my face, then walked out . . .

Then the head nurse was there.

"Mr. Bukowski," she said, "we can't let you have any blood. You don't have any blood credit."

She smiled. She was letting me know that they were going to let me die.

"All right," I said.

"Do you want to see the priest?"

"What for?"

"We have on your admissions card that you are a Catholic."

"I just put that down."

"Why?"

"I used to be. You put down 'no religion,' people always ask a lot of questions."

"We have you down as a Catholic, Mr. Bukowski."

"Listen, it's hard for me to talk. I'm dying. All right, all right, I'm a Catholic, have it your way."

"We can't let you have any blood, Mr. Bukowski."

"Listen, my father works for the county. I think they have a blood program. L.A. County Museum. A Mr. Henry Bukowski. He hates me."

"We'll check it out." . . .

There was something about my papers going down while I was upstairs. I didn't see a doctor until the fourth day and by then they found that my father who hated me was a good guy who had a job and who had a drunken dying son without a job and the good guy had given blood to the blood program and so they hooked up a bottle and poured it to me. 13 pints of blood and 13 pints of glucose without stop. The nurse ran out of places to stick the needle . . .

I awakened once and the priest was standing over me.

"Father," I said, "please go away. I can die without this."

"You want me to leave, my son?"

"Yes, Father."

"Have you lost the faith?"

"Yes, I've lost the faith."

"Once a Catholic always a Catholic, my son."

"Bullshit, Father."

An old man in the next bed said, "Father, Father, I'll talk to you. You talk to me, Father."

The priest went over there. I waited to die. You know god damned well I didn't die then or I wouldn't be telling you this now . . .

They moved me into a room with a black guy and a white guy. The white guy kept getting fresh roses every day. He raised roses which he sold to florists. He wasn't raising any roses right then. The black guy had busted open like me. The white guy had a bad heart, a very bad heart. We lay around and the white guy talked about breeding roses and raising roses and how he could sure use a cigarette, my god, how he needed a cigarette. I had stopped vomiting blood. Now I was just shitting blood. I felt like I had it made. I had just emptied a pint of blood and they had taken the needle out.

"I'll get you some smokes, Harry."

"God, thanks, Hank."

I got out of bed. "Give me some money."

Harry gave me some change.

"If he smokes he'll die," said Charley. Charley was the black guy.

"Bullshit, Charley, a couple of little smokes never hurt anybody."

I walked out of the room and down the hall. There was a cigarette machine in the waiting lobby. I got a pack and walked back. Then Charley and Harry and I lay there smoking cigarettes. That was morning. About noon the doctor came by and put a machine on Harry. The machine spit and farted and roared.

"You've been smoking, haven't you?" the doctor asked Harry.

"No doctor, honest, I haven't been smoking."

"Which of you guys bought him these smokes?"

Charley looked at the ceiling. I looked at the ceiling.

"You smoke another cigarette and you're dead," said the doctor.

Then he took his machine and walked out. As soon as he left I took the pack out from under the pillow.

"Lemme have one," said Harry.

"You heard what the doctor said," said Charley.

"Yeah," I said, exhaling a sheath of beautiful blue smoke, "you heard what the doctor said: 'You smoke another cigarette and you're dead.'"

"I'd rather die happy than live in misery," said Harry.

"I can't be responsible for your death, Harry," I said, "I'm going to pass these cigarettes to Charley and if he wants to give you one he can."

I passed them over to Charley who had the center bed.

"All right, Charley," said Harry, "let's have 'em."

"I can't do it, Harry, I can't kill you Harry."

Charley passed the cigarettes back to me.

"Come on, Hank, lemme have a smoke."

"No, Harry."

"Please, I beg you, man, just one smoke just one!"

"Oh, for Christ's sake!"

I threw him the whole pack. His hand trembled as he took one out.

"I don't have any matches. Who's got matches?"

"Oh, for Christ's sake," I said.

I threw him the matches . . .

They came in and hooked me to another bottle. About ten minutes my father arrived. Vicky was with him, so drunk she could hardly stand up.

"Lover!" she said, "Lover boy!"

She staggered up against the edge of the bed.

I looked at the old man. "You son of a bitch," I said, "you didn't have to bring her up here drunk."

"Lover boy, don't you wanna see me, huh? Huh, lover boy?"

"I warned you not to get involved with a woman like that."

"She's broke. You bastard, you bought her whiskey, got her drunk and brought her up here."

"I told you she was no good, Henry. I told you she was a bad woman."

"Don't you love me anymore, lover boy?"

"Get her out of here . . . NOW!" I told the old man.

"No, no, I want you to see what kind of a woman you have."

"I know what kind of woman I have. Now get her out of here now, or so help me Christ I'm going to pull this needle out of my arm and whip your ass!"

The old man moved her out. I fell back on the pillow.

"She's a looker," said Harry.

"I know," I said, "I know." . . .

I stopped shitting blood and I was given a list of what to eat and I was told that the first drink would kill me. They had also told me that I would die without an operation. I had had a terrible argument with a female Japanese doctor about operation and death. I had said "No operation" and she had walked out, shaking her ass at me in anger. Harry was still alive when I left, nursing his cigarettes.

I walked along in the sunlight to see how it felt. It felt all right. The traffic went by. The sidewalk was as sidewalks had always been. I was wondering whether to take a bus in or try to phone somebody to come and get me. I walked into this place to phone. I sat down first and had a smoke.

The bartender walked up and I ordered a bottle of beer.

"What's new?" he asked.

"Nothing much," I said. He walked off. I poured the beer into a glass, then I looked at the glass a while and then I emptied half of it. Somebody put a coin in the juke box and we had some music. Life looked a little better. I finished that glass, poured another and wondered if my pecker would ever stand up again. I looked around the bar: no women. I did the next best thing: I picked up the glass and drained it.

THE DAY WE TALKED ABOUT
JAMES THURBER

I was down on my luck or my talent was finished. It was Huxley, or one of his characters, I believe, who said in *Point Counter Point*: "Anybody can be a genius at twenty-five: at fifty it takes some doing." Well, I was forty-nine, which isn't fifty – short a few months. And my paintings weren't moving. There had recently been a small book of poems: *The Sky Is the Biggest Cunt of Them All*, for which I received a hundred dollars four months ago, and now the thing is a collector's item, listing at twenty-dollars at rare book dealers. I didn't even have a copy of my own book. A friend had stolen it while I was drunk. A friend?

My luck was down. I was known by Genet, Henry Miller, Picasso, so on and so on, and I couldn't even get a job as a dish-washer. I tried in one place but only lasted one night with my bottle of wine. A big fat lady, one of the owners, proclaimed, "Why this man doesn't know *how* to wash dishes!" Then she showed me how one part of the sink – it had an acid of some sort in it – was where you *first* put the dishes, *then* you transferred them over to the soap and water side. They fired me that night. But meanwhile I had drunk two bottles of wine and eaten half a leg of lamb which they had left just behind me.

It was, in a sense, terrifying to end up a zero, but what hurt more was that there was a five-year-old daughter of mine up in

San Francisco, the only person in the world I loved, who needed me, and shoes and dresses and food and love and letters and toys and an occasional visit.

I was forced to live with some great French poet who was now living in Venice, California, and this guy went *both* ways – I mean he fucked men and women and was fucked by men and women. He had likable ways, and a humorous and brilliant way of speaking. And he wore a little wig which kept slipping, and had to keep setting the damned thing straight as he talked to you. He spoke seven languages but he had to speak English while I was around. And he spoke each language as if it were his natural tongue.

"Ah, don't worry, Bukowski," he would smile, "I will take *care* of you!"

He had this twelve-inch dick, limp, and he had appeared in some of the underground newspapers when he had arrived in Venice, with notices and reviews of his power as a poet (one of the reviews had been written by me), but some of the underground papers had printed this photo of the great French poet – naked. He was about five feet tall and had hair all over his chest and arms. The hair ran all the way down from his neck to his balls – black, grizzly, stinking mass of stuff – and here in the middle of the photo was this monstrous thing hanging there, round-headed, thick: a bull's cock upon a tinkertoy of a man.

Frenchy was one of the greatest poets of the century. All he did was sit around and write his shitty little immortal poems and he had two or three sponsors who sent him money. Who wouldn't:(?): immortal cock, immortal poems. He knew Corso, Burroughs, Ginsberg, Kaja. He knew all that early hotel gang who lived at the same place, popped together, fucked together, and created separately. He'd even met Miro and Hem walking down the avenue, Miro carrying Hem's boxing gloves as they walked toward the battleground where Hemingway was hoping to kick the shit outa somebody. Of *course*, they all knew each other and paused a moment to flip off a little brilliant conversational crap.

The immortal French poet had seen Burroughs crawling along the floor "blind drunk" at B's place.

"He reminds me of you, Bukowski. There's no front. He drinks until he drops, until his eyes glaze. And this night he was crawling along the rug too drunk to get up and he looked up at me and he said to me, 'They fucked me! They got me drunk! I signed the contract. I sold all the movie rights to *Naked Lunch* for five-hundred dollars. Well, shit, it's too late!' "

Of course Burroughs was lucky – the option ran out and he had the five hundred dollars. I got hung up drunk for fifty bucks on some of my shit, two-year option, and I still have eighteen months to sweat. They caught Nelson Algren the same way – *Man With the Golden Arm*; they made millions, Algren got peanut shells. He had been drunk and failed to read the small print.

They played me good on movie rights to *Notes of a Dirty Old Man*. I was drunk and they brought in an eighteen-year-old cunt with a mini up to her hips, high heels, and long stockings. I hadn't had a piece of ass for two years. I signed away my life. And I probably could have driven a Railway Express truck through her vagina. I never even found out.

So there I was, down and out, fifty, outa luck and outa talent, couldn't even get a job as a newspaper boy, janitor, dishwasher, and the French poet immortal always had something going at his place – young men and young women always knocking at his door. And such a clean apartment! His john looked like nobody'd ever shit in it. All the tiles gleaming white clean, and with these little fat fluffy rugs everywhere. New sofas, new chairs. A refrigerator which shined like a mad and enlarged tooth that had been scrubbed until it cried. Everything, everything, touched of the delicacy of no-pain, no-worry, no-world out there at all. Meanwhile everybody knew what to say and do and how to act – it was a code – discreet and without sound: huge reamings and suckings and fingers up into the asshole and everywhere else. Men, women, children indulged. Boys.

And there was the Big C. Big H. And Hash. Mary. Name it.

It was an Art quietly done, everybody gently smiling, waiting, then doing. Leaving. Then coming back again.

There was even whiskey, beer, wine, for such clods as I – cigars and the stupidity of the past.

The immortal French poet went on and on with his various things. He rose early and did various yoga exercises, and would then stand looking at himself in the full-length mirror, brushing his hands over his tiny bit of sweat, and then, reaching and touching his huge cock and sacks – saving the cock and sacks for last – lifted them, savoring them, then letting them go: PLUNK.

About then I'd go into the bathroom and vomit. Come out.

"You didn't get any of it on the floor, did you, Bukowski?"

He didn't ask me if I were dying. He was only worried about his clean bathroom floor.

"No, Andre, I deposited all the vomit into the proper channels."

"Good boy!"

Then just to show off, knowing that I was sicker than seven hells, he would go over to the corner, stand on his head in his fucking bermuda shorts, cross his legs, look at me upside down like that, and say: "You know, Bukowski, if you would ever sober up and put on a tuxedo, I promise you this – if you ever walked into a room dressed that way, every woman in the room would faint."

"I don't doubt that."

Then he did a little flipover, landed on his feet: "Care for breakfast?"

"Andre, I haven't cared for breakfast for the last thirty-two years."

Then there'd be a knock on the door, lightly, oh so *delicately* you'd think it was a fucking bluebird tapping with one wing, dying, asking for a sip of water.

Mostly it would be two or three young men, with strawlike, shitty-looking beards.

It was *usually* men, although now and then it was a young girl, quite lovely, and I always hated to leave when it was a girl. But *he* had the twelve inches *limp* plus the immortality. So I always knew my role.

"Listen, Andre, this headache . . . I think I'll take a little stroll along the beach."

"Oh, no, Charles! No *need*, really!"

And even before I could get to the door, I'd look back and she'd already have Andre's fly open, or if the bermudas didn't have a fly, there it would be down around his French ankles, and she would be grabbing that twelve inches of *limp* to see what it could do if teased a bit. And Andre would always have her dress up around her hips by then and his finger fluttering, gorging, seeking the secret of the hole in that gap between her tight, cleanly washed pink panties. And for the finger, there was always something: the *seemingly* new melodramatic hole or asshole or if, master that he was, he could slip around and through the tight, washed pinkness, upward, there he was, preparing that cunt that had had only eighteen hours rest.

So I always had my walk along the beachfront. Since it was so early I did not have to view that giant spread of humanity wasted, stuffed side by side, gagging, croaking things of flesh, frogs' tumors. I didn't have to see them walking or lounging about with their horrible bodies and sold-out lives – no eyes, no voices, nothing, and not knowing it – just the shit of the waste, the smear along the cross.

But the mornings, early, were not bad, especially during the weekdays. Everything belonged to me, and the very ugly gulls – who became more ugly as the bags and crumbs began to vanish around Thursday or Friday – for this was the end of Life to them. They had no way of knowing that on Saturday and Sunday the mob would be back with their hotdog buns and various sandwiches. Well, I thought, maybe the gulls are worse off than I am? Maybe.

Andre got an offer to do a reading somewhere – Chicago, N.Y., Frisco, somewhere – one day, and so there he was gone and I was in the place, alone. I had a chance to use the typer. Not much good came out of that typer. Andre could make the thing work almost perfectly. it was strange that he was such a great writer and that I wasn't. It didn't seem as if there was *that* much difference between us. But there was – he knew how to lay down one word next to the other. But when I sat down that white sheet of paper just sat there and *looked* at me. Each man had his various hells but I had a three-length lead on the field.

So I drank more and more wine and waited on my death. Andre had been gone a couple of days when one morning about 10:30 a.m. there was this knock on the door. I said, "Just a moment," went into the bathroom, vomited, rinsed my mouth. Lavoris. I got into some shorts, then put on one of Andre's silken robes. I opened the door.

There was a young guy and a girl out there. She had on this very short skirt and high heels, and her nylons ran almost all the way up to her ass. The guy was just a guy, young, a kind of Cashmere Bouquet type – white T-shirt, thin, open-mouthed, holding his arms halfway up his sides as if he were going to take off and fly.

The girl asked, "Andre?"

"No. I'm Hank. Charles. Bukowski."

"You're making a joke aren't you, Andre?" the girl asked.

"Yeh. I'm a joke," I answered.

There was a light rain out there. They stood there.

"Well, anyhow, come on in out of the rain."

"You *are* Andre!" said the bitch. "I *recognize* you, that aged face – two hundred years old!"

"OK, OK," I said. "Come on in. I am Andre."

They had two bottles of wine. I went into the kitchen for the corkscrew and the glasses. I poured three wines. I was standing up drinking my wine, glancing up her legs best I could, when he reached out, unzipped my fly and began sucking at my dick. He made very much noise with his mouth. I patted him on top of the head, then asked the girl, "What's your name?"

"Wendy," she said, "and I've always admired your poetry, Andre. I think that you are one of the greatest living poets."

The guy kept working away, sucking and slopping it up, his head bobbing like some crazy thing with a lost mind.

"One of the greatest?" I asked. "Who are the others?"

"One other," said Wendy. "Ezra Pound."

"Ezra always bored me," I said.

"Really?"

"Really. He works too hard at it. Over-serious, over-learned, and finally just a dull craftsman."

"Why do you simply sign your work 'Andre'?"

"Because I feel like it."

The guy was working very hard then. I grabbed his head, pulled it forward into me and unloaded.

Then I zipped up, poured three more wines.

We simply sat and talked and drank. I don't know how long it went on. Wendy had beautiful legs and fine thin ankles which she kept twisting and turning as if she were on fire or something. They *did* know their literature. We talked of various things. Sherwood Anderson – *Winesburg*, all that stuff. Dos. Camus. The Cranes, the Dickeys, the Brontes; Balzac, Thurber, on and on . . .

We finished both wines and I found some more stuff in the refrigerator. We worked on that. Then, I don't know. I rather went crazy and began clawing at her dress – what there was of it. I saw a bit of underslip and panties; then I ripped the dress at the top, ripped the brassiere. I got a tit. I got a tit. It was fat. I kissed and sucked at the thing. Then I twisted it in my hand until she screamed, and as she did, I pushed my mouth against hers, gagging the screams.

I ripped the dress back – nylon, nylon legs knees flesh. And I picked her up out of the chair and ripped those chickenshit panties off and rammed it home.

"Andre," she said. "*Oh*, Andre!"

I looked over and the guy was watching us and jacking off in his chair.

I took her standing up, but we were all over the room. I was driving it in, and we knocked over chairs, broke lamps. At one time I had her across the coffee table, but I felt the legs giving under both of us, so I lifted her up before we could quite flatten the table to the floor.

"Oh, *Andre*!"

Then she quivered all over once, then once again, like something on a sacrificial altar. Then, knowing she was weakened and out of her senses, out of her being, I simply layed the whole thing into her like a hook, held it still, hung her there like some crazy sea-fish speared forever. In half a century I had learned a few tricks. She was out of consciousness. Then I leaned back and rammed rammed her, rammed her, had her head bobbing like some crazy puppet, and her ass, and she came again just as I did, and when we came I damn near died. Both of us damn near died.

To take someone standing up, their size must have a certain relationship to your size. I remember one time almost dying in a Detroit hotel room. I tried a standup and it didn't quite work. What I mean is, she took her legs *off* the floor and wrapped them around me. Which meant I was holding up two people on two legs. That's bad. I wanted to quit. I was only holding her up with two things: my hands under her asshole and my cock.

But she kept saying, "God, you've got powerful legs! God, you've got beautiful and strong legs!"

Which is true. The rest of me is mostly shit, including my mind and all the rest. But somebody had placed these huge and powerful legs upon my body. No bullshit. But it damned near killed me – that Detroit hotel fuck – because your leverage, the moving of the cock back and forth into that thing, takes a special movement from that position. You are holding up the weight of two bodies. All the motion must therefore be transferred to your spine or backbone. It's a rough and murderous maneuver. Finally we both came and I just tossed her off somewhere. Threw her away.

But with the one at Andre's, she kept her feet on the floor, which allowed me to do tricks – rotate, spearfish, slow down, speed up, and the various.

So there I finally finished her off. I was in a bad position – my pants and my shorts down there dripping around my shoes. I just let go of Wendy. I don't know where the hell she fell, nor did I care. Just as I was reaching down to pull up my shorts and my pants, the guy, the kid walked up and stuck the middle finger, right hand, straight and hard into my asshole. I screamed, turned around and punched him in the mouth. He went flying.

Then I got my shorts and pants up and sat in a chair, drinking wine and beer, glowering, not saying anything. They finally got themselves together.

"Good night, Andre," he said.

"Good night, Andre," she said.

"Watch the steps now," I said. "They get very slippery in the rain."

"Thank you, Andre," he said.

"We'll watch it, Andre," she said.

"Love!" I said.

"Love!" they both answered at once.

I closed the door. God, it was so nice to be an immortal French poet!

I walked to the kitchen, found a good bottle of French wine, some anchovies and some stuffed olives. I brought it all out and set it upon the wobbly coffee table.

I poured a tall glass of wine. Then I walked to the window which overlooked the world and the ocean. That ocean was nice: it kept on doing what it was doing. I finished that wine, had another, ate some of the stuff, then I was tired. I took my clothes off and got into the middle of Andre's bed. I farted, looking out at the sun, listening to the sea.

"Thank you, Andre," I said. "You're a pretty good guy after all."

And my talent was not yet finished.

ALL THE GREAT WRITERS

Mason had her on the phone. "yeh, well, listen, I was drunk. I don't remember WHAT I said to you! maybe it was true and maybe it wasn't! no, I'm NOT sorry, I'm tired of being sorry . . . you what? you won't? well, god damn you then!"

Henry Mason hung up. it was raining again. even in the rain there was always trouble with women, there was always trouble with . . .

it was the intercom buzzer. he picked up the phone.

"there's a Mr. Burkett, a James Burkett . . ."

"will you tell him that his manuscripts have been returned? we mailed them back yesterday. so sorry, all that."

"but he insists on seeing you personally."

"you can't get rid of him?"

"no."

"all right, send him in."

a bunch of damned extroverts. they were worse than clothing salesmen, brush salesmen, they were worse than . . .

in comes James Burkett.

"sit down, Jimmy."

"only my friends call me 'Jimmy.'"

"sit down, Mr. Burkett."

you could tell by looking at Burkett that he was insane. a great self-love covered him like a neon paint. there was no scrubbing it off. truth wouldn't do it. they didn't know what truth was.

"listen," said Burkett, lighting a cigarette and smiling around his cigarette like a temperamental & goofy bitch, "how come ya didn't like my stuff? your secretary out there sez ya sent it back? how come ya sent it back, man, huh? how come ya sent it back?"

then Mr. Burkett gave him the direct, the so direct look in the eye, playing at having SOUL. you were supposed to LOVE to do, so very hard to do, and *only* Mr. Burkett didn't realize this.

"it just wasn't any good, Burkett. that's all."

Burkett tapped his cigarette out in the ashtray. now, he *rammed* it out, jamming it and twisting it in the tray. then he lit another cigarette, and holding the match out in front of him, flaming, he said:

"hey, listen, man, don't give me that SHIT!"

"it was terrible writing, Jimmy."

"I said only my FRIENDS call me 'Jimmy'!"

"it was shitty writing, Mr. Burkett, in our opinion, only, of course."

"listen, man, I KNOW this game! you SUCK up right and you're in! but you've got to SUCK! and I don't SUCK, man! my work stands alone!"

"it certainly does, Mr. Burkett."

"if I were a Jew or a fag or a commy or black it would be all over, man, I'd be in."

"there was a black writer in here yesterday who told me that if his skin were white he'd be a millionaire."

"all right, how about the fags?"

"some fags write pretty good."

"like Genet, huh?"

"like Genet."

"I gotta suck dick, huh? I gotta write about sucking dick, huh?"

"I didn't say that."

"listen, man, all I need is a little promotion. a little promotion and I'll go. people will LOVE me! all they gotta do is SEE my stuff!"

"listen, Mr. Burkett, this is a business. if we published every writer who demanded that we do so because his stuff was so great, we wouldn't be here very long. we have to make the judgment. if we're wrong too many times we're finished. it's as simple as that. we print good writing that sells and we print bad writing that sells. we're in the selling market. we're not a charity, and frankly, we don't worry too much about the betterment of the soul or the betterment of the world."

"but my stuff will GO, Henry . . ."

"'Mr. Mason,' please! only my friends . . ."

"what are you trying to do, get SHITTY with me?"

"look, Burkett, you're a pusher. as a pusher, you're great. why don't you sell mops or insurance or something?"

"what's wrong with my writing?"

"you can't push and write at the same time. only Hemingway was able to do that, and then even he forgot how to write."

"I mean, man, what don't you *like* about my writing? I mean, be DEFINITE! don't give me a lot of shit about *Hemingway*, man!"

"1955."

"1955? Whacha mean?"

"I mean, you were good then, but the needle's stuck. you're still playing 1955 over and over again."

"hell, life is life and I'm still writing about LIFE, man! there *isn't* anything else! what the hell you giving me?"

Henry Mason let out a long slow sigh and leaned back. artists were intolerably dull. and near-sighted. if they made it they believed in their own greatness no matter how bad they were. if they didn't make it they still believed in their greatness no matter how bad they were. if they didn't make it, it was somebody *else's* fault. it wasn't because they didn't have talent; no matter how they stank they always believed in their genius. they could always trot out Van Gogh or Mozart or two dozen more who went to their graves *before* having their little asses lacquered with Fame. but for each Mozart there were 50,000 intolerable idiots who would keep on puking out rotten work. only the good quit the game – like Rimbaud or Rossini.

Burkett lit another cigarette, once again holding the flaming match in front of him as he spoke:

"listen, you print Bukowski. and he's slipped. you know he's slipped. *admit* it, man! hasn't Bukowski slipped, huh? hasn't he?"

"so, he's slipped."

"he writes SHIT!"

"if shit sells then we'll sell it. listen, Mr. Burkett, we aren't the *only* publishing house. why don't you try somebody else? just don't accept our judgment."

Burkett stood up. "what the hell's the use? you guys are *all* alike! you can't *use* good writing! the world has no use for REAL writing! you couldn't tell a human being from a fly! because you're dead! DEAD, ya hear? ALL YOU FUCKERS ARE DEAD! FUCK YOU! FUCK YOU! FUCK YOU! FUCK YOU!"

Burkett threw his burning cigarette on the rug, turned about, walked to the door, SLAMMED it and was gone.

Henry Mason got up, picked up the cigarette, put it in the tray, sat down, lit one of his own. no way of giving up smoking on a job like this, he thought. he leaned back and inhaled, so glad that Burkett was gone – those guys were dangerous – absolutely insane and vicious – especially those who were always writing about LOVE or SEX or the BETTER WORLD. jesus, jesus. he exhaled. the intercom buzzer rang.

he picked up the phone.

"a Mr. Ainsworth Hockley to see you?"

"what's he want? we sent him his check for LUSTS AND BUSTS ON THE CAMPUS."

"he says he has a new story."

"fine. tell him to leave it with you."

"he says he hasn't written it."

"o.k., have him leave the outline. I'll check it out."

"he says he doesn't have an outline."

"wutz he want, then?"

"he wants to see you personally."

"you can't get rid of him?"

"no, he just keeps staring at my legs and grinning."

"then, for Christ's sake. pull your dress down!"

"it's too short."

"all right. send him in."

in came Ainsworth Hockley.

"sit down," he told him.

Hockley sat down. then jumped up. lit a cigar. Hockley carried dozens of cigars. he was afraid of being a homosexual. that is, he didn't know whether he was a homosexual or not, so he smoked the cigars because he thought it was manly and also dynamic, but he still wasn't sure of where he was. he thought he liked women too. it was a mix-up.

"listen," said Hockley, "I just sucked a 36 inch COCK! gigantic!"

"listen, Hockley, this is a business. I just got rid of one nut. what do you want with me?"

"I want to suck your COCK, man! THAT'S what I want!"

"I'd rather you didn't."

the room was already smoggy with cigar smoke. Hockley really shot it out. he jumped out of the chair. walked around. sat down. jumped out of the chair. walked around.

"I think I'm going crazy," said Ainsworth Hockley. "I keep thinking of cock. I used to live with this 14 year old kid. huge COCK! god. HUGE! he beat his meat right in front of me once, I'll never forget it! and when I was in college, all these guys walking around the locker rooms, real cool-like ya know? why one guy even had BALLS down to his KNEES! we used to call him BEACHBALLS HARRY. after BEACHBALLS HARRY came, baby, it was all OVER! like a waterhose spurting curdled cream! when that stuff dried . . . why, man in the morning he'd have to beat the sheets with a baseball bat, shake the flakes off before he sent it to the laundry . . ."

"you're crazy, Ainsworth."

"I know, I know, that's what I'm telling YA! have a cigar!"

Hockley poked a cigar at his lips.

"no, no, thank you."

"maybe you'd like to suck MY cock?"

"I don't have the slightest desire. now what do you want?"

"I've got this idea for a story, man."

"o.k., write it."

"no, I want you to hear it."

Mason was silent.

"all right," said Hockley, "this is it."

he walked around shooting smoke. "a spaceship, see? 2 guys and 4 women and a computer. here they are shooting through space, see? days, weeks go by. 2 guys, 4 women, the computer. the women are getting real hot. they want it, see? got it?"

"got it."

"but you know what happens?"

"no."

"the two guys decide that they are homosexuals and begin to play with each other. they ignore the women entirely."

"yeah, that's kind of funny. write it."

"wait. I'm not done yet. these two guys are playing with each other. it's disgusting. no. it *isn't* disgusting! anyhow, the women walk over to the computer and open the doors. and inside this computer there are 4 HUGE cock and balls."

"crazy. write it."

"wait. wait. but before they can get at the cocks, the machine shows up with assholes and mouths and the whole damned machine goes into an orgy with ITSELF. god damn, can you imagine?"

"all right. write it. I think we can use it."

Ainsworth lit another cigar, walked up and down. "how about an advance?"

"one guy already owes us 5 short stories and 2 novels. he keeps falling further and further behind. if it keeps up, he'll own the company."

"give me half then, what the hell. half a cock is better than none."

"when can we have the story?"

"in a week."

Mason wrote out a check for $75.

"thanks, baby," said Hockley, "you're sure now that we don't want to suck each other's cocks?"

"I'm sure."

then Hockley was gone. Mason walked out to the receptionist. her name was Francine.

Mason looked at her legs.

"that dress is pretty short, Francine."

he kept looking.

"that's the style, Mr. Mason."

"just call me 'Henry.' I don't believe I ever saw a dress quite that short."

"they get shorter and shorter."

"you keep giving everybody who comes in here rocks. they come into my office and talk like crazy."

"oh, come on, Henry."

"you even give me rocks, Francine."

she giggled.

"come on, let's go to lunch," he said.

"but you've never taken me to lunch before."

"oh, is there somebody else?"

"Oh, no. but it's only 10:30 a.m."

"who the hell cares? I'm suddenly hungry. very hungry."

"all right. just a moment."

Francine got out the mirror, played with the mirror a bit. then they got up and walked to the elevator. they were the only ones on the elevator. on the way down, he grabbed Francine and kissed her. she tasted like raspberry with a slight hint of halitosis. he even pawed one of her buttocks. she offered a token resistance, pushing against him lightly.

"Henry! I don't know what's gotten *into* you!" she giggled.

"I'm only a man, after all."

in the lobby of the building there was a stand which sold candy, newspapers, magazines, cigarettes, cigars . . .

"wait a moment, Francine."

Mason bought 5 cigars, huge ones. he lit one and let out an immense spray of smoke. they walked out of the building, looking for a place to eat. it had stopped raining.

"do you usually smoke before lunch?" she asked.

"before, after and in between."

Henry Mason felt as if he were going just a bit insane. all those writers. what the hell was wrong with them?

"hey, here's a place!"

he held the door open and Francine walked in. he followed her.

"Francine, I sure like that dress!"

"you do? why thank you! I've got a dozen similar to this one."

"you have?"

"umm hummm."

he pulled up her chair and looked at her legs as she sat down. Mason sat down. "god, I'm hungry. I keep thinking of clams, I wonder why?"

"I think you want to fuck me."

"WHAT?"

"I said, 'I think you want to fuck me.'"

"oh."

"I'll let you. I think you're a very nice man, a very nice man, really."

the waiter came up and waved the smoke away with his menu cards. he handed one to Francine and one to Mason. and waited. and got rocks. how come some guys got nice dolls like that while he had to beat his meat? the waiter took their orders, wrote them down, walked through the swinging doors, handed the orders to the cook.

"hey," said the cook, "whatcha got there?"

"whadya mean?"

"I mean, ya got a horn! in *front* there! stay away from ME with that thing!"

"it's nothing."

"nothing? you'll kill somebody with that thing! go throw some cold water on it! it just don't look nice!

the waiter walked into the men's room. some guys got all the broads. he was a writer. he had a whole trunk full of manuscripts. 4 novels, 40 short stories. 500 poems. nothing published. a rotten world. they couldn't recognize a talent. they kept talent down. you have to have an "in," that's all there was to it. rotten cocksucking world. waiting on stupid people all day.

the waiter took his cock out, put it in the hand basin and began splashing cold water on it.

THE COPULATING MERMAID OF VENICE, CALIFORNIA

The bar had closed and they still had to make the walk to the rooming house, and there it was – the hearse had driven up across the street where the Stomach Hospital was.

"I think this is THE night," said Tony, "I can feel it in my blood, I really can!"

"The night for what?" asked Bill.

"Look," said Tony, "we know their operation well by now. Let's get one! What the fuck? You got the guts?"

"Whatsa matta? You think I'm a coward because that runty sailor whipped my ass?"

"I didn't say that, Bill."

"*You're* the coward! I can whip you, easy . . ."

"yeah. I know. I'm not talking about *that*. I say, let's grab a stiff just for laughs."

"Shit! Let's grab TEN stiffs!"

"Wait. You're drunk now. Let's wait. We know the operation. We know how they operate. We been watching every night."

"And you're *not* drunk, eh? You wouldn't have the GUTS otherwise!"

'Quiet now! Watch! Here they come. They've got a stiff. Some poor guy. Look at that sheet pulled over his head. It's sad."

"I *am* looking. And it *is* sad . . ."

"Okay, we know the operation: if it's just one stiff, they toss him in, light their cigarettes and drive off. But if it's two stiffs, they don't bother locking the hearse door twice. They're real cool boys. It's just old stuff with them. If it's two stiffs, they just leave the guy on the roller there behind the hearse, go in and get the other stiff, then toss them in together. How many nights have we watched it?"

"I dunno," said Bill, "sixty, at least."

"Okay, now there's the one stiff. If they go back in for another – that stiff belongs to us. *You game for grabs if they go in for another stiff?*"

"I'm game! I got double your guts!"

"Okay, then, watch. We'll know in a minute . . . Oops, there they go! *They're going in for another stiff!*" said Tony. "You game?"

"Game," said Bill.

They sprinted across the street and grabbed the corpse by the head and feet. Tony had the head, that sad head wrapped so tight in the sheet, while Bill grabbed the feet.

Then they ran across the street, the pure white sheet of the corpse floating in the momentum – sometimes you could see an ankle, an elbow, a thigh of flesh, and then they ran it up the rooming house front steps, got to the door and Bill said, "Jesus Christ, who's got the key? Look, I'm scared!"

"We don't have much time! Those bastards are gonna be out soon with the other stiff! Throw him in the hammock! Quick! We gotta find a goddamned key!"

They tossed the stiff into the hammock. It rocked back and forth in the hammock under the moonlight.

"Can't we take the body *back*?" asked Bill. "Good God oh Mother o Mighty, can't we take the body back?"

"No time! Too late! They'd see us. HEY! WAIT!" yelled Tony. "I found the key!"

"THANK JESUS!"

They unlocked the door, then grabbed the thing on the hammock and ran up the stairway with it. Tony's room was closest. Second floor. There was quite a bit of bumping with the corpse along the stairway wall and railing.

Then they had it outside Tony's door and stretched it out while Tony looked for his door key. They got the door open, plopped the stiff on the bed and then went to the refrigerator and got hold of Tony's cheap gallon of muscatel, had half a waterglass full each, then refilled, came back to the bedroom, sat down and looked at the stiff.

"Do you suppose anybody saw us?" asked Bill.

"If they had, I think the cops would be up here by now."

"Do you think they'll search the neighborhood?"

"How can they? How can they go knocking on doors at this time of the morning, asking, 'Do you have a dead body?'"

"Shit, I guess you're right."

"Sure, I'm right," said Tony, "still, I can't help wondering how those two guys felt when they came back and saw the body gone? It must have been kind of funny."

"Yeah," said Bill, "it musta been."

"Well, funny or not, we've got the stiff. There he *is*, right on the bed."

They looked at the thing under the sheet, had another drink.

"I wonder how long he's been dead?"

"Not very long, I don't think."

"I wonder when they begin to stiffen up? I wonder when they begin to stink?"

"That rigor mortis takes a bit of time, I think," said Tony. "But he'll probably begin to stink pretty soon. It's just like garbage left in the sink. I don't think they drain the blood until they reach the mortuary."

So, two drunks, they went on drinking the muscatel; they even forgot at times about the body, and they spoke of those vague and important other things in their rather inarticulate way. Then it was back to the body again.

The body was still there.

"What we gonna do with it?" asked Bill.

"Stand it up in the closet after it stiffens up. It seemed pretty loose when we were carrying it. Probably died about a half an hour ago or so."

"So, okay, we stand it up in the closet. Then what do we do when it starts to stink?"

"I never thought about that part," said Tony.

"Think about it," said Bill, pouring a good one.

Tony tried to think about it. "You know, we might go to jail for this. *If* we get caught."

"Sure. So?"

"Well, I think we made a mistake, but it's too late."

"Too late," repeated Bill.

"So," said Tony, pouring a tall one, "if we are stuck with this stiff we might as well have a look at him."

"Look at him?"

"Yeah, look at him."

"You got the guts?" asked Bill.

"I dunno."

"You scared?"

"Sure. No training in this sort of thing," said Tony.

"All right. *You* pull the sheet back," said Bill, "only fill my glass first. Fill my glass, then pull the sheet back."

"Okay," said Tony.

He filled Bill's glass. Then walked over.

"All right," said Tony, "here GOES!"

Tony pulled the sheet straight back over the body. He kept his eyes closed.

"Good GOD!" said Bill, "it's a woman! A *young* woman!"

Tony opened his eyes. "Yeah. *Was* young. Christ, look at that long blonde hair, goes way down past her asshole. But she's DEAD! Terribly and finally dead, forever. What a shame! I don't understand it.

"How old you figure she was?"

"She doesn't *look* dead to me," said Bill.

"She is."

"But look at those *breasts*! Those *thighs*! That *pussy*! That pussy: it still looks alive!"

"Yeah," said Tony, "the pussy, they say: it's the first thing to come and the last thing to go."

Tony walked over to the pussy, touched it. Then he lifted a breast, kissed the damned dead thing. "It's so sad, everything is so sad – that we live all our lives like idiots and then finally die."

"You shouldn't touch the body," said Bill.

"She's beautiful," said Tony, "even dead, she's beautiful."

"Yeah, but if she were alive she wouldn't even look at a bum like you twice. You know that, don't you?"

"Sure! And that's just the point! Now she can't say, 'NO!' "

"What the hell are you talking about?"

"I mean," said Tony, "that my cock is hard. VERY HARD!"

Tony walked over and poured a glassful from the jug. Drank it down.

Then he walked over to the bed, began kissing the breasts,

running his hands through her long hair, and then finally *kissing* that dead mouth in a kiss from the living to the dead. And then he mounted.

It was GOOD. Tony rammed and jammed. Never such a fuck as this in all his days! He came. Then rolled off, toweled himself with the sheet.

Bill had watched the whole thing, lifting the gallon muscatel jug in the dim lamplight.

"Christ, Bill, it was beautiful, beautiful!"

"You're crazy! You just fucked a dead woman!"

"And *you've* been fucking dead women all your life – dead women with dead souls and dead pussies – only you didn't know it! I'm sorry, Bill, she was a beautiful fuck. I have no shame."

"Was she *that* good?" asked Bill.

"You'll never believe it."

Tony walked to the bathroom to take a piss.

When he got back, Bill had mounted the body. Bill was going good. Moaning and groaning a bit. Then he reached over, kissed that dead mouth, and came.

Bill rolled off, hit the edge of the sheet, wiped off.

"You're right. Best fuck I *ever* had!"

Then they both sat in their chairs and looked at her.

"Wonder what her name was?" asked Tony. "I'm in love."

Bill laughed. "Now I *know* you're drunk! Only a damn fool falls in love with a living woman; now you gotta get hooked on a dead one."

"Okay, I'm hooked," said Tony.

"All right, you're hooked," said Bill, "whatta we do now?"

"Get her the hell outa here!" answered Tony.

"How?"

"Same way we got her in – down the stairway."

"Then?"

"Then into your car. We drive her down to Venice Beach, throw her into the ocean."

"That's cold."

"She won't feel it any more than she felt your cock."

"And how about your cock?" asked Bill.

"She didn't feel that either," answered Tony.

There she was, double-fucked, dead-laid on the sheets.

"Let's make it, baby!" screamed Tony.

Tony grabbed the feet and waited. Bill grabbed the head.

As they rushed out of Tony's room the doorway was still open. Tony kicked it shut with his left foot as they moved toward the top of the stairway, the sheet no longer wound about the body but, more or less, flopped over it. Like a wet dishrag over a kitchen faucet. And again, there was much bumping of her head and her thighs and her big ass against the stairway walls and stairway railings.

They threw her into the back seat of Bill's car.

"Wait, wait, baby!" screamed Tony.

"What for?"

"The muscatel jug, asshole!"

"Oh, sure."

Bill sat waiting with the dead cunt in the back seat.

Tony was a man of his word. He came running out with the jug of muski.

They got on the freeway, passing the jug back and forth, drinking good mouthfuls. It was a warm and beautiful night and the moon was full, of course. But it wasn't exactly night. By then it was 4:15 a.m. A good time anyhow.

They parked. Then had another drink of the good muscatel, got the body out and carried it that long sandy sandy walk toward the sea. They got down to that part of the sand where the sea reached now and then, that part of the sand that was wet, soaked, full of little sand crabs and air holes. They put the body down and drank from the jug. Now and then an excessive wave rolled a bit over all of them: Bill, Tony, the dead Cunt.

Bill had to get up to piss and having been taught nineteenth century morals he walked a bit up the shore to piss. As his friend did so, Tony pulled back the sheet and looked at the dead face in the seaweed twist and swirl, in the salty morning air. Tony looked at the face as Bill was pissing offshore. A lovely kind face, nose a little too sharp, but a very good mouth, and then with her body stiffening already, he leaned forward and kissed her very gently upon the mouth and said, "I love you, dead bitch."

Then he covered her with the sheet.

Bill finished pissing, came back. "I need another drink."

"Go ahead. I'll take one too."

Tony said, "I'm going to swim her out."

"Can you swim good?"

"Not too well."

"I'm a good swimmer. I'll swim her out."

"NO! NO!" screamed Tony.

"Goddamn it, stop yelling!"

"I'm going to swim her out!"

"All right! All right!"

Tony took another drink, pulled the sheet aside, picked her up and carried her step by step toward the breakers. He was drunker than he figured. Several times the big waves knocked them both down, knocked her out of his arms, and he had to get to his feet, run, swim, struggle to find the body. Then he'd see her – that long long hair. She was just like a *mermaid*. Maybe she *was* a mermaid. Finally Tony floated her out beyond the breakers. It was quiet. Halfway between moon and sunrise. He floated with her some moments. It was very quiet. A time within time and a time beyond time.

Finally, he gave the body a little shove. She floated off, half underwater, the strands of long hair whirling about the body. She was still beautiful, dead or whatever she was.

She began to float away from him, caught in some tide. The sea had her.

Then suddenly he turned from her, tried to swim back toward the shore. It seemed very far away. He made it in with the last stroke of his strength, rolling in with the force of the last breaker. He picked himself up, fell, got up, walked forward, sat down beside Bill.

"So, she's gone," said Bill.

"Yeh. Shark meat."

"Do you think we'll ever be caught?"

"No. Give me a drink."

"Go easy. We're getting close to the bottom."

"Yeah."

They got back to the car. Bill drove. They argued over the final drinks on the way home, then Tony thought about the mermaid. He put his head down and began to cry.

"You were always chickenshit," said Bill, "always chicken-shit."

They made it back to the rooming house.

Bill went to his room, Tony to his. The sun was coming up. The world was awakening. Some were awakening with hangovers. Some were awakening with thoughts of church. Most were still asleep. A Sunday morning. And the mermaid, the mermaid with that dead sweet tail, she was well out to sea. While somewhere a pelican dove, came up with a glittering, guitar-shaped fish.

TROUBLE WITH A BATTERY

I bought her a drink and then another drink and then we went up
the stairway behind the bar. there were several large rooms there.
she had me hot. sticking her tongue out at me. and we played all
the way up the stairway. I took the first one, standing up, inside
the door. she just slid back her panties and I put it in.

then we went into the bedroom and there was some kid in the
other bed. there were two beds, and the kid said, "hello."

"it's my brother," she said.

the kid looked real thin and vicious, but then almost everybody
in the world looked vicious when you thought about it.

there were several bottles of wine along the headboard. they
opened a bottle and I waited until they both drank from the
bottle, then I tried some.

I threw a ten on the dresser.

the kid really drank at the wine.

"his big brother is the great bullfighter, Jaime Bravo."

"I've heard of Jaime Bravo, he fights mostly out of T.," I said,
"but you don't have to give me any bullshit."

"o.k.," she said, "no bullshit."

we drank and talked for some time, just small easy talk, and
then she turned out the lights and with the brother there in the
other bed, we did it again. I had my wallet under her pillow.

when we finished she hit the light and went to the bathroom while her brother and I passed the bottle. while the brother wasn't looking I wiped off on the sheet.

she came out of the bathroom and she still looked good, I mean after two shots at it, she still looked good. her breasts were small but firm; what there was of them really jutted. and her ass was big, big enough.

"why did you come to this place?" she asked, moving toward the bed. she slid in beside me, pulled up the sheet, pulled from the bottle.

"I had to get my battery charged across the street."

"after *that* one," she said, "you'll need a charge."

we all laughed. even the brother laughed. then he looked at her: "is he all right?"

"sure he's all right," she said.

"what's all that?" I asked.

"we have to be careful."

"I don't know what you mean."

"one of the girls was almost murdered up here last year. some guy gagged her so she couldn't scream and then took a pen knife and cut these crosses all over her body. she almost bled to death."

the brother dressed very slowly, then left. I gave her a five. she threw it on the dresser with the ten.

she passed the wine. it was good wine, French wine. you didn't gag.

she put her leg up against mine. we were both sitting up in bed. it was very comfortable.

"how old are you?" she asked.

"damn near half a century."

"you can sure go, but you look real beat-up."

"I'm sorry. I'm not very pretty."

"oh *no*, I think you're a beautiful man, didn't anybody ever tell you?"

"I'll bet you say that to all the men you fuck."

"no, I don't."

we sat there a while, passing the bottle. it was very quiet except that you could hear a little music from the bar downstairs. I passed into a kind of dream-trance.

"HEY!" she yelled. she jammed a long fingernail into my bellybutton.

"ow! god damn!"

"LOOK at me!"

I turned and looked at her.

"what do you see?"

"a fine-looking Mexican-Indian girl."

"how can you see?"

"what?"

"how can you see? you don't open your eyes. you keep your eyes in little slits. why?"

it was a fair question. I took a good pull at the French wine.

"I don't know. maybe I'm afraid. afraid of everything. I mean, people, buildings, things, everything. mainly people."

"I'm afraid too," she said.

"but your eyes are open. I like your eyes."

she was hitting the wine. hard. I knew those Mexican-Americans. I was waiting for her to get nasty.

then there was a rapping on the door that damn near shitted me out. it was flung open, viciously, American-style, and there was the bartender – big red brutal banal bastard.

"ain't you through with that son of a bitch yet?"

"I think he wants some more," she said.

"do you?" asked Mr. Banal.

"I think so," I said.

his eyes eagled over to the money on the dresser and he slammed the door. a money society. they thought it was magic.

"that was my husband, sort of," she said.

"I don't think I want to go again," I said.

"why not?"

"first, I'm 48. second, it's kind of like fucking in the waiting room of a bus station."

she laughed. "I'm what you guys call a 'whore.' I must fuck 8 or ten guys a week, at least."

"that sure doesn't help my cause."

"it helps mine."

"yeh."

we passed the bottle back and forth.

"you like to fuck women?"

"that's why I'm here."

"how about men?"

"I don't fuck men."

she pulled at the bottle. she must have taken a good one-quarter of it.

"maybe you'd like it in the ass? maybe you'd like a man to fuck you in the ass?"

"you're talking crazy now."

she looked straight ahead. there was a little silver Christ on the further wall. she kept looking at the little silver Christ on his cross. he was very pretty.

"maybe you've been hiding it. maybe you want somebody to fuck you in the ass."

"o.k., have it your way – maybe that's what I really want."

I got the corkscrew and pulled out the top of a new French wine, meanwhile getting a bunch of cork and shit into the wine as I always did. only a waiter in the movies could open a French wine without that trouble.

I took the first good gulp. cork and all. I handed her the bottle. her leg had dropped away. she had a fish-like look on her face. she took a good swallow.

I took the wine back from her. the little splints of cork didn't seem to know where to go in the bottle. I got rid of some of them.

"you want *me* to fuck you in the ass?" she asked.

"WHAT?"

"I can DO it!"

she got out of bed and went to the top drawer of the dresser and strapped this belt around her waist and then faced me – and there, looking at me, was this BIG celluloid cock.

"ten inches!" she laughed, pushing out her belly, jutting the thing toward me, "and it never gets soft and it never wears out!"

"I liked you better the other way."

"you don't believe my big brother is Jaime Bravo the great bullfighter?"

there she was standing there with this celluloid cock on, asking me about Jaime Bravo.

"I don't think Bravo could cut it in Spain," I said.

"could *you* cut it in Spain?"

"hell, I can't cut it in Los Angeles. now please take that ridiculous artificial cock off . . ."

she unhooked the thing and put it back in the top dresser drawer.

I got out of bed and sat in a straight-backed chair, drinking the wine. she found another chair, and there we sat across from each other, naked, passing the wine.

"this reminds me somehow of an old Leslie Howard movie,

although they wouldn't shoot this part. wasn't Howard in the Somerset Maugham thing? OF HUMAN BONDAGE?"

"I don't know those people."

"that's right. you're too young."

"did you like this Howard, this Maugham?"

"they both had style. plenty of style. but, somehow, with both of them, hours or days or years later, you felt gypped, finally."

"but they had this thing you call 'style'?"

"yes, style is important. many people scream the truth but without style it is helpless."

"Bravo has style, I have style, you have style."

"now you're learning."

then I got back into bed. she came on in. I tried it again. I couldn't make it.

"you suck?" I asked.

"sure."

she took it in her mouth and got it out of me.

I gave her another five, dressed, took another drink of wine, and made it down the stairway, across the street to the gas station. the battery was fully-charged. I paid the attendant and then backed on out, hit up 8th ave. a cop on a bike trailed me for 2 or 3 miles. there was a pack of CLORETS in the glove compartment and I took them out, put in 3 or 4. the cop on the bike finally gave up and tailed after a Jap who made a sudden left turn without blinkers or hand signal on Wilshire blvd. they deserved each other.

when I got to my place the woman was asleep and the little girl wanted me to read to her from a book called BABY SUSAN'S CHICKEN. it was terrible. Bobby found a cardboard carton for the chicks to sleep in. he set it in a corner behind the kitchen stove. and Bobby put some of Baby Susan's cereal in a little dish and set it carefully in the carton, so the little chicks could have some dinner. and Baby Susan laughed and clapped her fat little hands.

it turns out later that the 2 other chicks are roosters and Baby Susan is a hen, a hen who lays a most wondrous egg. I'll say.

I put the little girl down and went into the bathroom and let the hot water run into the tub. then I got into the tub and thought, the next time I get a dead battery I'll go to a movie. then I stretched out into the hot water and forgot everything. almost.

The President of the United States of America entered his car, surrounded by his agents. He sat in the back seat. It was a dark and unimpressive morning. Nobody spoke. They rolled away and the tires could be heard on a street still wet from the preceding night's rain. The silence was more unusual than it had ever been before.

They drove along a while and then the President spoke:

"Say, this isn't the way to the airport."

His agents didn't answer. A vacation had been scheduled. Two weeks at his private home. His plane was waiting at the airport.

It began to drizzle. It looked as if it might rain again. The men, including the President, were dressed in heavy overcoats; hats; it made the car seem very full. Outside, the cold wind was steady.

"Driver," said the President, "I believe you're on the wrong course."

The driver didn't answer. The other agents stared straight ahead.

"Listen," said the President, "will somebody tell that man the way to the airport?"

"We're not going to the airport," said the agent to the President's left.

"We're not going to the airport?" the President asked.

The agents were again quiet. The drizzle became rain. The driver turned the wipers on.

"Listen, what is it?" asked the President. "What's going on here?"

"It's been raining for weeks," said the agent next to the driver. "It gets depressive. I'll certainly be glad to see a little sunshine."

"Yes, me too," said the driver.

"Something's wrong here," said the President, "I demand to know . . ."

"You are no longer in a position to demand," said the agent to the President's right.

"You mean? . . ."

"We mean," said the same agent.

"Is it to be an assassination?" asked the President.

"Hardly. That's old-fashioned."

"Then what . . ."

"Please. We have orders not to discuss anything."

They drove for some hours. It continued to rain. Nobody spoke.

"Now," said the agent to the President's left, "circle again, then turn in. We're not being followed. The rain has been very helpful."

The car circled the area, then turned up a small dirt road. It was muddy and now and then the tires spun, slipped, then gripped again and the car went on. A man in a yellow raincoat held a flashlight and directed them into an open garage. It was an isolated area with many trees. A small farmhouse sat to the left of the garage. The agents opened the car doors.

"Get out," they told the President. The President did so. The agents kept the President carefully between them, although there wasn't a human within miles except for the man with the flashlight and the yellow raincoat.

"I don't see why we couldn't have done the whole thing here," said the man in the yellow raincoat. "It certainly seems much riskier the other way."

"Orders," said one of the agents. "You know how it is. He's always gone a lot on intuition. He does so now, more than ever."

"It's very cold. Do you have time for a cup of coffee? It's ready."

"That's good of you. It's been a long drive. I presume the other car is all ready to go?"

"Of course. It's been checked again and again. Actually, we're about ten minutes ahead on the timetable. That's one reason I suggested the coffee. You know how he is about precision."

"O.K., then, let's go in."

Keeping the President carefully between them, they entered the farmhouse.

"You sit there," one of the agents told the President.

"It's good coffee," said the man in the yellow raincoat, "hand-ground."

He walked around with the pot. He poured himself one, then sat down, still in the yellow raincoat, only the headpiece thrown on the stove.

"Ah, it is good," said one of the agents.

"Cream and sugar?" one of them asked the President.

"All right," he said . . .

There wasn't much room in the old car but they all managed to get in, with the President again in the back seat. . . . The old car also slipped in the mud and rutholes but made it back to the road. Again, it was a silent ride most of the way. Then one of the agents lit a cigarette.

"Damn it, I just can't stop smoking!"

"Well, it's a hard thing to do, that's all. Don't worry about it."

"I'm not worried about it. Just disgusted with myself."

"Well, forget all that. This is a great day in History."

"I'll say so!" said the one with the cigarette.

Then he inhaled . . .

They parked outside an old roominghouse. It continued to rain. They sat there some moments.

"Now," said the agent next to the driver, "get him out. It's clear. Nobody on the streets."

They walked the President between them, first through the front door, then up 3 flights of steps, always keeping the President between them. They stopped and knocked at 306. The signal: one knock, pause, 3 knocks, pause, two knocks . . .

The door was opened and the men quickly pushed the President inside. The door was then locked and bolted. Three men were waiting inside. Two were in their 50's. The other sat in an outfit that consisted of an old laborer's shirt, 2nd-hand trousers that were too large and ten dollar shoes, scuffed and unpolished. He sat in a rocker in the center of the room. He was in his 80's but he smiled . . . and the eyes were those same eyes; the nose, the chin, the forehead hadn't changed much.

"Welcome, Mr. President. I've waited a long time on History and Science and You, and all have arrived, on schedule, today . . ."

The President looked at the old man in the rocker. "Great God! You're . . . you are . . ."

"You've recognized me! Others of your citizens have made jokes about the similarity! Too stupid to even realize that I was . . ."

"But it was proven that . . ."

"Of course, it was proven. The bunkers: April 30th, 1945. We wanted it that way. I've been patient. Science was with us but at times I had to speed-up History. We wanted the right man. You are the right man. The others were too impossible – too alienated from my political philosophy . . . You are far more ideal. By working through you it will be easier. But as I said, I had to speed-up the reel of History a bit . . . my age . . . I had to . . ."

"You mean . . .?"

"Yes. I had your president Kennedy assassinated. And then, his brother . . ."

"But why the 2nd assassination?"

"We had information that that young man would have won the presidential election."

"But what are you going to do with me? I've been told that I'm not to be assassinated . . ."

"May I introduce Drs. Graf and Voelker?"

The two men nodded at the President and smiled.

"But what is going to happen?" asked the President.

"Please. Just a moment. I must question my men. Karl, how did it go with The Double?"

"Fine. We phoned from the farm. The Double arrived at the airport on schedule. The Double announced, that due to weather conditions, he was canceling the flight until tomorrow. Then The Double announced that he would take a pleasure drive . . . that it pleased him to be driven about in the rain . . ."

"And the rest?" asked the old man.

"The Double is dead."

"Fine. Let's get on with it then. History and Science have arrived on Time."

The agents began walking the President toward one of the two operating tables. They asked him to disrobe. The old man walked to the other table. Drs. Graf and Voelker climbed into their medical gowns and made ready for the task . . .

The younger-looking of the 2 men arose from one of the operating tables. He dressed himself in the President's clothing, then walked to the full-length mirror on the north wall. He stood for a good 5 minutes. Then he turned.

"It *is* miraculous! Not even any operating scars . . . no recuperating period. Congratulations, gentlemen! How do you do it?"

"Well, Adolph," answered one of the doctors, "we've come a long way since . . ."

"WAIT! I am never to be addressed as 'Adolph' again . . . until the proper time, until *I* say so! . . . Until then, there will be no German spoken . . . I am *now* the President of the United States of America!"

"Yes, Mr. President!"

Then he reached and touched above his upper lip:

"But I *do* miss the old mustache!"

They smiled.

Then he asked:

"And the old man?"

"We've placed him in the bed. He will not awaken for 24 hours. At this moment . . . everything . . . all appendages of the operation have been destroyed, dissolved. All we need do is walk out of here," said Dr. Graf. "But . . . Mr. President, it is my suggestion that this man be . . ."

"No, I tell you, he's helpless! Let him suffer as I have suffered!"

He walked over to the bed and looked down at the man. A white-haired old man in his 80's.

"Tomorrow I'll be in his private home. I wonder how his wife will enjoy my lovemaking?" he gave a small laugh.

"I'm sure, mein Fuhrer . . . I'm sorry! Please! I'm sure, Mr. President, that she will enjoy your love-making very much."

"Let's leave this place, then. The doctors first, to go their way. Then the rest of us . . . one or two at a time . . . a transfer of cars, then a good night's sleep at the White House."

The old man with the white hair awakened. He was alone in the room. He could escape. He got out of the bed in search of his clothing and as he walked across the room he saw an old man in a full-length mirror.

No, he thought, oh my god, no!

He raised an arm. The old man in the mirror raised an arm. He moved forward. The old man in the mirror enlarged. He looked down at his hands – wrinkled, and not his hands! And he looked down at his feet! They weren't his feet! It wasn't his body!

"My God!" he said aloud, "OH MY GOD!"

Then he heard his voice. It wasn't even his own voice. They'd transferred the voice box also. He felt his throat, his head with his fingers. No scars! No scars anywhere. He got into the old man's clothing and ran down the stairway. At the first door he knocked on the door was marked "Landlady."

The door opened. An old woman.

"Yes, Mr. Tilson?" she asked.

" 'Mr. Tilson?' Lady, I am the President of the United States of America! This is an emergency!"

"Oh, Mr. Tilson, you're so funny!"

"Look, where's your telephone?"

"Right where it has always been, Mr. Tilson. Just to the left of the entrance door."

He felt in his pockets. They had left him change. He looked into the wallet. $18. He put a dime in the phone.

"Lady, what's the address here?"

"Now, Mr. Tilson, you *know* the address. You've lived here for years! You're acting very strange today, Mr. Tilson. And I want to tell you something else!"

"Yes, yes . . . what is it?"

"I want to remind you that your rent is due today!"

"Oh, lady, please tell me the address here!"

"As if you didn't know! It's 2435 Shoreham Drive."

"Yes," he said into the phone, "cab? I want a cab at 2435 Shoreham Drive. I'll be waiting on the first floor. My name? My name? All right, my name is Tilson . . ."

It's no use going to the White House, he thought, they have that covered . . . I'll go to the largest newspaper. I'll tell them. I'll tell the editor everything, everything that happened . . .

The other patients laughed at him. "See that guy? The guy that kinda looks like that dictator-fellow, what's-his-name, only a lot older. Anyhow, when he came in here a month ago he claimed that he was the President of the United States of America. That was a month ago. He doesn't say it too much now. But he sure likes to read the newspapers. I never saw a guy who was so eager to read a newspaper. He *does* know a lot about politics, though. I guess that's what drove him crazy. Too much politics."

The dinner bell rang. All the patients responded. Except one. A male nurse walked up to him.

"Mr. Tilson?"

There wasn't any answer.

"MR. TILSON!"

"Oh . . . yes?"

"It's time to eat, Mr. Tilson!"

The old white-haired man rose and walked slowly toward the patients' dining room.

POLITICS IS LIKE TRYING TO SCREW
A CAT IN THE ASS

"*Dear Mr. Bukowski:*
Why don't you ever write about politics or world affairs?
M.K."

"Dear M.K.:
What for? Like, what's new? – everybody knows the bacon
is burning."

our raving takes place quite quietly while we are staring down at
the hairs of a rug – wondering what the shit went wrong when
they blew up the trolley full of jellybeans with the poster of
Popeye the Sailor stuck on the side.

that's all that matters: the good dream gone, and when that's
gone it's all gone. the rest is horseshit games for the Generals and
money-makers. speaking of which – I see where another U.S.
bomber full of H-bombs fell out of the sky again – THIS time into
the sea near Iceland. the boys are mighty careless with their paper
birds while SUPPOSEDLY protecting my life. the State Dept. says
the H-bombs were "unarmed," whatever that means. then we
continue to read where one of the H-bombs (lost) had split open
and was spreading radioactive shit everywhere while supposedly
protecting me WHILE I hadn't even asked for protection. the

difference between a Democracy and a Dictatorship is that in a Democracy you vote first and take orders later; in a Dictatorship you don't have to waste your time voting.

getting back to the H-bomb dropout – a little while back the same thing happened off the coast of SPAIN. (we are everywhere, protecting me.) again the bombs get lost – careless little toys. it took them 3 months – if I remember properly – to find and lift that last bomb out of there. it may have been 3 weeks but to the people in that coast town it must have seemed 3 years. that last bomb – the god damned thing had gotten itself wedged on the edge of a sandhill far down in the sea. and everytime they tried to hook the thing, so tenderly, it would shake loose and roll a little further down the hill. meanwhile, all the poor people in that coast town were tossing in their beds at night wondering if they'd be blown to hell, courtesy of the Stars and Stripes. of course, the U.S. State Dept. issued a statement saying the H-bomb had no detonation fuse, but meanwhile the rich had left for other parts and the American sailors and townspeople looked very nervous. (after all, if the things couldn't blow up what were they flying them around for? might as well carry 2-ton salamis. fuse means "spark" or "trigger," and "spark" can come from anywhere, and "trigger" means "jolt" or any similar action that will set off the firing mechanism. NOW the terminology is "unarmed," which sounds safer but is the same thing.) anyhow, they hooked at the bomb but as the saying goes, the thing seemed to have a mind of its own. then a few undersea storms came about and our lovely little bomb rolled further and further down its hill. the sea is very deep, much deeper than our leadership.

finally, special equipment was designed just to haul bomb-ass and the thing was pulled from the sea. Palomares. yes, that's where it happened: Palomares. and you know what they did next? –

the American Navy had a BAND CONCERT in the town park in celebration of finding the bomb – if the thing wasn't dangerous they were really cutting loose. yes, and the sailors played the music and the Spanish people listened to the music and they all came together, one big sexual and spiritual release. whatever happened to the bomb they pulled out of the sea, I don't know, nobody (except the few) knows, and the band played on. while 1,000 tons of radioactive Spanish topsoil was shipped to Aiken, S.C. in sealed containers. I'll bet the rent is cheap in Aiken, S.C.

so now our bombs are swimming and sinking, chilled and "unarmed" about Iceland.

so what do you do when you've got the people's minds on something not so good? easy, you get their minds on something else. they can only think about one thing at a time. like, all right, headline of Jan. 23, 1968: B-52 CRASHES OFF GREENLAND WITH H-BOMBS; DANES IRKED. Danes irked? oh, mother!

anyhow, suddenly, Jan. 24, headline: NORTH KOREANS SEIZE U.S. NAVY SHIP.

oh boy, patriotism is back! why, those dirty bastards! I thought THAT war was over! ah ha, I see – the REDS! Korean puppets!

it says under the A.P. wirephoto, something like this – The U.S. intelligence ship Pueblo – formerly an army cargo ship, now converted into one of the Navy's secret spy ships equipped with electric monitoring gear and oceanographic equipment was forced into Wonsan Harbor off the coast of North Korea.

those dirty Red bastards, always fucking around!

but I DID notice that the lost H-bomb story got shoved into a small space: "Radiation Detected at B-52 Crash Site; Split Bomb Hinted."

we are told that the president was awakened between 2 a.m. and 2:30 a.m. and told of the capture of the Pueblo.

I presume he went back to sleep.

the U.S. says the Pueblo was in international waters; the Koreans say the ship was in territorial waters. one country is lying, one is not.

then one wonders, what good is a spy ship in international waters? it's like wearing a raincoat on a sunny day.

the closer you can get on in, the better your instruments pick up.

headline: Jan. 26, 1968: U.S. CALLS UP 14,700 AIR RESERVISTS.

the lost H-bombs off Iceland have completely disappeared from print as if it had never happened.

meanwhile :

Sen. John C. Stennis (D.-Miss.) said Mr. Johnson's decision (the call-up of Air Reserves) was "necessary and justified" and added, "I hope he will not hesitate to mobilize ground reserve components as well."

Senate minority leader, Richard B. Russell (D.-Ga.): "In the last analysis, this country must get the return of that ship and the men that were seized. After all, great wars have started from much less serious incidents than this."

House Speaker John W. McCormack (D: Mass.): "The American people have to wake up to the realization that communism is still bent on world domination. There is too much apathy about it."

I think that if Adolph Hitler were around now he would pretty much enjoy the present scene.

what's there to say about politics and world-affairs? the Berlin crisis, the Cuban crisis, spy planes, spy ships, Vietnam, Korea, lost H-bombs, riots in American cities, starvation in India, purge in Red China? are there good guys and bad guys? some that always lie, some that never lie? are there good governments and bad governments? no, there are only bad governments and worse governments. will there be the flash of light and heat that rips us apart one night while we are screwing or crapping or reading the comic strips or pasting blue-chip stamps into a book? instant death is nothing new, nor is mass instant death new. but we've improved the product; we've had these centuries of knowledge and culture and discovery to work with; the libraries are fat and crawling and overcrowded with books; great paintings sell for hundreds of thousands of dollars; medical science is transplanting the human heart; you can't tell a madman from a sane one upon the streets, and suddenly we find our lives, again, in the hands of the idiots. the bombs may never drop; the bombs might drop. eeney, meeney, miney, mo . . .

now if you'll forgive me, dear readers, I'll get back to the whores and the horses and the booze, while there's time. if these contain death, then, to me, it seems far less offensive to be responsible for your own death than the other kind which is brought to you fringed with phrases of Freedom and Democracy and Humanity and/or any or all of that Bullshit.

first post, 12:30. first drink, now. and the whores will always be around. Clara, Penny, Alice, Jo . . .

eeney, meeney, miney, mo . . .

MY BIG-ASSED MOTHER

they were two good girls, Tito and Baby. they both looked near 60 but they were closer to 40. all that wine and worry. I was 29 and looked closer to 50. all that wine and worry. I had gotten the apartment first and then they had moved in. it worried the apartment house manager who kept sending the cops up when we made the least bit of noise. it was jumpy. I was afraid to piss in the center of the bowl.

the best time was the MIRROR, watching myself, bloated belly, with Baby and Tito, drunk and sick for nights and days, all of us, the cheap radio playing, tubes all worn-out sitting there on that worn-down rug, ah my, the MIRROR, and I'd be watching, and I'd say:

"Tito, it's in your ass. feel it?"

"oh yes, oh my yes – SHOVE! hey! where ya GOING?"

"now, Baby, you got it in front there, umm? feel it? big purple head, like a snake singing arias! *feel* me love?"

"oooh, dahling, I think I'm gonna c... HEY! where ya GOING?"

"Tito, I am back in your rumble seat. I am parting you in two. you don't have a chance!"

"oooh god ooooh, HEY where ya GOING? get back in there!"

"I dunno."

"you dunno, what?"

"I dunno who I want to catch it. what can I do? I want you both, I can't HAVE you both! and while trying to make up my mind I am in a terror of demise and agony trying to hold it! doesn't anybody understand my suffering?"

"no, just give it to me!"

"no, me, me!"

THEN THE BIG FIST OF THE LAW.

bang! bAnG! BANG!

"hey, what's going on in there?"

"nuttin'."

"nothing? what's all that moaning and hollering and screaming? it's 3:30 a.m. you've got four floors of people wide awake and wondering . . ."

"it's nuttin'. I'm playing chess with my mother and sister."

"please go away. my mother has a bad heart. you are terrorizing her. and she's down to her last pawn."

"and YOU are too, buddy! in case you don't know, this happens to be the Los Angeles Police Department . . ."

"christ, I'd have never guessed . . ."

"now you've guessed. o.k. open up or we'll kick it down!"

Tito and Baby ran into the far corner of the dining room, crouched and shivering, holding, hugging their aging wrinkled and wino and insane bodies. they were stupidly lovely.

"open up here, buddy, we been up here four times in the past week and a half on the same call. you think we like to go around just throwing people in jail just because it makes us feel good?"

"yeah."

"Captain Bradley says he doesn't care whether you are black or white."

"you tell Captain Bradley that I feel the same way."

I kept quiet. the two whores shivering and clutching their wrinkled bodies by the corner lampshade. the bland and smothering silence of willow leaves in a chickenshit and unkind winter.

they had gotten the key from the manager and the door was open 4 inches but it was being held by the chain which I had on there. one of the cops talked to me while the other pushed with a screwdriver, trying to work the chain out of the slot-holder. I'd let the cop get it almost out, then I'd push the end of the chain all the way back in. while standing there naked with this hard-on.

"you are violating my rights. you need a search warrant to enter here. you can't force entry just on your own behest. what the hell's wrong with you guys."

"which one of those is supposed to be your mother."

"the one with the biggest ass."

the other cop almost had the chain off again. I pushed it back with my finger.

"come on, let us in, we'll just talk."

"what about? the wonders of Disneyland?"

"no, no, you sound like an interesting man. we just want to come in and talk."

"you must think I'm subnormal. if I ever get queer enough for bracelets I'll buy them at Thrifty's. I'm not guilty of a damn thing but a hard-on and a loud radio and you haven't asked me to shut either of them off."

"just let us in. all we want to do is talk."

"listen, you are attempting to break and enter without a permit. now, I've got the best lawyer in town . . ."

"a lawyer? whatta you got a lawyer for?"

"I've used him for years – draft dodging, indecent exposure, rape, drunk driving, disturbing the peace, assault and battery, arson – all bad raps."

"he won all those cases?"

"he's the best. now look, I'm giving you three minutes. either you stop trying to force the door and leave me in peace or I'm getting him on the phone. he won't like to be awakened at this time of the morning. he'll have your badges."

the cops stepped back, a little way down the hall. I listened.

"you think he knows what he's talking about?"

"yes, I think he does."

they came back.

"your mother sure has a big ass."

"too bad *you* can't have it, eh?"

"all right, we're leaving, but you keep it quiet in there. we want that radio off and all that moaning and hollering stopped."

"all right, we'll turn off the radio."

they left. what a pleasure to hear them leave. what a pleasure it was to have a good lawyer. what a pleasure it was to stay out of jail.

I closed the door.

"all right, girls, they're gone. 2 nice young boys on the wrong path. and now look!"

I looked down. "it's gone, all gone away."

"yes, it's all gone," said Baby. "where does it go? it's so sad."

"shit," said Tito, "it looks like a dead little vienna sausage."

I walked over and sat in a chair, poured a wine. Baby rolled us 3 cigarettes.

"how's the wine?" I asked.

"down to 4 bottles."

"fifths or gallons?"

"fifths."

"Jesus, we gotta get lucky."

I picked up a 4 day old newspaper. read the funnies. then went to the sports section. while I was reading, Tito came on over, dropped down to the rug. I felt her working. she had a mouth like one of those toilet plungers that unstopped toilets. I drank my wine and puffed at my cigarette.

they'd suck your brains out if you let them. I think they did it to each other when I wasn't around.

I got to the horse page. "look here," I told Tito, "this horse cut fractions of 22 and one fifth for the quarter, he's 44 and 4/5ths for the half, then one o nine for 6 furlongs, he must have thought it was a 6 furlong race –"

vurp   virp sloooom

vissaaa ooop

vop bop vop bop vop

"– it's a mile and a quarter, he's trying to sprint away from these routers, he's got 6 lengths turning the last curve and backing up, the horse is dying, he wants to be back in the stable –"

sllllurrrp

sllurrrrr vip vop vop

vip vop vop

"now check the jock – if it's Blum he'll win by a nose; if it's Volske he'll win by 3/4's of a length. it's Volske. he wins by 3/4's. a bet down from 12 to 8. all stable money, the public hates Volske. they hate Volske and Harmatz. so the stables use these guys 2 or 3 times a meet on the goodies to keep the public off. if it weren't for these two great riders, at the right time, I'd be down on East 5th Street –"

"oooh, you bastard!" Tito lifted her head and screamed, knocked the newspaper out of my hand. then went back to work. I didn't know what to do. she was really angry. then Baby walked over. Baby had very good legs and I lifted her purple skirt and

looked at the nylons. Baby leaned over and kissed me, gave me
the tongue down the throat, I got my palm on her haunch. I was
trapped. I didn't know what to do. I needed a drink. 3 idiots
locked together. o moaning and the flight of the last bluebird into
the eye of the sun, it was a child's game, a stupid game.

first quarter, 22 and 1/4, the half in 44 and 1/5, she smoked it
out, victory by a head, Calif. rain of my body. figs broken lovely
open like great red guts in the sun and sucked loose while your
mother hated you and your father wanted to kill you and the
backyard fence was green and belonged to the Bank of America,
Tito smoked it out while I fingered Baby.

then we separated, each waiting the bathroom's turn to wipe
the snot from our sexual noses. I was always last. I came out and
took one of the winebottles and went over to the window and
looked out.

"Baby, roll me another smoke."

we were on the top floor, the 4th. floor, high up on a hill. but
you can look out on Los Angeles and get nothing, nothing at all.
all those people down there sleeping, waiting to get up and go to
work. it was stupid. stupid, stupid and horrible. we had it right:
eye, say, blue on green staring deeply through shreds of beanfields,
into each other, come.

Baby brought me the cigarette. I inhaled and watched the
sleeping city. we sat and waited on the sun and whatever there
was to be. I did not like the world, but at cautious and easy times
you could almost understand it.

I don't know where Tito and Baby are now, if they are dead or
what, but those nights were good, pinching those high-heeled legs,
kissing nylon knees. all that color of dresses and panties, and
making the L.A. Police Force earn the green.

Spring or flowers or Summer will never be like that again.

A LOVELY LOVE AFFAIR

I went broke – again – but this time in the French Quarter, New Orleans, and Joe Blanchard, editor of the underground paper OVERTHROW took me down to this place around the corner, one of those dirty white buildings with green storm windows, steps that ran almost straight up. It was Sunday and I was expecting a royalty, no, an advance from a dirty book I had written for the Germans, but the Germans kept writing me this bullshit about the owner, the father, being a drunk, they were deep in the red because the old man had withdrawn their funds from the bank, no, overdrawn them for his drinking and fucking bouts and therefore, they were broke but they were kicking the old man out and as soon as . . .

Blanchard rang the bell.

This old fat girl came to the door, and she weighed about between 250 and 300 pounds. She kind of wore this vast sheet as a dress and her eyes were very small. I guess that was the only small thing about her. She was Marie Glaviano, owner of a cafe in the French Quarter, a very small cafe. That was another thing that was not very big about her – her cafe. But it was a nice cafe, red and white tablecloths, expensive menus and no people about. One of those old-time black mammy dolls standing near the entrance. The old black mammy doll signified good times, old times, good old times, but the good old times were gone.

The tourists were walkers now. They just liked to walk around and look at things. They didn't go into the cafes. They didn't even get drunk. Nothing paid anymore. The good times were over. Nobody gave a shit and nobody had any money and if they had any, they kept it. It was a new age and not a very interesting one. Everybody kind of watched the revolutionaries and the pigs rip at each other. That was good entertainment and it was free and they kept their money in their pockets, if they had any money.

Blanchard said, "Hello, Marie. Marie, this is Charley Serkin. Charley, this is Marie."

"Hi," I said.

"Hello," said Marie Glaviano.

"Let us come in a minute, Marie," said Blanchard.

(There are only two things wrong with money: too much or too little. And there I was down at the "too little" stage again.)

We climbed the steep steps and followed her down one of those long long sideways-built places – I mean all length and no width, and then we were in the kitchen, sitting at a table. There was a bowl of flowers. Marie broke open 3 bottles of beer. Sat down.

"Well, Marie," said Blanchard, "Charley's a genius. He's up against the knife. I'm sure he'll pull out, but meanwhile ... meanwhile, he's got no place to stay."

Marie looked at me. "Are you a genius?"

I took a long drag at the beer. "Well, frankly, it's hard to tell. More often, I feel like some type of subnormal. Rather like all these great big white blocks of air in my head."

"He can stay," said Marie.

It was Monday, Marie's only day off and Blanchard got up and left us there in the kitchen. Then the front door slammed and he was out of there.

"What do you do?" asked Marie.

"Live on my luck," I said.

"You remind me of Marty," she said.

"Marty?" I asked, thinking, my god, here it comes. And it came.

"Well, you're ugly, you know. Well, I don't mean ugly, I mean beat-up, you know. And you're really beat-up, you're even more beat-up than Marty was. And he was a fighter. Were you a fighter?"

"That's one of my problems: I could never fight worth a damn."

"Anyhow, you got that same look as Marty. You been beat but you're kind. I know your type. I know a man when I see a man. I like your face. You got a good face."

Not being able to say anything about her face, I asked, "You got any cigarettes, Marie?"

"Why sure, honey," she reached down into that great sheet of a dress and pulled a full pack out from between her tits. She could have carried a week's worth of groceries in there. It was kind of funny. She opened me another beer.

I took a good drain, then told her, "I could probably fuck you until I made you cry."

"Now look here, Charley," she said, "I won't have you talking that way. I'm a nice girl. My mother brought me up right. You keep talking that way and you can't stay."

"Sorry, Marie, I was just kidding."

"Well, I don't like that kind of kidding."

"Sure, I understand. You got any whiskey?"

"Scotch."

"Scotch is fine."

She brought out an almost full fifth. 2 waterglasses. We had ourselves some scotch and water. That woman had been around. That was obvious. She's probably been around ten years longer than I. Well, age wasn't any crime. It was only that most people aged badly.

"You're just like Marty," she said again.

"And you're not like anybody I've ever seen," I said.

"Do you like me?" she asked.

"I've got to," I said, and she didn't give me any snot over that one. We drank another hour or two, mostly beer but with a bit of scotch here and there, and then she took me down to my bed. And on the way down we passed a place and she was sure to say, "That's my bed." It was quite wide. My bed was next to another one. Very strange. But it didn't mean anything. "You can sleep in either bed," said Marie, "or both of them."

There was something about that that felt like a putdown . . .

Well, sure, I had a head in the morning and I heard her rattling in the kitchen but I ignored it as any wise man would, and I heard her turn on the tv for the morning news, she had the tv on the breakfast nook table, and I heard the coffee perking, it smelled rather good but the smell of bacon and eggs and potatoes I didn't like, and the sound of the morning news I didn't like, and I felt like pissing and I was thirsty, but I didn't want Marie to know that I was awake, so I waited, mildly pissed (haha, yes), but wanting to be alone, wanting to own the place alone and she kept fucking around fucking around and finally I heard her running past my bed . . .

"Gotta go," she said, "I'm late."

"Bye, Marie," I said.

When the door slammed I got up and walked to the crapper and I sat there and I pissed and I crapped and I sat there in New Orleans, far from home, wherever my home was, and then I saw a spider sitting in a web in the corner, looking at me. Now that spider had been there a long time, I knew that. Much longer than I had. First, I thought of killing him. But he was so fat and happy and ugly, he owned the joint. I'd have to wait some time, until it was proper. I got up and wiped my ass and flushed. As I left the crapper, the spider winked at me.

I didn't want to play with what was left of the 5th, so I sat in the kitchen, naked, wondering, how can people trust me so? Who was I? People were crazy, people were simple. That gave me an edge. Hell yes, it did. I'd lived for ten years without a trade. People gave me money, food, places to stay. Whether they thought I was an idiot or a genius, that didn't matter. I knew what I was. I was neither. What made people give me gifts didn't concern me. I took the gifts and I took them without a feeling of victory or/and coercion. My only premise was that I couldn't *ask* for anything. On top of it all, I rather had this little phonograph record spinning around on top of my brain and it kept playing the same tune: don't try don't try. It seemed like an all right idea.

Anyhow, after Marie left I sat in the kitchen and drank 3 cans of beer I found in the refrigerator. I never cared much for food. I'd heard of people's love for food. But food only bored me. Liquid was o.k. but bulk was a dragdown. I liked shit, I liked to shit, I liked turds but it was such terrible work creating them.

After the 3 cans of beer I noticed this purse on the seat next to me. Of course, Marie had taken another purse to work. Would she be foolish enough or kind enough to leave money? I opened the purse. There at the bottom was a ten dollar bill.

Well, Marie was testing me and I'd prove worthy of her test.

I took the ten, walked back to my bedroom and dressed. I

felt good. After all, what did a man need to survive? Nothing. It was true. And I even had the key to the place.

So I stepped outside and *locked* the door to keep out the thieves, hahaha, and there I was out on the streets, the French Quarter, and what a stupid place that was, but I had to make it do. Everything had to serve me, that's the way it went. So ... oh yes, I was walking down the street, and the trouble with the French Quarter was that there just weren't any liquor stores around like in other decent parts of the world. Maybe it was deliberate. One had to guess that it helped those horrible shit holes on every corner that were called bars. The first thing I ever thought of when walking into one of those "quaint" French Quarter bars was vomiting. And I usually did, running back to some urine-stinking pisspot and letting go – tons and tons of fried eggs and half-cooked greasy potatoes. And walking back in, after heaving, and looking upon them: the only thing more lonely and inane than the patrons was the bartender, especially if he also owned the place. O.k., so I walked around, knowing that the bars were the lie, and you know where I found my 3 six packs? A little grocery with stale bread and all about it, even peeling into the paint, this half-sex smile of loneliness ... help me, help me, help me ... terrible, yes, and they can't even light the place up, electricity costs money, and here I was, the first guy to buy a 6 pack in 17 days and the first guy to buy three six packs in 18 years, and my god, she almost came across the top of the cash register ... It was too much. I grabbed my change and 18 tall cans of beer and ran out into the stupid French Quarter sunlight ...

I placed the remainder of the change back in the purse in the breakfast nook and then left the purse open so Marie could see it. Then I sat down and opened a beer.

It was good being alone. Yet, I wasn't alone. Each time I had to piss I'd see that spider and I thought, well, spider, you've got to go, soon. I just don't like your looks in that dark corner, catching bugs and flies and sucking the blood out of them. You see, you're bad, Mr. Spider. And I'm o.k. At least, that's the way I like to see it. You're nothing but a frigging dark brainless wart of death, that's what you are. Suck shit. You've had it.

I found a broom in the backporch and came back in there and I crashed him out of his web and brought him his own death. All right, that was all right, he was out there ahead of me, somewhere, I couldn't help that. But how could Marie put her big ass down on the rims of that lid and shit and look at that thing? Did she even see it? Perhaps not.

I went back in the kitchen and had some more beer. Then I turned on the tv. Paper people. Glass people. I felt as if I were going insane and turned the thing off. I drank some more beer. Then I boiled 2 eggs and fried two strips of bacon. I managed to eat. You forgot about food sometimes. The sun came through the curtains. I drank all day. I threw the empties in the trash. Time went. Then the door opened. It flew open. It was Marie.

"Jesus Christ!" she screamed, "you know what happened?"

"No, no, I don't."

"Oh, god damn it!"

"Whatssa matta, honey?"

"I burned the strawberries!"

"Oh, yes?"

She ran around the kitchen in little circles, that big ass bobbing. She was crazy. She was out of it. Poor old fat cunt.

"I had this pot of strawberries going in the kitchen and one of these tourists came in, rich bitch, first customer of the day, and she likes the little hats I make, you know ... Well, she's kinda cute and all the hats look good on her and so she's got a problem, and then we get to talking about Detroit, she knew somebody in Detroit that I knew, you know, and we're talking and then all of a sudden I SMELL IT!!! THE STRAWBERRIES ARE BURNING! I ran into the kitchen, but it's too late ... what a mess! The strawberries have boiled over and they are everywhere and it stinks, it's burned, it's sad, and nothing can be saved, nothing! What hell!"

"I'm sorry. But did you sell her a hat?"

"I sold her two hats. She couldn't make up her mind."

"I'm sorry about the strawberries. And I killed the spider."

"What spider?"

"I didn't think you'd know."

"Know what? What's this spiders? They're just bugs."

"They tell me a spider isn't a bug. Something to do with the number of legs ... I really don't know or care."

"A spider ain't a bug? What kinda shit is that?"

"Not an insect. So they say. Anyhow, I killed the damn thing."

"You been in my purse."

"Sure. You left it there. I had to have beer."

"You have to have beer all the time?"

"Yes."

"You're going to be a problem. You had anything to eat?"

"2 eggs, 2 slices of bacon."

"You hungry?"

"Yes. But you're tired. Relax. Have a drink."

"Cooking relaxes me. But first I gotta have a hot bath."

"Go ahead."

"O.k.," she reached over and turned on the tv and then went to the bathroom. I had to listen to tv. A news broadcast. Perfectly ugly bastard. 3 nostrils. Perfectly hateful bastard dressed like a little inane doll, sweating, and looking at me, saying words I hardly understood or cared about. I knew that Marie would be looking at tv for hours, so I had to adjust to it. When Marie came back I was looking directly into the glass, which made her feel better. I looked as harmless as a man with a checkerboard and the sports page.

Marie had come out, dolled in another outfit. She might have even looked cute, but she *was* so god damned fat. Well, anyhow, I wasn't sleeping on a park bench.

"You want me to cook, Marie?"

"No, it's all right. I'm not so tired now."

She began preparing the food. When I got up for the next beer, I kissed her behind the ear.

"You're a good sport, Marie."

"You got enough to drink for the rest of the night?" she asked.

"Sure, kid. And there's still that 5th. Everything's fine. I just want to sit here and look at the set and listen to you talk. O.k?"

"Sure, Charley."

I sat down. She had something going. It smelled good. She was evidently a fine cook. The whole walls crawled with this warm smell of cooking. No wonder she was so fat: good cook, good eater. Marie was making a pot of stew. Every now and then she'd get up and add something to the pot. An onion. A piece of cabbage. A few carrots. She knew. And I drank and looked at that big sloppy old gal and she sat there making these most magic hats, her hands working into a basket, picking up first this color, then that, this length of ribbon, then that, and then twisting it so, sewing it so, placing it against the hat, and that 2 bit straw was just more magic. Marie created masterpieces that would never be discovered – walking down the street on top of bitches' heads.

As she worked and tended stew, she talked.

"It's not like it used to be. People don't have any money. Everything's Traveler's checks and checkbooks and credit cards. People just don't have money. They don't carry it. Credit's everything. A guy gets a paycheck and it's already taken. They mortgage their whole lives away to buy one house. And then they've got to fill that house with shit and have a car. They're hooked on house and the legislators know this and tax them to death with property taxes. Nobody has any money. Small businesses just can't last."

We sat down to the stew and it was perfect. After dinner we brought out the whiskey and she brought me two cigars and we looked at tv and didn't talk much. I felt as if I had been there for years. She kept working on the hats, talking now and then, and I'd say, yeh, that's right, or, is that so? And the hats kept flying off of her hands, masterpieces.

"Marie," I told her, "I'm tired. Got to go to bed."

She told me to take the whiskey with me, so I did. But instead of going down to my bed, I threw back the cover of Marie's bed and crawled in. After undressing, of course. It was a fine mattress. It was a fine bed. It was one of those old-fashioned highpost jobs with a wooden roof, or whatever they called them. I guess if you fucked until the roof came down, you made it. I'd never bring that roof down without help from the gods.

Marie kept looking at tv and making hats. Then I heard her turn off the set, switch out the kitchen light and she came into the bedroom, right past the bedroom and she didn't see me, she went right on down to the crapper. She was in there a while and then I watched her switch out of her clothes and into this big pink nightie. She fucked with her face a bit, gave up, put on a couple of curlers, then turned around and walked toward the bed and saw me.

"My god, Charley, you're in the wrong bed."

"Uh uh."

"Listen, honey, I'm not that kind of woman."

"O, cut the horseshit and climb in!"

She did. My god, she was nothing but meat. Actually, I was a bit frightened. What did you do with all that stuff? Well, I was trapped. Marie's whole side of the bed sank down.

"Listen, Charley . . ."

I grabbed her head, turned it, and she seemed to be crying, and then my lips were on hers. We kissed. Damn it, my cock was getting hard. Good god. What was it?

"Charley," she said, "you don't have to."

I took one of her hands and placed it around my cock.

"O shit," she said, "o shit!"

Then *she* kissed me, tongued me. She had a small tongue – at least *that* was small – and it ripped in and out, rather full of saliva and passion. I pulled away.

"Whatza matta?"

"Wait uh minute."

I reached over and got the fifth and took a good long pull, then I sat it down again and I reached on under and lifted that huge pink nightie. I got to feeling and I didn't know what I had but it seemed to be it, very small though, but in the right place. Yes, it was her cunt. I poked at it with my pecker. Then she reached down and guided me in. Another miracle. That thing was tight. It almost ripped the skin off of me. We started working. I was looking for the long ride but I didn't care. She had *me*. It was one of the best fucks of my life. I moaned and hollered, then finished, rolled off. Unbelievable. When she came back from the bathroom we talked a while, then she went to sleep. But she snored. So I had to go down to my own bed. And I awakened the next morning as she went to work.

"Gotta hurry, Charley," she said.

"Sure, baby."

As soon as she left I went to the kitchen and drank a glass of water. She'd left a purse there. Ten dollars. I didn't take it. I walked back to the bathroom and took a good crap, without the spider. Then I took a bath. I tried to brush my teeth, vomited a bit. I dressed and walked into the kitchen. I'd gotten hold of a piece of paper and a pen:

> Marie:
>   I love you. You are very good to me. But I must leave. And I don't know exactly why. I'm crazy, I guess. Goodbye.
>   Charley

I propped the note up against the television set. I didn't feel good. I felt like crying. It was quiet in there, it was quiet in there the way I liked it. Even the stove and the refrigerator looked human, I mean good human – they seemed to have arms and voices and they said, hang around, kid, it's good here, it can be very good here. I found what was left of the 5th in the bedroom. I drank that. Then I found a can of beer in the refrigerator. I drank that. Then I got up and made the long walk down that narrow place, it seemed like a hundred yards. I got to the door and then I remembered I had the key. I walked back and put the key with the note. Then I looked at the ten in the purse again. I left it there. I made the walk again. When I got to the door, I knew that when I closed it there would be no going back. I closed it. It was final. Down those steps. I was alone again and nobody gave a damn. I walked south, then took a right. I walked along, I walked along and got out of the French Quarter. I crossed Canal Street. I walked along for some blocks and then I turned this way and then I crossed another street and turned that way. I didn't know where I was going. I passed a place to my left and a man was standing in the doorway and he said,

"Hey, man, you want a job?"

And I looked into the doorway and here were these rows of men lined up at wooden tables and they had hammers and they were hitting at things in shells, they looked like clam shells and they broke the shells and did something with the meat, and it was dark in there; it seemed as if the men were beating at themselves with hammers and tossing away what was left of them, and I told the man,

"No, I don't want a job."

I was facing the sun as I walked.

I had 74 cents.

The sun was all right.

ALL THE PUSSY WE WANT

Harry and Duke. The bottle sat between in a cheap hotel in downtown L.A. It was Saturday night in one of the cruellest towns in the world. Harry's face was quite round and stupid with just a tip of a nose looking out and you hated his eyes; in fact, you hated Harry when you looked at him, so you didn't look at him. Duke was a little younger, a good listener, with just the slightest of smiles on when he listened. He liked to listen; people were his biggest show and there wasn't any admission charge. Harry was unemployed and Duke was a janitor. They'd both done time and would be in jail again. They knew it. It didn't matter.

The 5th was about one-third finished and there were empty beercans on the floor. They rolled their cigarettes with the easy calm of men who had lived hard and impossible lives before the age of 35 and were still alive. They knew it was all a bucket of shit but they refused to quit.

"See," said Harry, taking a drag, "I chose you, man. I can trust you. You won't panic. I think your car can make it. We split it right down the middle."

"Tell me about it," said Duke.

"You won't believe it."

"Tell me."

"Well, there's gold out there, laying on the ground, real gold. All you gotta do is walk out and pick it up. I know it sounds crazy, but it's there, I've seen it."

"What's the catch?"

"Well, it's an army artillery grounds. They shell all day, and sometimes at night, that's the catch. It takes guts. But the gold is there. Maybe the shells broke it out of the earth, I don't know. But they usually don't shell at night."

"We go in at night."

"Right. And just pick the stuff up off of the ground. We'll be rich. All the pussy we want. Think of it – all the pussy we want."

"It sounds good."

"In case they start shelling we leap into the first shell hole. They ain't gonna aim there again. If they hit the target, they're satisfied. If they haven't, the next shot will be somewhere else."

"That sounds logical."

Harry poured some whiskey. "But there's another catch."

"Yeah?"

"There's snakes out there. That's why we need two men. I know you're good with a gun. While I pick up the gold you watch for the snakes and blow their heads off. There are rattlers out there. I think you're the man to do it."

"Why the hell not?"

They sat smoking and drinking, thinking about it.

"All that gold," said Harry, "all that pussy."

"You know," said Duke, "it mighta been that those guns blew open an old treasure chest."

"Whatever it is, there's gold out there."

They thought about it a while longer.

"How do you know," asked Duke, "that after you gather all the gold I won't shoot you out there?"

"Well, I just gotta take that chance."

"Do you trust me?"

"I don't trust any man."

Duke opened another beer, poured another drink.

"Shit, there's no use of me going to work Monday is there?"

"Not now."

"I feel rich already."

"I kind of do too."

"All a man needs is some kind of break," said Duke, "then people treat him like a gentleman."

"Yeah."

"Where's this place at?" asked Duke.

"You'll see when we get there."

"We split down the middle?"

"We split down the middle."

"You're not worried about me shooting you?"

"Why do you keep bringing that up, Duke? I might shoot you."

"Jesus, I never thought of that. You wouldn't shoot a pal, would you?"

"Are we friends?"

"Well, yes, I'd say so, Harry."

"There'll be enough gold and pussy for both of us. We'll be set for life. No more parole officers. No more dish washing gigs. The Beverly Hills whores will be chasing us. Our worries are over."

"Do you really think we can bring it off?"

"Sure."

"Is there really gold down there?"

"Listen, man, I told you."

"O.k."

They drank and smoked some more. They didn't talk. They were both thinking of the future. It was a hot night. Some of the roomers had their doors open. Most of them had a bottle of wine. The men sat in their undershirts, easy and wondering and beaten. Some of them even had women, not too much as ladies but they could hold their wine.

"We better get another bottle," said Duke, "before they close."

"I don't have any money."

"I'll get it."

"O.k."

They got up and walked out the door. They turned right down the hall and went toward the back. The liquor store was down the alley and to the left. At the top of the back steps a man in stained and wrinkled clothing was stretched across the back doorway.

"Hey, it's my old pal Franky Cannon. He really hung one on tonight. Guess I'll move him out of the doorway."

Harry picked him up by the feet and dragged him out of the way. Then he bent over him.

"Wonder if anybody's got to him yet?"

"I don't know," said Duke, "check him out."

Duke pulled all Franky's pockets inside out. Checked the shirt. Opened his pants, checked him around the waist. All he found was a matchbook that said:

LEARN
DRAFTING
AT HOME

Thousands of top pay
jobs waiting

"I guess somebody got him," said Harry.

They walked down the back steps and into the alley. "Are you sure that gold is there?" asked Duke.

"Listen," said Harry, "you're pissing me off! You think I'm crazy?"

"No."

"Well, don't ask me that no more then!"

They walked into the liquor store. Duke ordered a fifth of whiskey and a tall six pack of malt beer. Harry stole a bag of mixed nuts. Duke paid for his stuff and they walked out. Just as they got to the alley a young woman walked up; well, young for that area, she was about 30 with a good figure, but her hair was uncombed and she slurred a bit.

"What you guys got in that bag?"

"Cats' tits," said Duke.

She got up near Duke and rubbed against the bag.

"I don't wanna drink no wine. You got whiskey in there?"

"Sure, baby, come on up."

"Lemme see the bottle."

She looked good to Duke. She was slim and her dress was tight, real shit ass tight, god damn. He pulled the bottle out.

"O.k.," she said, "let's go."

They walked up the alley, the girl between them. Her haunch bumped Harry as she walked. Harry grabbed her and kissed her. She broke off.

"You son of a bitch!" she screamed, "lemme alone!"

"You're gonna spoil everything, Harry!" said Duke. "You do that again and I'm gonna punch you out!"

"You can't punch me out."

"Just don't do it again!"

They walked up the alley and up the stairways, opened the door. The girl looked at Franky Cannon laying there but didn't say anything. They walked on up to the room. The girl sat down and crossed her legs. She had nice legs.

"My name's Ginny," she said.

Duke poured the drinks.

"I'm Duke. He's Harry."

Ginny smiled and took her drink.

"Some son of a bitch I'm stayin' with, he kept me naked, kept my clothes locked in the closet. I was in there a week. I waited until he passed out, took the key off him, got this dress and ran off."

"That's a nice dress."

"It's all right."

"It brings out the best in you."

"Thanks. Hey, listen, what do you guys do?"

"Do?" asked Duke.

"Yeah, I mean how do you make it?"

"We're gold prospectors," said Harry.

"Oh, come on, don't give me that shit."

"That's right," said Duke, "we're gold prospectors."

"We've struck it. We're gonna be rich inside a week," said Harry.

Then Harry had to get up to piss. The can was down the hall. When Harry left Ginny said, "I wanna fuck you first, Honey. I'm not too crazy about him."

"That's o.k.," said Duke.

He poured three more drinks. When Harry came back Duke told him.

"She's gonna lay me first."

"Says who?"

"Says us," said Duke.

"That's right," said Ginny.

"I think we ought to take her with us," said Duke.

"Let's see how she lays first," said Harry.

"I drive men crazy," said Ginny. "I make men scream. I've got the tightest pussy in the state of California!"

"All right," said Duke, "let's find out."

"Gimme another drink first," she said, draining her glass.

Duke gave her a refill. "I've got something too, baby, I'll probably rip you wide open!"

"Not unless you stick your foot in there," said Harry.

Ginny just smiled as she drank. She finished her drink.

"Come on," she said to Duke, "let's make it."

Ginny walked over to the bed and pulled her dress off. She had on blue panties and a faded pink brassiere held together by a safety pin in the back. Duke had to undo the safety pin.

"Is he gonna watch?" she asked Duke.

"He can if he wants," said Duke, "what the hell."

"O.k.," said Ginny.

They got into the sheets together. There were some minutes of warmup and maneuvering as Harry watched. The blanket was on the floor. All Harry could see was movement under a rather dirty sheet.

Then Duke mounted. Harry could see Duke's butt bobbing under the sheet.

Then Duke said, "Oh shit!"

"What'sa matter?" asked Ginny.

"I slipped out! I thought you said you had a tight box!"

"I'll put you in! I don't even think you were in!"

"I was in *somewhere*!" said Duke.

Then Duke's butt was bobbing again. I never should have told that son of a bitch about the gold, thought Harry. Now we've got this bitch on our hands. They might team against me. Of course, if he happened to get killed, she might like me better.

Then Ginny moaned and started talking. "Oh, honey, honey! Oh, Jesus, honey, oh my gawd!"

What a bunch of bullshit, thought Harry.

He got up and walked over to the back window. The back of the hotel was right near the Vermont turnoff on the Hollywood freeway. He watched the headlights and tail lights of the cars. It always amazed him that some people were in such a hurry to go in one direction while other people were in such a hurry to go in another. Somebody had to be wrong, or else it was just a dirty game. Then he heard Ginny's voice:

"I'm gonna COME! O, my gawd I'm gonna COME! O, my gawd! I'm . . ."

Bullshit, he thought and then turned to look at them. Duke was really working. Ginny's eyes did seem glazed; she stared straight up into the ceiling, straight up into an unshaded lightbulb; glazed, seemingly glazed she stared up past Duke's left ear . . .

I might have to shoot him out on that artillery field, thought Harry. Especially if she's got a tight box. gold, all that gold.

THE BEGINNER

Well, I got off the deathbed and came out of the county hospital and got a job as a shipping clerk. I had Saturdays and Sundays off and I talked it over with Madge one Saturday:

"Look, baby, I'm not in a hurry to go back to that Charity ward. I ought to find something that can get in the way of the drinking. Like today. There's nothing to do but get drunk. And I don't like the movies. Zoos are stupid. We can't screw all day. It's a problem."

"Have you ever been to a race track?"

"What's that?"

"They run horses. You bet on them."

"Is there a track open today?"

"Hollywood Park."

"Let's go."

Madge showed me how to get there. It was an hour before the first race and the parking lot was almost full. We had to park about a half mile from the track entrance.

"Seems a lot of people come here," I said.

"Yes, they do."

"What do we do when we get there?"

"You bet on a horse."

"Which one?"

"Anyone you want."

"Can you win money?"

"Sometimes."

We paid our way in and here were all these newsboys waving papers at us: "Get your winners here! You like money? Get your longshot plays here!"

There was a booth with 4 people in it. 3 of them sold you their selections for 50 cents, the other went for a dollar. Madge told me to buy 2 programs and a Racing Form. The Racing Form gave you a record, she said, of what the horses had been doing. Then she explained win, place and show betting to me, and across the board betting.

"Do they serve beer here?" I asked.

"Oh yeah. And they have bars too."

When we walked in we found all the seats were taken. We found a bench in back where they had a kind of park-like area, got 2 beers and opened the Racing Form. It was just a bunch of numbers.

"I just bet the horses' names," she said.

"Pull your skirt down. Everybody's looking at your ass."

"Woops! Sorry, daddy."

"Here's 6 dollars. That's your bets for the day."

"You're all heart, Harry," she said.

Well, we studied and studied, I mean I did, and we had another beer and then we walked underneath the grandstand to the front of the track. The horses were coming out for the first race. They had these little guys on them dressed in these very flashy silk shirts. Some of the fans screamed things at the jocks but the jocks were quite at ease. They ignored the fans and even seemed a little bored.

"That's Willie Shoemaker," she pointed at one of them. Willie Shoemaker looked as if he were about to yawn. I was bored too. There were too many people around and there was something about the people that was depressing.

"Now you bet," she said.

I told Madge where I'd meet her and then I stepped into one of the 2 dollar win lines. All the lines were very long, and I had a feeling that the people didn't want to bet. They seemed listless. I just got my ticket when the announcer said, "They're at the gate!"

I found Madge. It was a mile race and we were at the finish line.

"I've got GREEN FANG," I told her.

"I have him too," she told me.

I felt as if we were going to win. With a name like that and the last race he had run, it looked like we were in. And at 7 to one.

They jumped out of the gate and the announcer began making the calls. When he called GREEN FANG quite late, Madge screamed.

"GREEN FANG!" she screamed.

I couldn't see anything. There were people everywhere. There were more calls and then Madge started jumping up and down screaming, "GREEN FANG! GREEN FANG!"

Everybody else was screaming and leaping. I didn't say anything. Then the horses came by.

"Who won?" I asked.

"I don't know," said Madge. "Isn't it exciting?"

"Yeah."

Then they put the numbers up. The 7/5 favorite had won, a 9/2 shot was second and a 3 to one third.

We tore up our tickets and walked back to our bench.

We looked at the Form for the next race.

"Let's get away from the finish line so we can see something next time."

"O.k.," said Madge.

We got a couple of beers.

"This whole game is stupid," I said. "All those fools leaping and screaming, each calling on a different horse. What happened to GREEN FANG?"

"I don't know. He had such a nice name."

"But do horses know their names? Does it make them run any differently?"

"You're just mad because you lost a race. There are plenty more races."

She was right. There were.

We kept losing. As the card wore on the people began looking very unhappy, even desperate. They looked stunned, ugly. They walked into you, bumped into you, walked over your feet and never said, "Pardon me." Or, "Sorry."

I bet almost out of rote, just because I was there. Madge's 6 bucks were gone after the first 3 races and I didn't give her any more. I could see that it was very hard to win. Whichever horse you picked, some other horse won. I no longer took notice of the odds.

In the feature race I bet a horse called CLAREMOUNT III. He'd won his last easily and was getting ten pounds off for the handicap race. I had Madge down by the final curve by that time and I didn't have much hope of winning. I looked at the board and CLAREMOUNT III was 25 to one. I drained my beercup and threw it away. They came around the curve and then the announcer said, "Here comes CLAREMOUNT III!"

And I said, "Oh, no!"

And Madge said, "You got him?"

And I said, "Yeah."

CLAREMOUNT passed the 3 horses in front of him and drew out by what looked like 6 lengths. He was all alone.

"Jesus Christ," I said, "I've got him."

"Oh, Harry! Harry!"

"Let's go get a drink," I said.

We found a bar and ordered. No beer this time. Whiskey.

"He had CLAREMOUNT III," Madge told the barkeep.

"Yeah," he said.

"Yup," I said, trying to act like an old-timer. Whatever they looked like.

I turned around to look at the board. CLAREMOUNT had paid 52.40.

"I think this game can be beat," I told Madge. "You see, if you bet win, it is not necessary to win every race. One good hit or two can put you over."

"That's right, that's right," said Madge.

I gave her two dollars and then we opened the Form. I felt confident. I ran over the horses, looked at the board.

"Here it is," I said, "LUCKY MAX. He's 9 to one right now. If you don't bet LUCKY MAX, you're crazy. He's obviously the best and he's 9 to one. These people are stupid."

We walked over while I collected my 52.40.

Then I went to bet LUCKY MAX. Just for fun I got 2 two dollar win tickets on him.

It was a mile and one-sixteenth. And a cavalry charge ending. There must have been 5 horses at the wire. We waited on the photo. LUCKY MAX was number 6. They flashed the top horse:

6.

Good god o mighty. LUCKY MAX.

Madge went crazy, hugging and kissing me, jumping around.

She'd bought the horse too. It had risen to ten to one. It paid $22.80. I showed Madge the extra win ticket. She screamed. We went back to the bar. They were still serving. We just managed to get 2 drinks before they closed down.

"Let's let the lines simmer down," I said, "then we'll cash in."

"Do you like horses, Harry?"

"They can," I said, "they can definitely be beat."

We stood there with our cool drinks in our hands and watched the mob gang up down in the tunnel going to the parking lot.

"For Christ's sake," I said to Madge, "pull your stockings up. You look like a washerwoman."

"Woops! Sorry, daddy!"

As she bent over I looked at her and thought, soon I'll be able to afford something just a little bit better than that.

uh huh.

THE FIEND

Martin Blanchard had married twice, divorced twice, shacked up many times. Now he was forty-five, lived alone on the fourth floor of an apartment house and had just lost his twenty-seventh job through absenteeism and disinterest.

He was living on his unemployment checks. His desires were simple – he liked to get drunk as much as possible, alone, and he liked to sleep long hours and stay in his apartment, alone. Another odd thing about Martin Blanchard was that he was never *lonely*. The longer he could remain separated from the human race, the better he felt. The marriages, the shackjobs, the one-night stands had made him feel that the sex act was not worth what the female demanded in return. Now he lived without the female and masturbated frequently. His education ended in the first year of high school, and yet when he listened to his radio – his closest contact with the world – he listened to symphony only, Mahler preferred.

One morning he awakened rather early for him – about 10:30 a.m. – after a night of heavy drinking. He had slept in his undershirt, shorts, socks; he got out of a rather dirty bed, walked into the kitchen and looked into the refrigerator. He was in luck. There were two bottles of port wine there, and it was not cheap wine.

Martin went to the bathroom, shit, pissed, then walked back to the kitchen and opened the first bottle of port, poured a good fat glassful. Then he sat at the kitchen table, which gave him a good view of the street, looking north. It was summertime, hot and lazy. Down below, there was a small house in which two old people lived. They were on vacation. Though the house was small, it was preceded by this very long and large green lawn, well kept, all that green. It gave Martin Blanchard this strange feeling of peace.

Since it was summertime the children were not in school, and as Martin looked down at the long green lawn while drinking the good chilled port, he noticed this little girl and two boys playing some type of game. They seemed to be shooting at each other. *Pow! Pow!* Martin recognized the little girl. She lived in the court across the way with her mother and older sister. The male of the family had either left or died. The little girl, Martin had noted, was a very saucy type – always sticking her tongue out at people and saying nasty things. He had no idea what her age was. Somewhere between six and nine. Vaguely, he had been watching her throughout the early summer. When Martin passed her on the sidewalk now and then, she always seemed *frightened* of him. He could never understand this.

As he watched, he noticed that she was dressed in a kind of sailor's jacket, white, and over the jacket, hung in straps was this very *short* red skirt. As she crawled along the grass, it pulled back what there was of the very short red skirt, and she had on the most interesting *panties* – red, a bit paler than the skirt. And the panties had these little series of red ruffles.

Martin stood up and had a drink, kept staring at those little panties as the girl crawled along. His cock got hard very fast. He didn't know what to do. He circled out of the kitchen, back into the front room, then found himself in the kitchen again, looking. Those panties. Those *ruffles.*

Jesus Christ under the naked sun, he couldn't stand it!

Martin poured another full glass of wine, drank it down at once, then looked again. Those panties showed more than ever! *Jesus!*

He took his cock out of his shorts, spit into the palm of his right hand and began rubbing his cock. God, it was beautiful! No grown woman had ever heightened him like that! His cock was harder than it had ever been, purple and ugly. Martin felt as if he were inside the very secret of life. He leaned against the screen, beating and moaning, looking down at that little ruffled ass.

Then he came.

All over the kitchen floor.

Martin walked to the bathroom, got some toilet paper, cleaned up the floor, got the wad of greasy stuff and flushed the come away. Then he sat down. Poured another wine.

Thank God, he thought, that's over. It's out of my mind. I'm free again.

Still looking north, he could see the Griffith Park Observatory up there in the blue-purple Hollywood Hills. It was nice. He lived in a nice place. Nobody ever came to his door. His first wife had said he was simply neurotic but not insane. Well, to hell with his first wife. With all wives. Now he paid the rent and people left him alone. He sipped gently at the wine.

He watched as the little girl and the two boys kept playing their game. He rolled a cigarette. Then he thought, well, I should at least eat a couple of boiled eggs. But he wasn't interested in food. Seldom was.

Martin Blanchard watched out the window. They were still at it. The little girl crawled along the ground. *Pow! Pow!*

What a dull game.

Then his cock began to get hard again.

Martin noticed that he had drunk one complete bottle of wine and had begun on another. The cock curved up like something beyond him.

Little saucy. Her tongue out. Little saucy, crawling on the grass.

Martin was always worried when he got down to one bottle of wine. And he needed cigars. He liked to roll his cigarettes. But there was nothing like a good cigar. A good 2-for-27-cent cigar.

He began to dress. Looked at his face in the mirror – four-day beard. It didn't matter. The only time he shaved was when he went down to get his unemployment check. So he put on some dirty clothing, opened the door and went down the elevator. Once on the sidewalk, he began to walk toward the liquor store. As he did, he noticed that the children had gotten the garage doors open and were inside, her and the two boys: *Pow! Pow!*

Martin found himself walking down the driveway toward the garage. They were in there. He walked into the garage and swung the doors shut.

It was dark in there. He was in there with them. The little girl screamed.

Martin said, "Now *shut up* and nobody will get hurt! You make *any* noise and you'll get hurt, I promise you!"

"Whatcha gonna do, mister?" Martin heard a boy's voice.

"*Shut up! Goddamnit, I told you to shut up!*"

He lit a match. There it was – a single electric light bulb with a long string attached. Martin pulled the string. Just enough light. And, like in a dream, there was this small hook inside the garage doors. He hooked the doors shut.

He looked around.

"All right! You boys go stand over in the corner and you won't get hurt! *Now go on! Hurry up!*"

Martin Blanchard pointed to the corner.

The boys went over there.

"Whatcha gonna do, mister?"

"*I told you to shut up!*"

Little saucy with her sailor's blouse and her short red skirt and ruffled panties was in another corner.

Martin moved toward her. She ran left, then right. Each time he moved toward her, he got her further into the corner.

"Leeme alone! You leeme alone! You ugly old fart-thing, you leeme *alone*!"

"*Shut up! If you scream, I'll kill you!*"

"Leeme alone! Leeme alone! Leeme alone!"

Martin finally caught her. She had straight ugly uncombed hair and an almost vicious face for a little girl. He held her legs between his, like a vise, then leaned down and put his big face against her small one, kissing and sucking at her mouth again and again as her fists beat against his face. His cock felt as large as his body. He kept kissing, kissing, seeing her skirt fall away, seeing those ruffled panties.

"He's kissing her! Look, he's kissing her!" Martin heard one of the boys in the corner say.

"Yeah," said the other one.

Martin's eyes looked into her eyes and it was a communication between two hells – one her's, the other his. He kissed, wildly out of mind, a hunger beyond the seas, a spider kissing the fly. With his hands he began to feel those ruffled panties.

Ah Jesus, save me, he thought, nothing so beautiful, that red-pink, and more than that – the *ugliness* – a rosebud held tight against his total rot. He couldn't stop himself.

Martin Blanchard got her panties off, but at the same time he couldn't seem to stop kissing that small mouth, and she was in a faint, had stopped hitting his face, but the different lengths of their bodies made it difficult, awkward, very, and being in passion, he couldn't think. But his cock was out – large, purple, ugly, like some stinking insanity run away with itself, and no place to go.

And all the time – under this small light bulb – Martin heard the boys' voices saying, "Look! Look! He's got that big thing and he's trying to stick that big thing into her slit!"

"I hear that's how people have babies."

"Are they going to have a baby right here?"

"I guess so."

The boys moved in close, watching them. Martin kept kissing that face while trying to get the head of it in. It just didn't work. He couldn't think. He was just hot hot hot. Then he saw an old straight-backed chair, one rung missing in the back. He carried her over the chair, still kissing, kissing, thinking all the time of the ugly strands of her hair, that mouth up against his.

This was it.

Martin got to the chair, sat down, still kissing that small mouth and small head again and again, and then he worked her legs apart. How old *was* she? Would it work?

The boys were very close now, watching.

"He's got the front part in."

"Yeah. Look. Are they gonna have a baby?"

"I donno."

"Now look! He's got it almost halfway in!"

"A *snake*!"

"*Yeah! A snake!*"

"Look! Look! He's moving it back and forth!"

"Yeah. It's going deeper in!"

"It's all the way in!"

It's in her body now, Martin thought. Jesus, my cock must be half the length of her body!

Bent over her in the chair, at the same time kissing and ripping, he didn't care, he would have just as soon ripped her head off.

Then he came.

They hung together on that chair under the electric lightbulb. They hung.

Then Martin placed her body upon that garage floor. Unhooked the doors. Walked out. Went back to his place. Pushed the elevator button. Got off at his floor, got to the refrigerator, got a bottle, poured a glass of port, sat down and waited, watched.

Soon there were people everywhere. Twenty, twenty-five, thirty people. Outside the garage. Inside the garage.

Then an ambulance ran up the driveway.

Martin watched as they carried her out on a stretcher. Then the ambulance was gone. Just more people. More people. He drank the wine, poured another.

Maybe they don't know who I am, he thought. I seldom leave this place.

It wasn't somehow so. He hadn't locked the door. Two cops came in. Big boys, rather handsome. He almost liked them.

"Okay, *shit!*"

One of them ripped him a good one across the face. As Martin stood up to hold his hands out for the handcuffs the other one took his billyclub and ripped him full in the belly. Martin fell to the floor. He couldn't breathe or move. They got him up. The other one hit him in the face again.

There were people everywhere. They didn't take him down the elevator, they walked, pushed him down the steps.

Faces, faces, faces, out of doors, faces on the street.

In the squad car it was very strange – there were two cops up front and two cops in the back seat with him. Martin was being given special treatment.

"I could kill a son of a bitch like you," one of the cops in the rear said to him. "I could kill a son of a bitch like you without even trying . . ."

Martin began to cry without sound, the ticks of tears running down like wild things.

"I've got a five-year-old daughter," said one of the cops in back. "I could kill you without even thinking about it!"

"I couldn't help it," said Martin, "I tell you, so help me Christ, I couldn't help –"

The cop started beating Martin across the head with his club. Nobody stopped him. Martin fell forward, vomited wine and blood, the cop straightened him up, clubbed him across the face, the mouth, knocked out most of Martin's front teeth.

Then they left him alone for a while, driving toward the station.

THE MURDER OF RAMON VASQUEZ

They rang the doorbell. Two brothers, Lincoln, 23 and Andrew, 17.

He came to the door himself.

There he was. Ramon Vasquez, the old star of the silent screen and the beginning of the talkies. He was in his 60's now, but still had the same delicate look. In those days, on screen and off, his hair was smeared heavily with vaseline and combed straight back, hard. And with the long thin nose and the tiny mustache and the way he looked deeply into the ladies' eyes, well, it was too much. He had been called "The Great Lover." The ladies swooned when they saw him on the screen. "Swooned," that's what the movie columnists said. But actually, Ramon Vasquez was a homosexual. Now his hair was a stately white and the mustache a bit thicker.

It was a chilly California night and Ramon's place was set off in a hilly area by itself. The boys were dressed in army pants and

---

This story is fiction, *and any events or near-similar events in actual life which* did *transpire have not prejudiced the author toward any figures involved or uninvolved; in other words, the mind, the imagination, the creative facilities have been allowed to run freely, and that means* invention, *of which said is drawn and caused by living one year short of half a century with the human race* ... *and is not narrowed down to any specific case, cases, newspaper stories, and was not written to harm, infer or do injustice to any of my fellow creatures involved in circumstances similar to the story to follow.*

white T-shirts. Both of them were on the muscular side and had rather pleasant faces, pleasant and apologetic faces.

Lincoln did the talking. "We've read about you, Mr. Vasquez. I'm sorry to bother you but we're deeply interested in Hollywood idols, and we found out where you lived, and we were driving by and just couldn't help ringing your doorbell."

"Isn't it cold out there, boys?"

"Yes, yes, it is."

"Won't you step in for a moment?"

"We don't want to disturb you, we don't want to interrupt anything."

"That's all right. Do come in. I'm alone."

The boys walked in. Stood in the center of the room, looking rather awkward and confused.

"Ah, *please* sit down!" said Ramon. He pointed to a couch. The boys walked over, sat down, rather stiffly. There was a small fire going in the fireplace. "I'll get you something to warm you up. Just a moment, please."

Ramon came back with some good French wine, opened the bottle, left again, then returned with 3 chilled glasses. He poured 3 drinks.

"Have a bit. Very nice stuff."

Lincoln downed his rather quickly. Andrew, watching, did the same thing. Ramon refilled the glasses.

"You are brothers?"

"Yes."

"I thought so."

"I'm Lincoln. He's my younger brother, Andrew."

"Ah, yes. Andrew has a very delicate and fascinating face. A brooding face. Something a bit cruel about it too. Perhaps just the right *amount* of cruel. Hmmm, might get him into the movies. I still have a bit of pull, you know."

"How about my face, Mr. Vasquez?" asked Lincoln.

"Not as delicate, and crueler. So cruel as to have almost an animal beauty; that, and with your . . . body. Forgive, but you are built like some damned ape who has had most of his hair shaven off. But . . . I like you very much – you *radiate* . . . something."

"Maybe it's hunger," said Andrew, speaking for the first time, "We just got into town. We drove in from Kansas. Flat tires. Then we threw a god damned piston. It ate up all our money – tires and repairs. It's sitting outside now – a '56 Plymouth – we couldn't even junk it for ten bucks."

"You're hungry?"

"And how!"

"Well, wait, good heavens, I'll get you something, I'll fix you something. Meanwhile, drink up!"

Ramon went into the kitchen.

Lincoln picked up the bottle, drank from it. For a long time. Then handed it to Andrew: "Finish it off."

Andrew had just emptied the bottle when Ramon came back with a large platter – pitted and stuffed olives; cheese, salami, pastrami, white crackers, green onions, ham and deviled eggs.

"Oh, the wine! You've finished it! Fine!"

Ramon left, came back with two chilled bottles. Opened them both. The boys snatched at the food. It didn't take them long. The plate was clean.

Then they started on the wine.

"Did you know Bogart?"

"Ah, only slightly."

"How about Garbo?"

"Of course, don't be silly."

"How about Gable?"

"Only slightly."

"Cagney?"

"I never knew Cagney. You see, most of those you mention came from different eras. I sometimes believe that some of the later Stars resented, *do* resent that I made most of my money before the tax-bite became too deep. But they forget, that in terms of money-earned, I have never earned their kind of inflationary money. Which they are now learning to protect through the advice of tax-experts who show them all the tax-loopholes – re-investment, all that. Anyhow, at parties, all that, it makes for mixed feelings. They think that I am rich; I think that they are rich. We all worry too much about money and fame and power. Me, I only have enough left to live comfortably upon until I die."

"We've read up on you, Ramon," said Lincoln. "One writer, no, two writers claim you always keep 5 grand in cash hid in your house. A kind of pocket-money. And that you really have this mistrust of banks and the banking system."

"I don't know where you got that. It's not true."

"SCREEN," said Lincoln, "September issue, 1968; THE HOLLYWOOD STAR, YOUNG AND OLD, January issue, 1969. We have the magazines in the car right now."

"It's untrue. The only money I have in the house is what I have in my wallet, and that's it. 20 or 30 dollars."

"Let's see."

"Surely."

Ramon took out his wallet. There was one twenty and three ones. Lincoln grabbed the wallet. "I'll take that!"

"What's the matter with you, Lincoln? If you want the money take it. Only give me my wallet back. There are my things in there – a driver's license, all those necessary things."

"Fuck you!"

"What?"

"I said, 'FUCK YOU!'"

"Listen, I'll have to ask you boys to leave the house. You are becoming unruly!"

"Is there more wine?"

"Yes, yes, there's more wine! You can have it all, ten or twelve bottles of the best French wines. Please take them and leave! I beg you!"

"Worried about your 5 grand?"

"I tell you sincerely, that there isn't any hidden 5 grand. I tell you sincerely from my heart that there isn't any 5 grand!"

"You lying cocksucker!"

"Why must you be so rude!"

"Cocksucker! COCKSUCKER!"

"I offered my hospitality, my kindness to you. Now you become brutal and unkindly."

"That plate of fucking food you gave us! You call *that* food?"

"What was wrong with it?"

"QUEER FOOD!"

"I don't understand?"

"Little pickled olives . . . stuffed eggs. *Men* don't eat that kinda shit!"

"You ate it."

"Oh, you giving me lip, COCKSUCKER?"

Lincoln got up from the couch, walked over to Ramon in his chair, slapped him across the face, hard, with his open palm. 3 times. Lincoln had big hands.

Ramon dropped his head, began to weep. "I'm sorry. I was only trying to do what I could."

Lincoln looked at his brother. "See him? Fucking pansy! CRYING LIKE A BABY! MAN, I'LL MAKE HIM CRY!

I'LL REALLY MAKE HIM CRY UNLESS HE COUGHS UP
THAT 5 GRAND!"

Lincoln picked up a wine bottle, drank heavily from it.

"Drink up," he told Andrew. "We got work to do."

Andrew drank from his bottle, heavily.

Then while Ramon wept, they each sat sipping at the wine,
looking at each other, and thinking.

"You know what I'm gonna do?" Lincoln asked his brother.

"What?"

"I'm gonna make him suck my cock!"

"Why?"

"Why? Just for laughs, *that's* why!"

Lincoln took another drink, then walked over to Ramon, got
him under the chin and lifted his head.

"Hey mother . . ."

"What? Oh please, PLEASE LEAVE ME ALONE!"

"You are going to suck my cock, COCKSUCKER!"

"Oh no, please!"

"We know you are a homo! Get ready, mother!"

"NO! PLEASE! PLEASE!"

Lincoln ran down his fly.

"OPEN YOUR MOUTH!"

"Oh, no, please!"

This time when Lincoln hit Ramon his fist was closed.

"I love you, Ramon: Suck!"

Ramon opened his mouth. Lincoln put the tip of his dick into
the lips.

"You bite me, mother, I'LL KILL you!"

Ramon began to suck while weeping.

Lincoln slapped him across the forehead.

"Gimme some ACTION! Put some life into it!"

Ramon bobbed harder, worked his tongue. Then just as Lincoln
felt himself coming, he grabbed the back of Ramon's head and
jammed it all the way in. Ramon gagged, choked. Lincoln left it
in there until it was emptied.

"Now! Suck my brother!"

Andrew said, "Linc, I'd rather not."

"You chickenshit?"

"No, it's not that."

"No guts?"

"No, no . . ."

"Have another drink."

Andrew drank. Thought a while. "O.K., he can suck my dick."

"MAKE HIM DO IT!"

Andrew got up, unzipped.

"Get ready to suck mother."

Ramon just sat there weeping.

"Lift his head. He really likes it."

Andrew lifted Ramon's head. "I don't want to hit you, old man. Open your lips. It won't take long."

Ramon opened his lips.

"There," said Lincoln, "see, he's doing it. No trouble at all."

Ramon bobbed his head, tongued, and Andrew came.

Ramon spit it out on the rug.

"Bastard!" said Lincoln, "you're supposed to swallow it!"

He walked over and slapped Ramon, who had stopped crying, who looked as if he were in a trance of some sort.

The brothers sat down again, finished their wine bottles. Found more in the kitchen. Brought them out, uncorked them, and drank some more.

Ramon Vasquez already looked like a wax figure of a dead Star in the Hollywood Museum.

"We're gonna get the 5 grand and then we're gonna split," said Lincoln.

"He said it ain't here," said Andrew.

"Queers are natural-born liars. I'll get it out of him. You just sit here and enjoy your wine. I'll take care of this punk."

Lincoln picked up Ramon and threw him over one of his shoulders and carried him into the bedroom.

Andrew sat there drinking the wine. He heard some talking and shouting from the bedroom. Then he saw the telephone. He dialed a New York City number, charged it to Ramon's phone. That's where his chick was. She'd left Kansas City for the big time. But she still wrote him letters. Long ones. She wasn't making it yet.

"Who?"

"Andrew."

"Oh, Andrew, is something wrong?"

"Were you asleep?"

"I was just going to bed."

"Alone?"

"Of course."

"Well, there's nothing wrong. This guy is going to get me into the movies. He says I have a delicate face."

"Oh wonderful, Andrew! You have a beautiful face, and I love you, you know that."

"Sure. How's it going with you, kitten?"

"Not so good, Andy. New York is a cold town. Everybody tries to get into your panties, that's all they want. I'm working as a waitress, it's hell, but I think I'm getting a part in an off-Broadway play."

"What kinda play?"

"Oh, I don't know. It seems a little corny. Something written by a nigger."

"Don't you trust those niggers, babe."

"I don't. It's just for the experience. And they've got some big name actress working her part for free."

"Well, that's all right. But don't trust those niggers!"

"I'm no damn fool, Andy. I don't trust anybody. It's just for experience."

"Who's the nigger?"

"I don't know. Some playwright. All he does is sit around and smoke grass and talk revolution. It's the thing now. We gotta go with it until it blows over."

"That playwright, he ain't fucking with you?"

"Don't be a damn fool, Andrew. I treat him nicely, but he's nothing but a pagan, a beast ... And I'm so tired of being a waitress. All these wise-guys pinching your ass because they left a quarter tip. It's hell."

"I think of you all the time, baby."

"And I think of you, ol' pretty face, ol' big-dick Andy. And I love you."

"You talk funny sometimes, funny and real, that's why I love you, babe."

"Hey! What's all that SCREAMING I hear?"

"Just a joke, babe. Big wild party here in Beverly Hills. You know these actors."

"It sounds like somebody getting killed."

"Don't worry, babe. It's just a gag. Everybody drunk. Somebody practicing his lines. Love you. I'll phone or write again soon."

"Please do, Andrew, I love you."

"Night, sweets."

"Goodnight, Andrew."

Andrew hung up and walked toward the bedroom. He walked into the bedroom. There was Ramon on the big double bed. Ramon was very bloody. The sheets were very bloody.

Lincoln had this cane in his hand. It was the famous cane that The Great Lover used in the movies. The cane had blood all over it.

"Son of a bitch won't cop out," said Lincoln. "Get me another bottle of wine."

Andrew came back with the wine, uncorked it, and Lincoln took a long haul.

"Maybe the 5 grand ain't here," said Andrew.

"It's here. And we need it. Queers are worse than Jews. I mean Jews would rather die than give up a penny. And queers LIE! Get me?"

Lincoln looked again at the body on the bed.

"Where you got the 5 grand hidden, Ramon?"

"I swear . . . I swear . . . from the bottom of my soul, there's no 5 grand, I swear! I swear!"

Lincoln brought the cane down again across the face of the Great Lover. Another slash. The blood ran. Ramon became unconscious.

"No good this way. Put him under a shower," Lincoln told his brother. "Revive him. Get all the blood off. We'll start all over again. This time – not only his face but also his cock and balls. He'll talk. Any man will talk. Go clean him up while I have myself a few drinks."

Lincoln walked out. Andrew looked at the mass of bleeding red, gagged for a moment, then vomited on the floor. He felt better after vomiting. He picked the body up, walked it toward the bathroom. Ramon seemed to revive for a moment.

"Holy Mary, Holy Mary, Mother of God . . ."

He said it once more as they walked toward the bathroom.

"Holy Mary, Holy Mary, Mother of God . . ."

When Andrew got him to the bathroom he took off Ramon's blood soaked clothes, saw the shower stall, put Ramon upon the floor and tested the water until he got it to the proper warmth. Then taking off his own shoes and stockings, pants, shorts and T-shirt, he got into the shower with Ramon, held him up under the water. The blood began washing off. Andrew looked at the water plastering the grey hairs flat upon the head of this once-idol of Womanhood. Ramon just looked like a sad old man, dropping within the mercy of himself.

Then, suddenly, upon impulse he turned off the hot water, just left on the cold.

He put his mouth up against Ramon's ears.

"All we want, old man, is your 5 grand. We'll split. Just give us the 5 grand, then we'll leave you alone, understand?"

"Holy Mary . . ." said the old man.

Andrew brought him out of the shower. Took him back to the bedroom, put him upon the bed. Lincoln had a new bottle of wine. Was working at it.

"O.K.," he said, "this time he *talks*!"

"I don't think he's got the 5 grand. I wouldn't take a beating like that for 5 grand."

"He's got it! He's a homo-kike-nigger bastard! This time, he TALKS!"

Lincoln handed the bottle to Andrew who immediately drank from it.

Lincoln picked up the cane:

"Now! Cocksucker! WHERE'S THE 5 GRAND?"

There wasn't any answer from the man on the bed. Lincoln inverted the cane, that is, he took the straight end in his hand, then took the curved end and came down upon Ramon's cock and balls.

There was very little sound from the man except for a continual series of moans.

Ramon's sexual organs were almost completely erased.

Lincoln took off for a moment for a good drain of wine and then took the cane and began beating everywhere – upon Ramon's face, belly, hands, nose, head, everywhere, no longer asking the question about the 5 grand. Ramon's mouth was open and the pouring of the blood from a broken nose and other parts of the face flowed into his mouth. He swallowed it down and drowned in his own blood. Then he was very still and the thrashing of the cane had very little effect.

"You've killed him," said Andrew from his chair, watching, "and he was going to get me into the movies."

"I didn't kill him," said Lincoln, "you killed him! I sat there and watched you beat him to death with his own cane. The cane that made him famous in his movies!"

"What the fuck," said Andrew, "you're really talking like a wino-nut now. The main thing is to get out of here. We'll settle the rest later. This guy's dead! Let's move!"

"First," said Lincoln, "I've read crime mags on this sort of stuff. First we throw them off. We dip our fingers into his blood and write various things on the walls, all that."

"What?"

"O.K. Like: 'FUCK PIGS! DEATH TO PIGS!' Then, write some name above the headboard, a man's name – say like 'Louie.' O.K.?"

"O.K."

They dipped their fingers into his blood and wrote their little slogans. Then went outside.

The '56 Plymouth started. They rolled south with Ramon's 23 dollars plus his stolen wine. At Sunset and Western they saw two young mini's standing near the corner hitchhiking. They pulled up. There was some clever rejoinder, then the two girls got in. The car had a radio. That's about all it did have. They turned it on. There were bottles of expensive French wine rolling all around the car.

"Hey," said one of the girls, "I think these guys are a couple of swingers!"

"Hey," said Lincoln, "let's drive down to the beach and lay on the sand and drink this wine and watch the sun come up!"

"O.K.," said the other girl.

Andrew managed to uncork one, it was tough – he had to use his pocketknife, thin blade – they'd left Ramon and Ramon's nice corkscrew behind – and the pocketknife didn't quite work like a corkscrew – everytime you drank a bit of wine you had to drink a bit of cork.

Up front, Lincoln was having a bit of a time, but having to drive, he was mainly mentally conning his. In the back seat, Andrew had already run his hand up her legs, then he slid away part of the panty, it was hard work, and he had gotten his finger into there. Suddenly she withdrew, shoved him off, and said, "I think we should get to know each other better first."

"Sure," said Andrew, "We've got 20 or 30 minutes before we hit the sand and get busy. My name," said Andrew, "is Harold Anderson."

"My name is Claire Edwards."

They embraced again.

The Great Lover was dead. But there would be others. Also plenty of un-great. Mostly those. It was the way things worked. Or didn't work.

A DRINKING PARTNER

I met Jeff at an auto parts warehouse on Flower street or maybe it was Figueroa street, I always get the two mixed. Anyhow, I was the receiving clerk and Jeff was more or less the flunky. He'd unload used parts, sweep the floors, hang paper in the crappers and so forth. I'd had flunky jobs like that all over the country, so I never looked down on them. I was coming off a bad run with a woman who had almost finished me. I wasn't in the mood for any more women for a while and as a substitute I played the horses, jacked-off and drank. Frankly, I was always happier doing that, and each time I got into that I thought, no more women, ever, god damn it all. Of course, another always came long – they hunted you down, no matter how indifferent you were. I guess it was when you got real indifferent they put it to you, to bring you down. Women could do that; no matter how strong a man was, women could do that. But, anyhow, I was in this calm free state when I met Jeff – womanless – and there was nothing homosexual in it. Just two guys who lived on their luck, traveled about, had been burned by the ladies. I remember one time sitting in The Green Light, I had a beer to myself, I was at a table reading the race results and that gang was talking about something when I heard somebody say, "... and, yeah, Bukowski was burned good by little Flo. Didn't she burn ya good, Bukowski?"

I looked up. People laughed. I didn't smile. I just raised my beer, "Yeah," I said, had a drink, sat it down.

When I looked up again a young black girl had brought her beer over. "Look, man," she said, "look man . . ."

"Hello," I said.

"Look, man, don't let this little Flo bring you down, don't let her shoot you down, man. You can make it."

"I know I can make it. I don't intend to toss it in."

"Good. You just looked sad, that's all. You just looked so sad."

"Of course, I am. She got into me, inside. But it will wear away. Beer?"

"Yeah. But on me."

We made it that night at my place but that was my farewell to women – for maybe around 14 or 18 months. If you don't hunt it you can get these rest periods.

So I drank every night after work, alone, up at my place and I had enough left for a day at the track on Saturday, and life was simple and without too much pain. Maybe without too much reason, but getting away from pain was reasonable enough. I knew Jeff right off. Although he was younger than I, I recognized a younger model of myself.

"You got a hell of a hangover for yourself there, kid," I said to him one morning.

"There's no other way," he said, "a man has to forget."

"I guess you're right," I said, "a hangover is better than a madhouse."

That night we hit a nearby bar after work. He was like me, he didn't worry about food, a man never thought about food. For it all, we were two of the strongest men in the plant but we never examined it. Food was simply boring. I was plenty bored with bars at that time – all those lonely male idiots hoping some woman would walk in and carry them off to wonderland. The two most sickening crowds are the racetrack crowd and the bar crowd, and I mean mostly the male of the species. The losers who kept losing and couldn't make a stand and gather themselves. And there *I* was, right in the center of them. Jeff made it easier for me. By that, I mean, the thing was newer to him and he pepped it up, almost made it realistic, as if we were doing something meaningful instead of throwing our poor salaries away on drink and gambling and cheap rooms, and losing jobs and finding jobs and getting burned by women, and always in hell, and ignoring it. All of it.

"I want you to meet my buddy Gramercy Edwards," he said.

"Gramercy Edwards?"

"Yeah, Gram's been in more than he's been out."

"Stir?"

"Stir and madhouse."

"Sounds great. Tell him to come down."

"I gotta get the desk phone. If he's not too drunk, he'll make it . . ."

Gramercy Edwards came in about an hour later. By then, I was feeling more able to handle things, and that was good, for here came Gramercy walking through the door – a victim of reform schools and prisons. His eyes seemed to keep rolling back into the inside of his head as if he were trying to look into his brain to see what had gone wrong. He was dressed in rags and a large wine bottle was jammed into the ripped pocket of his pants. He stank, and a rolled cigarette dangled. Jeff introduced us. Gram pulled his wine bottle out of his pocket and offered me a drink. I took it. We stayed in there drinking until closing time.

Then we walked down the street to Gramercy's hotel. In those days, before industry moved into that area, there were old houses that rented out rooms to the poor, and in one of these houses the landlady had a bulldog that she let out each night to guard her precious property. He was one mean son of a bitch; he had frightened me many a drunken night until I learned which side of the street was his and which side was mine. I got the side he didn't want.

"All right," said Jeff, "we're going to get that son of a bitch tonight. Now, Gram, it's up to me to catch him. Now if I catch him, it's up to you to cut him."

"You catch him," said Gramercy, "I've got the steel. Just had it sharpened."

We walked along. Soon there was this growling sound and the bulldog was bounding toward us. He was good at nipping at the calves. He was one hell of a watchdog. He came bounding out with much aplomb. Jeff waited until the bulldog was almost upon us, then he turned sideways and leaped over the top of the bulldog. The bulldog skidded, turned back quickly and Jeff grabbed him as he passed underneath his leap. He locked his arms under the bulldog's front legs and then stood up. The bulldog kicked and snapped helplessly, his belly exposed.

"Hehehehe," went Gramercy, "hehehehe!"

And he poked his knife in and sliced a rectangle. Then he divided it into 4 parts.

"Jesus," said Jeff.

Blood was everywhere. Jeff dropped the bulldog. The bulldog didn't move. We walked on.

"Hehehehehe," went Gramercy, "that son of a bitch won't ever bother anybody again."

"You guys make me sick," I said. I walked up to my room thinking about that poor bulldog. I remained angry at Jeff for 2 or 3 days, then forgot it . . .

I never saw Gramercy again but I kept getting drunk with Jeff. There didn't seem to be anything else to do.

Each morning, down at work, we would be sick . . . it was our private joke. Each night we would get drunk again. What is a poor man to do? The girls don't search out the common laborers; the girls search out the doctors, the scientists, the lawyers, the businessmen, so forth. We get the girls when they are through with the girls, and they are no longer girls – we get the used, the deformed, the diseased, the mad. After a while, instead of taking seconds and thirds and fourths, you give it up. Or you try to give it up. Drinking helps. And Jeff liked the bars so I went with him. Jeff's trouble was that when he got drunk he liked to fight. Luckily, he didn't fight me. He was very good at it, he was a good duker, and he was strong, perhaps the strongest man I had ever seen. He wasn't a bully, but after drinking a while he'd just seem to go crazy. I saw him put down 3 guys in a fight one night. He looked at them stretched in the alley there, put his hands in his pockets, then looked at me:

"Well, let's go get another drink."

He never bragged on it.

Of course, Saturday nights were best. We had Sunday off to get over the hangover. Most of the time we just got another one but at least on a Sunday morning you didn't have to be in an auto parts warehouse working for slave wages on a job you would either finally quit or be fired from.

This Saturday night we were sitting in The Green Light and we finally got hungry. We walked up to the Chinaman's, which was a rather clean class place. We walked up the stairway to the second floor and took a table in the back. Jeff was drunk and knocked over a tablelamp. It broke with a great crash. Everybody looked. The Chinese waiter at another table gave us a particularly distasteful look.

"Take it easy," said Jeff, "put it on the bill. I'll pay for it."

A pregnant woman was staring at Jeff. She seemed quite unhappy with what he had done. I couldn't understand it. I couldn't see it as all that bad. The waiter wouldn't serve us, or he was keeping us waiting and this pregnant woman kept staring. It was as if Jeff had committed the most heinous of crimes.

"Whatsa matta, baby? Ya need a little love? I can go in the back door for you. Ya lonely, honey?"

"I'm gonna call my husband. He's downstairs in the men's room. I'm gonna call him, I'm gonna get him. He'll show you something!"

"What's he got?" asked Jeff, "A stamp collection? Or butterflies under glass?"

"I'm gonna get him! Now!" she said.

"Lady," I said, "please don't do it. You need your husband. Please don't do it, lady."

"I'm gonna do it," she said, "I'm gonna do it!"

She got up and ran toward the stairway. Jeff ran after her, caught her, spun her and said, "Here, I'll send you on your way!"

Then he hit her on the chin and she went bouncing and rolling down the stairway. It sickened me. It was as bad as the night of the dog.

"God o mighty, Jeff! You've knocked a pregnant woman down the stairway! That's chickenshit and stupid! You might have killed 2 people. You get so vicious man, what are you trying to prove?"

"Shut up," said Jeff, "or you'll get it too!"

Jeff was insanely drunk, standing at the top of the stairway, weaving. Downstairs they gathered about the woman. She still seemed alive, no parts broken, but I didn't know about the child. I hoped the child was o.k. Then the husband came out of the restroom and saw his wife. They explained to him what had happened then pointed to Jeff. Jeff turned and walked back toward the table. The husband rocketed up the steps. He was a big guy, as big as Jeff and as young. I wasn't too happy with Jeff so I didn't warn him. The husband leaped upon Jeff's back, then got a stranglehold upon Jeff. Jeff choked and his whole head flushed scarlet but under it all he grinned, the grin came out. He loved fights. He got one hand on the guy's head, then he reached back with the other hand and he had the guy's body parallel to the floor. The husband still had a grip about Jeff's neck as Jeff walked him to the top of the stairway, stood there, and then simply snapped the guy off his neck, lifted him in the air and threw him into space. When the lady's husband stopped rolling he was very still. I began to think about getting out of there.

There were some Chinamen circling down there. Cooks, waiters, owners. They seemed to run about talking to each other. Then they started running up the stairway. I had a half pint in my coat and sat down at a table to watch the fun. Jeff met them at the top of the stairway and punched them back down. There were more and more of them. Where all those Chinamen came from, I don't know. Just the force of them all moved Jeff back from the stairway and then he was stepping about in the center of the room knocking them down. I would have helped Jeff otherwise, but I kept thinking about that poor dog and that poor pregnant woman and I sat there drinking from the half pint and watching.

Finally a couple of them got Jeff from the back, another grabbed one arm, two others got the other arm, another had a leg, another had him about the neck. He was like a spider being brought down by an ant-swarm. Then he was down and they were trying to hold him down, hold him still. As I said, he was the strongest man I had ever seen. They held him down but they couldn't hold him still. Every now and then a Chinaman would come flying off the pile as if he had been ejected by some invisible force. Then he would leap back on. Jeff simply would not give up. And although they had him there, there was nothing they could do with him. He kept struggling and the Chinamen seemed very confused and unhappy that he would not give up.

I had another drink, put the bottle in my coat, got up. I walked over there.

"If you'll hold him still," I said, "I'll knock him out. He'll kill me for it, but it's the only way out."

I got down in there and sat on his chest.

"Hold him still! Now hold his head still! I can't hit him when he's moving like that! Hold him still, god damn it! God damn it, there are a dozen of you! Can't you even hold one man still? Hold him still, god damn it, hold him still!"

They couldn't do it. Jeff kept rocking and rolling. His strength seemed endless. I gave up and sat down at the table again and had another drink. It must have gone on for another 5 minutes.

Then, suddenly, Jeff became very still. He stopped moving. The Chinamen held him and watched. I began to hear crying. Jeff was crying! The tears washed over his face. His whole face shone like a lake. Then he screamed out, very woefully – one word:

"MOTHER!"

It was then that I heard the sirens. I got up and walked past them and down the stairway. Half way down the stairway I met the police.

"He's up there, officers! Hurry!"

I walked slowly out the front door. Then I passed an alley. When I got to the alley I cut in and began to run. I came to the other street and as I did I could hear the ambulances coming. I got to my room, pulled down all the shades and cut the light. I finished the bottle in bed.

Monday Jeff wasn't at work. Tuesday Jeff wasn't at work. Wednesday. Well, I never saw him again. I didn't check out the jails.

Not much later I was fired for absenteeism and moved to the west side of town where I found a job as a stockboy for Sears-Roebuck. The Sears-Roebuck stockboys never had a hangover and were very tame, slightly built. Nothing seemed to disturb them. I ate lunch alone and said very little to the rest of them.

I don't suppose Jeff was a very good human being. He made a lot of mistakes, brutal mistakes, but he *had* been interesting, interesting enough. I suppose he's doing time now or somebody has killed him. I'll never find another drinking partner like him. Everybody's asleep and sane and proper. A real son of a bitch like him is needed now and then. But like they say in the song – Where has everybody gone?

THE WHITE BEARD

And Herb would drill a hole in a watermelon and fuck the watermelon and then force Talbot, little Talbot to eat it. We got up at 6:30 a.m. to pick the apples and the pears and it was near the border and the bombing shook the earth as you yanked at the apples and the pears, trying to be a good guy, trying for the ripe ones only, and then climbing down to piss – it was cold in the mornings – and having a bit of hash in the john. What it all meant, nobody knew. We were tired and we didn't care; we were thousands of miles from home in a foreign country and we didn't care. It was as if they had simply dug an ugly hole in the earth and thrown us into it. We only worked for lodging and food and a very small salary and what we could steal. Even the sun didn't act right; it seemed covered with this thin red cellophane and the rays couldn't get through so we were always sick, in the infirmary, where all they knew how to do was feed you these huge cold chickens. The chickens would taste like rubber and you'd sit up in bed eating these rubber chickens, one after the other, the snot running out of your nose and down your face, the big-ass nurses farting at you. It was so bad in there you just had to get well and back into those stupid pear and apple trees.

Most of us had run away from something – women, bills, babies, the inability to cope. We were resting and tired, we were sick and tired, we were done.

"You shouldn't make him eat that watermelon," I said.

"Go ahead, eat it," said Herb, "eat it or so help me I'll rip your head off your shoulders!"

Little Talbot would bite into that melon, swallowing seeds and Herb's come, crying silently. Bored men liked to think of things to do to keep from going crazy. Or maybe they went crazy. Little Talbot used to teach Algebra in highschool in the States but something had gone wrong and he'd run off to our slop pit and now he was eating come laced with watermelon juice.

Herb was a big guy, steam-shovel hands, black wire beard, and he was full of farts like those nurses. He carried this huge hunting knife in a leather holder on his side. He didn't need it, he could kill anybody without it.

"Look, Herb," I said, "why don't you go out there and end this one-quarter of a war? I'm tired of it."

"I don't want to upset the balances," said Herb.

Talbot was finished with the watermelon.

"Ah, why don't you check your shorts for shit?" he asked Herb.

Herb answered him: "One more word out of you and you'll be carrying your bunghole in a knapsack."

We went out on the street and here were all these thin-assed people in shorts, carrying guns and needing shaves. Even some of the women needed shaves. There was the faint smell of shit everywhere, and every now and then, VURUMB – VURUMB!, you'd hear the bombing. It was one hell of a cease-fire agreement . . .

We went underneath a place to a table and ordered some cheap wine. They burned candles in there. Some Arabs sat on the floor, dazed and listless. One had a raven on his shoulder and every now and then he'd lift the palm of his hand. The palm had one or two seeds in it. The raven would peck at them sickly and seemed to have trouble swallowing. Hell of a cease-fire. Hell of a raven.

Then a young girl of 13 or 14, origin unknown, came and sat at our table. Her eyes were a milky blue, if you can imagine a milky blue, and the poor child was hung with nothing but breasts. She was simply a body – arms and head and everything else hung to those breasts. The breasts were more enormous than the world and the world was killing us. Talbot looked at her breasts, Herb looked at her breasts, I looked at her breasts. It was as if we had been visited by the last miracle, and we knew that all the miracles had ended. I reached out and touched one of her breasts. I couldn't help myself. Then I squeezed it. The girl laughed and said in English:

"They make you hot, don't they?"

I laughed. She was dressed in a yellow see-through. Purple bra and panties; green high-heeled shoes, green large earrings. Her face shone as if it had been varnished and her skin was somewhere between pale brown and dark yellow. Who knows? I'm not a painter. She had tits. She had breasts. It was quite a day.

The raven flew around the room once in an untrue circle, landed again on the Arab's shoulder. I sat there thinking about the breasts, and about Herb and Talbot too. About Herb and Talbot: how they never mentioned what had brought them there and how I never mentioned what had brought me there and how we were such terrible failures, fools in hiding, trying not to think or feel, but still not killing ourselves, hanging on. We belonged there. Then a bomb landed in the street and the candle on our table fell out of its holder. Herb picked it up and I kissed the girl, mauling her breasts. I was going crazy.

"You want to fuck me?" she asked.

When she mentioned the price, it was too high. I told her we were just fruit pickers and when that was over we had to go work the mines. The mines weren't a hell of a lot of fun. Last time the mine had been in the mountain. Instead of digging into the ground we brought the mountain down from the sky. The ore was in the mountaintop and the only way to get it out was from the bottom. So we drilled these holes upward in a circle, cut the dynamite, stuck the fuses in and stuck the dynamite in this circle of holes. You laced all the fuses together to one fuse hanging down, lit it and split. You had two and one half minutes to get as far away as possible. Then, after the blast, you came back and shoveled all that shit out of there and repeated the process. You ran up and down this ladder like a monkey. Every now and then they'd just find a hand or a foot and nothing else. The 2 and one half minutes hadn't been enough. Or one of the fuses had been improperly constructed, the flame running right up. The manufacturer had fucked-up but he was too far away to care. It was kind of like jumping in a parachute – if it didn't open, there really wasn't anybody to bitch to.

I went upstairs with the girl. The place had no windows, and again a candle. There was a mat on the floor. We both sat on the mat. She lit the hash pipe and passed it to me. I took a hook and passed it back, looked at those breasts again. She looked almost ridiculous tied to those two things. It was almost a crime. I said, almost. And, after all, there are other things besides breasts. The things that go with them, for instance. Well, I'd never seen anything like that in America. But in America, of course, when there was something like that the rich boys took it and hid it until it spoiled or changed, then they let the rest of us have a run at it.

But there I was bitching about America because they'd run me out. They were always trying to kill me over there, bury me. There was even a poet I'd known, Larsen Castile, he'd written this long poem about me and in the end they find a mound in the snow one morning and they pile back the snow and it's me. "Larsen, you half-ass," I told him, "that's just wishful thinking."

Then I was on the breasts, sucking first one, then the other. I felt like a baby. At least I felt like I imagined a baby might feel. I felt like weeping because it was so good. I felt as if I could stay there sucking at those breasts forever. The girl didn't seem to mind. In fact, a tear did come down! It was so good, a tear did come down. A tear of placid joy. Sailing, sailing. My god, what men had to learn! I had always been a leg man, my eyes always fastened to the legs. Women climbing out of cars always goofed me up entirely. I didn't know what to do. Like, my god, there's a woman climbing out of a car! I see her LEGS! WAY UP! All that nylon, trappings, all that shit ... WAY UP! Too much! Can't stand it! Mercy! Stamp me down with oxen! – Yes, it was always too much. – now I was sucking breast. O.K.

I got my hands under the breasts, lifted them. Tons of meat. Meat without mouth or eye. MEAT MEAT MEAT. I slammed it into my mouth and flew into heaven.

Then I was on her mouth and working at the purple panties. Then I mounted. Steamships sailed by in the dark. Elephants squirted my back with sweat. Blue flowers shook in the wind. Turpentine burned. Moses belched. A rubber innertube rolled down a green hill. It was over. I hadn't lasted long. Well ... hell.

She took a little bowl and washed me off and then I put my clothes on and marched down the stairway. Herb and Talbot waited. The eternal question:

"How was it?"

"Well, much the same as any other."

"You mean you didn't fuck the breasts?"

"Damn it. I knew I fucked-up somewhere."

Herb walked on up. Talbot told me, "I'm going to kill him. I'm going to kill him while he sleeps tonight. With his own knife."

"Tired of eating watermelon?"

"I never did like watermelon."

"You going to try her?"

"I might as well."

"The trees are almost empty. I guess we'll be going to the mines soon."

"At least Herb won't be there smelling up the shafts with his farts."

"Oh yes, I forgot. You're going to kill him."

"Yes, tonight with his own knife. You won't spoil it, will you?"

"It's none of my business. I figured you told me in secrecy."

"Thanks."

"Think nothing of it . . ."

Then Herb came down. The steps shook as he walked. The whole place shook. You couldn't tell the bombing from Herb. Then *he* bombed. You could hear it, FLURRRRRPPP, then you could smell it all over. An Arab who had been sleeping against the wall awakened, swore and ran out into the street.

"I rammed it between her breasts," said Herb. "Then a *sea* of come under her chin. When she stood up it hung there like a white beard. She needed two towels to mop it up. When they built me, they threw away the mould."

"When they built you they forgot to flush," said Talbot.

Herb just grinned at him. "You going to try her, little titmouse?"

"No, I've changed my mind."

"Chicken, eh? That figures."

"No, I've got something else on my mind."

"Probably some guy's cock."

"Maybe you're right. You've given me an idea."

"It doesn't take much imagination. Just stick it in your mouth. Do what you want to."

"That isn't what I had in mind."

"Yeh? What'd you have in mind? Up your butt, then?"

"You'll find out."

"I'll find out, eh? What do I care what you do with some guy's cock?"

Then Talbot laughed.

"The little titmouse is crazy. He's been eating too much watermelon."

"Maybe he has," I said.

We had a couple of rounds of wine, then got out. It was our day off but our money was gone. Nothing to do but go back, lay on our bunks, wait for sleep. It got cold there at night and there wasn't any heat and they just gave you two thin blankets. You just put all your clothes on top of the blankets – coats, shirts, shorts, towels, everything. Dirty clothes, clean clothes, everything. And when Herb farted you pulled it all over your head. We walked back on in and I felt very sad. There was nothing I could do. The apples didn't care, the pears didn't care. America had tossed us out or we had run away. A shell landed on top of a schoolbus two blocks up. They had been bringing children back from a picnic. As we walked by, there were pieces of children everywhere. The blood was heavy on the road.

"Poor kids," said Herb, "they'll never get laid."

I figured they had been. We walked on.

A WHITE PUSSY

bar near the train depot, has changed ownership 6 times in a year. it went from a topless joint to a Chinaman to a Mexican to a cripple and back and forth like that, but I knew it best sitting there looking out at the tower clock of the train station through a half-open side door. it's a fair enough bar – there aren't any women there to bother you. just a bunch of cassava-eaters and badminton players and they left me alone. most of the time they sat watching a dull game of some sort on tv. it's better in your room, of course, but we've learned through years of drinking that if you use it all alone inside the 4 walls, then the 4 walls will not only destroy you but help THEM destroy you. no need giving them easy victories. knowing the proper balance of solitude vs. the crowd – that was the trick, the con needed to keep you from the padded walls.

so I am sitting there being dull when this Mexican with the Perpetual Grin sits down beside me.

"I need 3 g's. can you get me 3 g's?"

"the boys say 'no' – for a while. lot of trouble lately."

"but I need it."

"we all need it. buy me a beer."

the Perpetual Mexican Grin buys me a beer.

a) he's putting me on.

b) he's crazy.

c) he wants to suck pipe.

d) he's a cop.

e) he doesn't know anything.

"I can get you 3 g's, maybe," I tell him.

"I hope so. lost my partner. he knew how to get through a safe on the thin side, just applying the vise-wedge from a blocked-in setup, just screwed up the pressure until the side buckled. nice, no noise. now he's busted. now I gotta use the sledge, bust off the combo and dynamite the hole. too noisy and old-fashioned. but I need 3 g's to lay up until I can spot a lark."

he tells me all this very quietly, close in, so nobody can hear. I can hardly hear.

"how long you been a fucking cop?" I ask him.

"you got me wrong. I'm a student. night school. taking advanced trig now."

"you gotta bust safes to do that?"

"sure. and when I'm done I'm gonna own some safes of my own and a place in Beverly Hills where the riots can't touch me."

"my friends tell me that the word is Rebellion, not Riot."

"what kind of friends you got?"

"all kinds, and none. maybe when you get into upper calculus you'll understand better what I mean. I think you got a long way to go.

"that's why I need the 3 g's."

"a 3 g loan means 4 g's in 35 days."

"how do you know I won't skip?"

"nobody ever has, you know what I mean."

2 more beers come along. we watch the ballgame.

"how long you been a fucking cop?" I ask again.

"I wish you'd stop that. mind me asking YOU something?"

"uhhuhh," I say.

"I saw you walking along outside one night about 2 weeks ago, around one a.m., your face covered with blood. it was all over your shirt, too. a white shirt. I wanted to help you but you didn't seem to know where you were at. and you scared me: you didn't stagger but it was like you were walking in a dream. then I watched you go into this phone booth and later a cab picked you up."

"uhhuhh," I say.

"was that you?"

"I think so."

"what happened?"

"I was lucky."

"what?"

"sure. they just touched me up a bit. this is the Roaring Decade of the Assassins. Kennedy. Oswald. Doc King. Che G. Lumumba. sure that I have forgotten several. I was lucky. I wasn't important enough to kill."

"who did it to you?"

"everybody."

"everybody?"

"uhhuhh."

"what do you think of the King-thing?"

"a real chickenshit play, like any assassination from Julius Caesar on down."

"you think the blacks are right?"

"I don't think that I deserve to die at the hands of a black man, though I think there are some fantasy-sick whites who do, I mean, THEY want to die at the hands of a black. but I think that one of the finest things about the Black Revolution is that they are TRYING; most of us white panty-waists have forgotten how to, including me. what's this got to do with 3 g's?"

"well, I was told you had the 'inside' and I need bread but I think you're some kind of nut."

"F.B.I."

"sir?"

"are you the F.B.I.?"

"are you paranoid?" he asks.

"of course. what sane man is not?"

"you're nuts!" he seems pissed and pushes his stool back and walks out. Teddy, the new owner, comes up with another beer.

"who was that?" he asks.

"some guy shoveling me a bit of shit."

"yeah?"

"yeah. so I shoveled a little shit back."

Teddy walks off unimpressed but that's the way bartenders are. I finish the beer, walk outside and go down to that big barn Mexican bar with the all-brass rail. they wanted to kill me in there. I was a bad actor when drunk. it felt good to be white and screwy and easy. she comes up. the barmaid. I remember the face. the band strikes up "Happy Days Are Here Again." they are giving me the finger. that beats the switchblade.

"I need my keys back."

she reaches into her apron (she looks good in that apron; women always do; some day I am going to fuck a woman with nothing but an apron on. I mean on HER) and she flips the keys out onto the bar. there they were – car keys, apt. keys, keys to the inside of my skull.

"you said you were coming back last night."

I look around, 2 or 3 guys were just laying around over the bar. knocked out. the flies circling around over their heads, their wallets gone. it smelled like Mickeys. well, a gringo's got it coming, except for me. but the Mexicans were cool – we stole their land but they just kept playing the brass. and I say:

"I forgot to come back."

"the drink's on me."

"o.k., pretend I'm Bob Hope telling Christmas jokes to the soldiers. One Mickey, strong."

she laughs and goes over to mix the poison. I turn my head to make it easy for her. she sits it in front of me.

"I like you," she says. "I want to fuck you again. you do good tricks for an old man."

"thank you. it's that white wig you wear. I'm a freak: I like young women who pretend they are old, old women who pretend they are young. I like garter belts, high heels, thin pink panties, all that ribald trapping."

"I've got one scene where I dye my pussy white."

"perfect."

"drink your poison."

"oh yes, thank you."

"you're welcome."

I drink the Mickey but I fool them, I walk right out and luck it, see a cab sitting right there on Sunset in the sunshine, get in, and by the time he gets me to my place, I am just barely able to pay him, get the door open, close the door and then I am paralyzed. a white pussy. yes she had wanted to fuck me, all right. I make it to the couch and then I am frozen, except for the thought, oh yes, 3 g's, who couldn't use it? interest and final penalty be damned. 35 days. how many men ever had 35 free days in their lives? and then it got dark so I couldn't answer my own question.

uhhuhh.